The Ditty Chasers

By John Buckner

John Buckner

ISBN 13: 978-0-9978949-2-9
ISBN 10: 0-9978949-2-X

The Ditty Chasers

Introduction

What we know as Morse code today was devised by Samuel F.B. Morse and first used on railroads in the middle of the 19th Century. The code was later adapted to accommodate countries on an international basis and modified slightly. During the 1920s and 1930s the practice of sending messages over the airwaves was common.

Businesses and governments could communicate with distant locations almost instantaneously and the airwaves were filled with the sound of 'dits' and 'dahs', or dots and dashes as they appear visually.

Corey Ward was a 1934 graduate of the U.S. Naval Academy and during his time at sea, serving his obligated active duty, he learned to copy Morse code as a means of keeping up with the news while in the middle on one ocean or another. His final assignment was in naval intelligence and he started to study the Japanese language.

Upon his release from active duty he took a job with the government and became a watch supervisor for the navy's communications intelligence effort at the Navy Yard in Washington, D.C. The objective of the group was to copy the Morse code messages off the airwaves and attempt to extract any worthwhile intelligence.

As early as 1930, the navy had been devoting a small amount of manpower to copying Japanese radio traffic, which they had learned to decrypt. Because of the differences in the English and Japanese languages the Japanese developed four letter groups to represent different interpretations of the arcane Katakana language.

The U.S. Navy communicators had learned to decipher the groups they used and with a bit of effort could convert the coded groups to the old language, which could then be read by anyone who knew the dialect of the language they used.

A small group of Navy and Marine Corps operators, somewhere around 200, carried on the job from 1930 to 1941, going through three iterations of changes to the code system the Japanese were using.

The events leading up to the Japanese attack on Pearl Harbor were cataloged by the naval ditty chasers, even to the point of suspecting the targets the Japanese were going to attack on that fatal day.

Throughout the war years the Japanese steadfastly refused to modify or change their communications codes. The reason remains a mystery to this day, but their stubbornness provided the U.S. a decided advantage in determining force compositions and intentions.

This is the story of the role the Morse code intercept operators played during WWII. Though the story is fictional as far as the characters and their actions are concerned, the events portrayed as they relate to the different battles of that era are more accurate than not.

Chapter 1

My name is Corey Ward. I live in a suburb of Washington, D.C. and work for the federal government. The year is 1941 and Hitler is trying to gobble up more of Europe before winter sets in. I follow the news headlines, but I also work for a secret organization that has better information than the newspapers most of the time.

I work for the Department of the Navy as an intelligence analyst. I attended the Naval Academy from 1930 to 1934, and did my six years of active duty through the summer of 1940. I had worked in the intelligence field for the final two years of my active duty time and found the work challenging, with little or no guidance about how to do the work.

I look at the work as a never ending jigsaw puzzle with no picture and an infinite number of pieces, which could change from day to day, sometimes hour to hour. Just when I thought I was getting close to some break through, something would happen to screw up my thought process.

My specialty was cryptographic codes. Ever since Samuel F.B. Morse proved the concept of sending code in an understandable fashion, people, especially governments and military forces, have attempted to use the airwaves to issue time critical orders.

There are many documented instances where intercepted communications provided a decided advantage to one side or another in a battle or confrontation.

Sometimes just the knowledge of who is sending a message and who is receiving it can be very useful. Even if the message is encoded, the chatter between operators sometimes provides valuable information.

I had been intrigued with cryptography from the start of my tour of active duty. My major subject of study at the

Academy had been mathematics, and I was told that most cryptographic systems were mathematically based. I found that to be one of those questions with both a yes and no answer. Most of the high level codes are indeed mathematically based, but a lot of the lesser ones are not.

Some are simple substitution codes where one letter, say A, represented a different letter, say W. Every time the letter A appears in the message, it actually means W. Each letter in the alphabet will have a substitute letter. Sometimes the numbers zero through nine will also be represented in a like manner.

Such a code is not very sophisticated and with even a moderate amount of intercepted message traffic the code would be fairly simple to break. Where the math comes into play is in the frequency of letters of the alphabet appearing. E is of course the most used letter in the English alphabet, so it is a simple matter of counting the number of times each letter appears in the message(s). If you have ten messages using the same system and the most frequently appearing letter in all the traffic is K, then K most likely equates to E in the actual message.

The same holds true for other letters of the alphabet, so once the most heavily used letters are decoded, the remainder of the messages can be filled in through trial and error.

The fly in the ointment is that you have to know what language the code is in. You then have to have someone with knowledge of the language.

The belligerent countries involved in the current world troubles are very different in terms of their cryptographic security. In simpler terms, some countries are more worried than others about letting people know about their business and future plans.

Germany, which gets most of the British attention, and certainly has a lot to lose if their messages are being read, spends a lot of time and effort devising cryptographic systems that are as secure as they can make them.

The Enigma code machine is the end product of a lot of research by Polish and German mathematicians. Without one of the machines and the key for the message sent, it is almost impossible to break the code.

The Japanese, on the other hand, rely on the Katakana code, which is nothing more than substituting numbers for the symbols of the arcane Japanese written language. I suppose they might think that westerners are incapable of deciphering the numbers used for substitutes and they continue the practice.

While a lot of the British work is on the German communications America devotes a lot of time to Japanese communications. The first step in the process is to have someone capable of copying the code off the air. That assumes, number one, that you have a trained operator capable of copying the code, and number two, that he or she can recognize the code when they hear it on the air. Neither of those chores are easy.

It takes several months to train a Morse code operator, and there is very little in the way of structure to the process of pulling the signals off the air. In most cases the end product that the analyst sees is dependent upon the skill of the operator.

I took the time to learn Morse code during my first tour of sea duty, not because I intended to go into the intelligence field, but because I enjoyed it and could get more news that way. When you are in the middle of the ocean every little bit of news is welcome. I took to making carbon copies for the wardroom, where the officers ate, the Chief's quarters, and the enlisted mess decks.

My spending so much time in the radio shack caused me to be given the extra duty as cryptographic officer. That meant that every time a message had to be encoded or decoded, I had the chore.

Of course we looked at other material as well. We had people in the diplomatic corps who routinely took photographs of anything they thought might be interesting to the American intelligence community.

We also got information from others, the British in particular, related to both Europe and the Far East, though we didn't have any treaty agreements to cover the intelligence exchanges.

While the Germans are pounding the British Isles almost daily, the Japanese are gobbling up China and Korea like so much elixir. Some of the reports coming out of the Far East are almost too gruesome to believe for the average person.

I had taken Japanese language instruction on my own, and went to a formal school run by the University of California for a semester, so while not fluent, I did have enough skill to get through the basics.

My group has offices in one of the buildings at the Navy Yard. Our spaces are on the top floor and entry is restricted to those actually working in the area. A guard sits at a desk baring entry to anyone who does not have the proper identification. The emergency exit leading to the outside stairs is locked.

Our spaces are manned around the clock by intelligence watch standers. We operate on an eve/day/mid rotation. That means that we work eight hours in the evening, come back in the morning for another eight, then come in at midnight for the final eight. We then have the remainder of the day from eight AM plus the next full day, plus the first sixteen hours of the third day off. Seasoned watch standers call this eve/day/mid/56.

It really isn't a bad way to work when the job requires around the clock manning.

I am one of four watch supervisors. I have the responsibility for what goes on during my watch time, from ensuring that people are gainfully employed, and that anything of importance gets to the right people in a timely manner, to assigning cleaning crews. The people who work in the sections are the best we can get based on the qualities we are told to look for. That process works most of the time, but once in a while someone will come along who seems to be the absolute opposite of what we are told to look for and this person proves to be a natural at intelligence collection.

That's especially true with the Morse code operators. The intercept operator cannot ask for repeats if he misses it the first time, and the airwaves are filled with manmade interference and natural atmospheric noise. Very seldom does an operator get a clean copy of a message unless the intended recipient asks for repeats of part of the message.

John Clarence Carter, J.C. to his friends, was one of those people who could copy code at 40 words per minute and carry on a conversation while doing it. Even the side garbage didn't seem to deter him. He was simply the best Morse operator I have ever seen.

J.C. could recognize the operating signals the Japanese used as well as the international Q and Z signals which were published as a constant standard of shortening frequently asked questions, such as, 'how's my signals strength', or 'do you have traffic for me?

Most of the things to do with radio operation are listed in a book put out by the International Telecommunications

Union, which regulates communications, from Geneva, Switzerland.

The publication is in English and countries whose alphabets or pictographs did not lend themselves to the Q and Z signals devise their own. Such was the case with the Japanese.

J.C. is so good that he can tell you which operator is sending the message he is copying. Operators have rhythms and other characteristics to their "fists". They are almost like voice characteristics to good Morse code operators.

September had turned to October and my section was closely following the exchanges between the U.S. and Japan as they related to finding some mutual ground for opening discussions about peaceful coexistence. Japan has been taking over China since the early 1930's, and several incidents, from the attack on USS Panay, a U.S. Navy gun boat on the Yangtze River, to the Rape of Nanking, an incident in which more than 200,000 Chinese civilians were reportedly killed, were stumbling blocks. The Japanese were not bashful about taking what they needed, which was primarily natural resources. Japan was very dependent on foreign imports for most of the major minerals, especially oil products.

That was the single most important factor in almost every move they made. My section tracked the trends and also the diplomatic exchanges. Unless meetings were held face to face the important parts were sent in message format to government officials. In many cases we had the information quicker than the people the message was addressed to.

Sometime around 1930, the Admiral in charge of the Asiatic Fleet became aware that his radio operators were copying the Japanese fleet's communications. Instead of chastising them for wasting their time he asked what they learned from the communications. They showed him how they could tell different things about the fleet operations by the message traffic. He was impressed and became the first operational commander to request COMINT support.

His message received the attention of the Fleet Admiral and a limited effort was set up to train operators in Morse code and the Japanese language.

One of the early pioneers of Navy COMINT was a young naval officer by the name of Joseph Wenger. He labored long and hard for the formal recognition of Signals Intelligence as a discipline comparable to other navy ratings, such as engineman or yeoman. The early training was conducted in a block house on the roof of the navy building and during the next three or four years from 1929 they trained a total of 176 operators. They sent some to Hawaii and some to the Philippines. Others stayed in Washington to review the reports they produced. The important thing was that we could read the decrypted version of Japanese messages.

Because of the characteristics of radio wave propagation we didn't copy much of the Japanese communications in Washington. We were supposed to get the raw product from other places by courier, and try to make sense of it when added to the mix of other intelligence bits and pieces.

The high frequency spectrum, which is from two to thirty megacycles, is where most of the military communications are to be found. With the time of day the frequencies are changed. Higher frequency signals were used during day time hours, while the lower frequencies were better suited to nighttime use. Don't ask me to go into a scientific explanation, just accept the statement as true. The signals, depending on the power output, travel a long way in a straight line, even considering the curvature of the earth. The signals also bounce off the ionosphere, which is denser with the elements needed to bounce signals off that layer.

So if you want a signal to travel from Washington, D.C. to Tokyo, for example, you will need a lot of power at the right time of day or night in which there will be multiple skips before the signal reaches the intended recipient. Another little item that comes into play is what is called the skip distance of the signal. As the signal reaches the ionosphere it is strong enough to burn through directly overhead, but as the angle decreases the signal is not strong enough to burn through and it is reflected back to earth. It is reflected at the same angle. That means that the area directly beneath the location where the signal bounces back to earth is not very good for signal reception. So someone nearer the point at which the signal is generated will not hear the signal as well as someone who is in the pattern for receiving the skipped signal.

I know you probably don't care much about that anyway, but it helps to understand how and why intercept stations are located in specific places. WWI had taught most civilized nations a great deal about wireless communications and the important part they play in exercising command and control of belligerent forces engaged in combat.

The Zimmerman telegram, intercepted by the British in January, 1917, played a prominent role in getting the U.S. involved in WWI. The communication, originated by, who else, a German by the same name who was a ranking member of the ruling party in Germany.

The message was a proposal to the Mexican President to restore the land that the United States had taken over during the past two centuries if the Mexicans would support Germany against the Americans.

The importance of keeping the U.S. from actively participating in the hostilities in Europe was seen as a must in order for Germany's plan to bring the English to their knees to succeed. They simply didn't have the forces to engage the British Isles, Russia, and the United States at the same time. They viewed their success on the eastern front as an indicator that they could keep the Russians in line with a minimum of forces, which was a military blunder.

The message also said that Germany would initiate unrestricted warfare against anyone supporting their enemies, a somewhat veiled threat to sink American shipping bound for the British Isles, with their submarine fleet. The date given for that event was February 1, 1917.

The British had copied the "Zimmerman message" off the diplomatic circuit operated between Germany and Copenhagen. The message would then be sent via the Atlantic cable to the Germany Embassy in the United States. (The U.S. had agreed to allow the Germans use of the cable system for diplomatic messages.)

The British had intercepted the original version of the message and also got it off the Atlantic Cable. They were in a very precarious position relative to just how to handle the message. The U.S. had no idea that Britain was pilfering the traffic off the Atlantic Cable. Within a day of acquiring the message they had decrypted a large portion of it.

Two factors came into play in deciding how to handle the situation. Number one, the British monitoring U.S. cable traffic between the U.S. and Europe, and number two, revealing the plain text of the message would let the world know that they were able to read some of Germany's codes where they hadn't a clue to that point.

The British simply had to make the U.S. President aware of the message, with the hope of drawing us into the war.

Many historians feel that this played as large a role in involving the U.S. in the shooting war as did the sinking of two merchant ships by German submarines in early February of 1917.

Zimmerman himself helped the British by confirming that he had in fact sent the telegram after it was made public.

The Mexicans refused to do the German's bidding because they saw no way that Germany could live up to the agreement. In addition, the Germans didn't even have enough gold to prop up the German bank in Mexico just a year before.

Even with this background the U.S. did not place a lot of emphasis on exploiting other nation's communications. However, the Navy was way ahead of the Army, and the Marine Corps took what the navy provided them.

This sets the stage for the dramatic increase in the U.S. Armed Forces attention to communications intelligence.

Chapter 2

Armed couriers were dispatched almost daily from CINCPACFLT with the 'take' of messages intercepted off Japanese circuits by the intercept operators who operated from CINCPACFLT headquarters or most probably Wahiawa in the mountains of Oahu where they had ample room for antennae. Like most functions in a military organization, when a task needed to be done those in charge looked around at their assets to decide who under their charge could most likely do the job best. When the higher-ups were educated to some degree about signal characteristics, and the fact that the Japanese were using the Katakana code, which could be read by a Japanese linguist, they immediately stripped the best Morse code operators out of the Radioman rating and put them to work on the secret project to try to learn what the Japanese were up to.

Because the higher ranking officers recognized the importance of keeping their efforts secret, even from their own government, the functions performed by these people pulled from other jobs was known by very few.

The Commander in Chief of the Pacific Fleet, had been moved from San Diego to Hawaii in February 1941, under very strong protests from Admiral Richardson, then Commander of the Pacific Fleet. He was relieved of his command and the move was made anyway, with Admiral Husband E. Kimmel assuming command.

When the couriers arrived from Hawaii, the bags, stuffed with intercepted Japanese messages, were delivered to my humble working spaces at the navy yard.

What they delivered was added to what our own people had collected and looked at by our analysts, some of whom were Japanese linguists.

15

John Buckner

The one single thing that the Navy, and Army to a lesser degree did that made sense early on was to recognize the need for not only Japanese linguists, but German, Chinese, Russian, and Italian as well.

The first group had entered the training cycle in summer of 1940. That group had come into the duty pipeline just a year later and were now employed in the different watch sections. We always kept at least one German, and one Japanese linguist in each duty section. The others worked days to finalize the reports that would be used to brief senior officers and put out to field units as intelligence product.

Because the information was so sensitive it was encrypted in separate codes and handled separately from other intelligence information.

Some of the intercepted message traffic from Hawaii indicated a heavier than usual training schedule for the Japanese carriers. The analysis of this bit of information was considered significant by one of the linguists in Hawaii. He thought that with the shortage of petroleum products, which was substantiated by message reports of low supplies from major Japanese supply depots, that the Japanese were planning something big but had no indications as to what.

Others who viewed the raw traffic speculated that the Japanese might be planning an invasion of the Philippines. If that should happen there was no way that the small garrison in the Philippines under General MacArthur could prevent the Japanese from taking Manila, and probably the rest of Luzon.

One of the things that we did with our watch sections was to keep an order-of-battle for German and Japanese naval units. It was just one of those things that someone started and it seemed to take hold.

Basically it just kept track of when different units were heard from in a visual medium. The units were broken down into individual task groups. We knew the names of all their carriers, and carriers always had screening units and oilers as part of their make-up.

On the German side, we were particularly concerned with their submarines and battleships.

The courier who brought the latest bag of intercepts was about ready for his return trip. We sent our combined intelligence reports back to Hawaii with him and the bag was almost full.

The analysts had divided up the material from Hawaii and were trying to fit it into the overall picture.

"Look at this Mr. Ward," one of the analysts said to me.

He handed me the intercept. It wasn't even a message but was chatter between operators.

"What am I looking for?" I asked.

"The reference to sunny beaches," he said.

I looked at the entire page, having to ask the meaning of a couple of the groups. The comment the analyst had highlighted was a response to a question from the distant operator about when they would meet again.

The response was, "maybe on a sunny beach in a week."

The operators were both on aircraft carriers, one the Akagi, and the other Kaga. The analyst had highlighted the comment and I added a question of my own. "Does this possibly refer to ship movements to Indo-China or maybe Singapore?" and handed it back.

I made the rounds to the operating positions and stopped to talk to J.C. about the comment between the two carrier radiomen.

"Tell me about circuit discipline in the Japanese navy," I said, and explained the reference to 'sunny beaches'.

"I don't think they would behead them, but they certainly are capable of public flogging on the flight deck. They are, for the most part, very disciplined but I don't think the Japanese officers know code and consider it beneath their dignity to learn. The operators use abbreviations just like our people do. The most popular in both navies is FU, which meaning is obvious."

"They use things like CUL, which is also obvious, but I don't recall ever seeing them doing something disregarding circuit discipline this obviously."

"Do you think they are still in home waters?"

"You're talking about the carriers?" J.C. asked.

"Yeah," I said.

"From the tempo of operations I would say yes, but that's nothing you can take to the bank. Usually when they are doing carrier qualifications for new pilots they start off with daylight operations. They report the number of takeoffs and landings and any accidents. If they are doing daylight operations the message is sent just after dark over there. If night time ops are being conducted they send the message just after daybreak. I haven't been able to see the reason for that procedure. It seems to me that one message a day, at the end of the GMT day would be the most logical thing to do, but then you would think they would encrypt their traffic too," J.C. said.

"If you notice any other anomalies, let me know. Things have begun to get a bit dicey with the diplomatic efforts to try to tone the Japanese aggression down and they invaded Indo-China so they might be preparing to send some air power down that way to keep the natives in line," I said.

That became a very moot point from that moment forward. The carriers were not heard from for two days.

Two days after I had the conversation with J.C. about the chatter he stopped me as I was walking by his position.

"Mr. Ward, something funny is going on with the Japanese," he said.

"What do you mean?"

"I mean that something is not right. All the carriers are off the air. Not a peep for two days. Even if they are in port they still send messages and keep their communications schedules. They aren't even doing that now. And the other men-of-war are silent as well. We are still getting traffic from the ships near China and Russia, but other than that we only hear the service ships, and all they do is broadcast their traffic. They don't even wait for their messages to be acknowledged. It's like the entire fleet went to radio silence."

"And what conclusion do you draw from that?"

"That something important is going on. I don't know what, but I believe we will find out in as little as two weeks, maybe even sooner."

I trusted J.C.'s instincts and his ability and I agreed with him that the Japanese were up to something important, but I didn't know what.

When I got back to my desk I put a new sheet of paper into the typewriter and started organizing my thoughts.

I described the anomalies in the Japanese procedures.

First they had very hectic work-ups for six aircraft carriers. They conducted daylight and nighttime landing operations.

Even though the supply centers were reporting dangerously low levels of petrol based products, they didn't slow their tempo of operations.

More accidents had been reported during the previous two weeks than any I could remember.

Then the chatter between two radio operators about beachfront property, which certainly wasn't on the home islands.

Then the radios went silent.

I finished with J.C.'s comment that something big was about to happen.

When I started I had no idea what I was doing, other than trying to make sense of disparate facts relating to the same subject. Now with the individual items listed I felt a cold stab of fear in my stomach. I had just concluded that the Japanese were about to attack the Philippines!

I took the sheet from my typewriter and put in a blank form for an intelligence assessment. That was an official document based on facts from different sources that someone thought meant something in particular.

As I started to fill out the form I was less sure of my conclusion. Still, something unusual was going on and nobody had said anything about it. At least this would get some people thinking about the problem other than the COMINT section.

I tried to present the facts in a logical progression from the communications standpoint.

The tempo of operations was the single most important factor and was supported by reports from supply depots of very low petrol inventories.

Next was the fact that all the important pieces of their navy was working up for something at the same time.

An almost blatant disregard for casualties during the work-up.

That was the point at which I slid in the chatter between two Japanese radio operators on different aircraft carriers.

I postulated that the exchange had to do with some new real estate the Japanese hoped to acquire shortly.

The clincher was the radio silence for the past three days.

My conclusion was that the Japanese were about to invade some islands, probably Luzon in the Philippines or even one of the southern islands in what they called the southern resource area.

My section was on the evening watch and I signed the report. There were four carbon copies in addition to the original. The original was sent up the chain of command and the carbon copies were meted out to working groups, depending on the subject.

I would get off at midnight and have to come back to work at 0800, so when the heavies got to read their morning traffic I would be available to explain my reasoning. Tomorrow would be the fourth day of radio silence if it held.

When my section came on watch at 0800 there was a note for me to report to Captain Baxter. He was the head of the intelligence watch sections and had probably read the report I put together already.

I went down the hallway to his office and knocked on the door frame.

He looked up and said, "Come on in Corey and explain this to me."

He handed me the assessment I had written the night before.

"First, get yourself a cup of coffee and sit down," he said.

I did as ordered and took a sip of the very hot and very black coffee.

He shook the report again and raised his eyebrows.

"Captain, I think the facts speak for themselves. Something is going on that is very important to the Japanese and I believe it has to do with a coming invasion of some as yet unknown island(s) in the Pacific."

"Why do you think Luzon might be their choice?"

"Because it is closer than anything else and if they take it they can garrison troops and homeport warships in Manila or Subic Bay. That will give them a choke point to patrol the entrance to the South China Sea, and by extension, the seas in the southern pacific," I said.

"You really believe this is going to happen?"

"Yes sir, and very soon."

"How soon?"

"Not later than the 10th of December. If I was in a position of command I would be sending reconnaissance flights out from all the major bases in the Philippines right now until the Japanese are detected, or it was determined that they were going someplace else," I said.

"I wonder why nobody else put these facts together?" the Captain asked.

"I probably wouldn't have without the prodding of probably the best Morse operator in the entire navy. This kid is so good he can copy code at 40 words a minute and carry on a conversation while he is doing it. He recognizes communicators as you and I would visually recognize someone. He told me that the chatter between the Japanese radio operators was unusual."

"His comment was they probably wouldn't be beheaded for the breach of procedure, but they might very well get a flogging on the flight deck if they were found out."

"Your operator thinks something heavy is going down too?"

"Yes sir. And the radio silence confirms that something unusual is in the wind. We may be off on the target, but the timing depends on the logistic chain, and I don't think that will change. I make it seven to ten days before something big happens."

"You might as well go tell your assistant supervisor to take charge of the section. You are probably going to be tied up in briefings all morning, perhaps even all day," the Captain said.

After another cup of coffee the Captain called his boss and suggested that he had an interesting report he might want to look over.

We made our way to the appropriate office and the Captain handed the report to the Admiral.

He quickly read it and did much as the Captain had done and raised an eyebrow.

I didn't wait for the invitation but started to explain how the facts came to my attention. "Had it not been for the chatter between Japanese radio operators I probably would not have even considered what you are looking at. The reference to a beach was so out of character for the Japanese I discussed it with a young intercept operator in my section, who copied it, and he thought it was unusual enough that he commented on other anomalies. The end result was what you are holding."

"Would it surprise you to learn that our government has been holding secret negotiations with the Japanese to try to curtail their expansion in the South Pacific?"

"I knew that negotiations were going on from some of the intercepts that come across my desk, but I didn't know the reason," I replied.

"The Japanese have already gobbled up a large chunk of China, most of Korea, some of Manchuria, and a great deal of Indo-china. It is felt that they will make a play for Singapore and Burma next. If they aren't stopped the ultimate goal is Australia, so your report helps put that in better perspective. They are afraid that if they attack British assets, or Australian for that matter, that we will intervene on their behalf. So taking the Philippines makes sense from a strategic standpoint to keep us from staging out of there."

"I know the Fleet Admiral is going to want to see this, and I might as well take you along to provide the background," he said.

The Fleet Admiral is the most senior person in the navy hierarchy. I might need to qualify that and say usually, because there was another Navy Admiral who was senior to Admiral Stark, who was the current big cheese. The other was Admiral Leahy, who was serving as the U.S. Ambassador to France.

Many in the upper reaches of the military rank structure felt that Roosevelt had given him the job to keep him informed about the war efforts of the allies in the European theater of operations. Since we weren't at war with any of the belligerents he had to walk a fine line in both the private and public sectors.

The Admiral's door was open and he was alone, so we knocked on the door frame and he motioned us in.

"What have you got?" Admiral Stark asked.

"A prediction that the Japanese are going to take Luzon," he said with a chuckle.

He handed him the report. Admiral Stark read it slowly.

"Well, I have to say that it makes sense the way it is presented, but there's nothing concrete except the reference to the beach in a week."

"Admiral, the pieces all fit. They are up to something that is big even for them. My best intercept operator says their activity has been unusual for several weeks. They have had six aircraft carriers doing work-ups at the same time, even when their supply depots tell them that stocks are dangerously low. Their activities in other areas have been very low key during all this time. If they are not going to attack the Philippines, which we should know in the next day or two, then I don't know where they are going, but it will be to the south of them."

"A lot of people believe the only reason they haven't attacked Singapore and other points south is because they are afraid we will come in with our traditional allies and they will be biting off more than they can chew. I agree with your assessment. It is a good piece of work and you have enough to support your theory to raise some eyebrows. Having said that, I don't know what we can do. We certainly don't have enough time or assets to reinforce General MacArthur in Manila. If that is their plan, then we might as well start planning how we are going to take the Philippines back from them somewhere down the road. One thing I can do, without ruffling any feathers is have our carriers put to sea between Hawaii and Midway. It is not inconceivable that the Japanese will attack the fleet in Hawaii. That was the reason for the change of command in PACFLT. Richardson complained too strongly about the move and Roosevelt had no option but to fire him. I have to agree with Richardson's way of thinking to a point. The fleet is certainly more vulnerable sitting in the middle of the Pacific, but if we need to deploy those units we can do it a lot quicker from Hawaii than from San Diego."

"I don't think the Japanese are crazy enough to attack Pearl Harbor, but I don't want the carriers there if they should try it. How long will it be before we know for sure?"

"Even if they have supply ships within the task groups it is still a good two to four days steaming to get to Hawaii. They are now in their fourth day of radio silence and if the Philippines are the objective they should be showing up any time now. If we don't hear anything by tomorrow I guess my prediction was in error," I said.

"Son, I don't think you are in error regardless of the intentions of the Japanese. You picked up on anomalies that indicate something important is going to happen. Just because your crystal ball doesn't reveal the location of the target doesn't mean that the report was in error. I believe this is important enough to have the President have a look. Would you two do the honors if I can set up an appointment for you this morning?"

Admiral Kennan said, "If that is your wish sir."

The Admiral picked up the phone and asked to speak with the President.

"I have a couple of gentlemen in my office with a report that I think you should see. I have the gentleman who wrote it and his boss in my office now. If I send them over can you give them about 10 minutes of your time?"

"Yes sir. Admiral Kennan and a civilian by the name of Corey Ward. He is one of our COMINT watch supervisors. They will be there as soon as possible."

"Go gentlemen and brief me when you get back."

I had been around the military enough to not get the jitters when I was to meet someone much senior to me, but the President himself was a horse of a different color. My knees were not knocking, but I was highly excited.

The Admiral had a driver take us to the White house entrance and told him we would make our own way back. I had a .45 strapped around my waist because I was the junior man, and one of us had to be armed in order to carry the classified message.

The President's keepers insisted that I give up the weapon before joining the President, which I did.

When we were shown into the office President Roosevelt was stuffing a cigarette into his trademark holder. He stood and shook hands with each of us and I took the report out of the briefcase chained to my wrist.

I placed the report on the desk and he picked it up for a quick look.

"Tell me what this means," he said.

The Admiral looked at me and nodded slightly.

I took a deep breath and went over the mechanics again. I finally wound it up with, "So the conclusion that they are going to attack the Philippines is because it is the most logical target. While I don't know for certain what the target is, I know that within the next week an attack is going to be carried out by six Japanese aircraft carriers on what they believe is a very strategic target."

"So if you were General MacArthur what would you be doing now?" the President asked.

At first I thought he was talking to Admiral Keenan, but he continued to look at me.

I finally said, "I would have reconnaissance flights in the air around the clock until I either found the Japanese, or they were discovered by someone else."

"What is your background?" the President asked.

"I attended the Naval Academy from 1930 to 1934. When I finished my military commitment last year I went to work for the government. I learned to copy Morse code while aboard my first ship. I also started to study the Japanese language. I got into the intelligence arm of the Navy Department and became a watch supervisor for the COMINT section."

"Are you still a reservist?"

"I suppose so. I never resigned my commission but was transferred to the inactive reserve," I said.

"How good are your Japanese language skills?"

"I am not fluent, but I know enough to get the meaning of most things related to naval affairs," I said.

"I believe we are going to have to fight Japan sooner or later. The world is in such a mess now that it is hard to decide how to use our resources. Germany is a much larger worry than the Japanese right now. If they manage to subdue the British they can take the remainder of Europe at their leisure. The Japanese are too far away to cause us much trouble at home. If we get into this war we are going to have to fight Germany first and a lot of people are not going to like that decision. I wish there was some other way but I don't believe there is."

I just nodded my head. I didn't know if he was talking to the Admiral, me, or to himself.

He was still looking at me but I couldn't imagine the comments he just made to be directed to me.

"Do you understand the reasoning behind what I just said?" he asked, this time no doubt talking to me.

"Yes sir, I believe so. The closest the Japanese can get to us is the Hawaiian Island chain unless they want to come down the Aleutian Islands and through Alaska. The supply chain would be so long that they couldn't effectively wage war against us at home. The Germans on the other hand are much better suited in terms of resources, both natural and human. They don't have to travel far to engage their enemies and have many more options than the Japanese have. They are also technologically superior to the European countries they are engaging."

"That's about what Admiral Leahy is telling me. He's in France trying to keep me up to date about what is happening over there."

"Are you married?" the President asked, obviously changing the subject.

"No sir. The right one hasn't come along yet," I responded.

"Then you are pretty much unencumbered by family responsibilities that would preclude your travelling on short notice," the President said.

"Yes sir. That is correct."

"Thank you for bringing this to my attention. I will be in touch later through Admiral Stark."

Admiral Kennan and I headed back to the Navy Yard after I retrieved my .45 from the Secret Service detail.

"You handled that very well. I think the President was impressed with your analytical ability. I also have a feeling that he has something in mind for you personally. He has a habit of using people for things that other people would not even consider. Admiral Leahy is a good example of that. They are very close friends, and Leahy will tell him the truth, even if it isn't what the President wants to hear. He also knows that Admiral Leahy will gather information from the right kind of people."

"I can't imagine what he could use me for that other people would not be better suited to handle," I said.

"You never know. A lot will depend on how accurate your speculation is about the Japanese target," Admiral Kennan said.

Chapter 3

It was almost lunch time when I got back to the work area. We had a cafeteria of sorts on the ground floor of the building and that is where I usually got my lunch. I stopped by and picked up a package of chips and a sandwich.

I was sitting at my desk eating when J.C. left his position and came to the desk. I had a mouth full of sandwich and lifted my coffee cup in greeting.

He pulled up a chair and sat down by my desk.

"I'm not sure if I should bring this to your attention or not, but I have been copying the Japanese propaganda network. You know how they use it to discredit the U.S. and also as a means to let their sailors send messages to the home folks. One of the radio operators from Kaga sent a message on the circuit."

"What did the message concern?"

"I don't know. I don't read Japanese, but it was kind of like their normal family-grams where a bunch of the crew of a ship sends personal greetings to their folks. I imagine the information is censored before they allow it to be transmitted, but still...." He left the sentence unfinished.

"Do you have the copy?" I asked.

"Be right back," he said and returned to his position in the back row.

He was back with the message copy in less than a minute.

He handed me the copy. "The entire message was sent by the same party. I suspect he is probably the senior radioman on the ship. He is very steady and has a rhythm to his fist. He sent that at about 30 words per minute. I think he did so to avoid having to repeat sections of the message. He is normally faster than what he showed here."

I looked the message over. It was in the katakana code and the four number groups had to be decoded to form the Japanese characters.

Once the transliteration was complete I read what I could of the message. It dealt with greetings to several people from members of the crew, and closed with a wish for prayer to the spirits for the success of their mission which would be a great blow against the Gaijin.

I had only ever heard the term Gaijin used to refer to westerners. It was a mild pejorative and I was surprised to see it used in even unofficial communications.

I said to J.C., "What do you think this means?" I slid the message to him. I had written the English translation on a separate sheet of paper.

J.C. said, "They wouldn't refer to Filipino's as Gaijin. That term is only used for round eyes. It means that the target of their operations is either Australia, New Zealand, or the U.S."

"How long have they been under radio silence?"

J.C. made a show of looking at his wrist and said, "Just over 96 hours."

"If they were going to attack the Philippines they would be on station today," I said.

"There's a possibility that the ships are going to different locations. They might be preparing to attack several places at once," J.C. said.

"Six carriers are a bit much for a single attack now that you mention it. If they are going to attack multiple locations then Hawaii, Guam, Midway, and the Philippines are the most likely targets," I said.

"We need eyeballs on at least one of the carriers before we can tell how they are organized," J.C. said.

"How did you get onto the circuit anyway?" I asked.

"Just sampling through the band and ran across it. They use different frequencies every day and I recognized the "fist" of the guy sending the message."

"Do you think the guys in Hawaii got this?"

"I have no way of knowing, but they do the same as we do. When the change-over occurs they sample the activity until they find the new frequency."

"I'm going to write another assessment based on what you got. Help me out here," I said.

Between the two of us we articulated the facts upon which the prediction would be based.

The single fact that repudiated our suppositions was that the Kaga would even allow a message to be sent while under total radio silence.

J.C. handled that one. "They are just like us. I mean as far as their radio operators are concerned. Many of us are members of the Amateur Radio Relay League. That means we build our own transmitters and receivers from scratch. In many cases they are better than the official radios. I will place a small wager with you that the transmitter used to send that message is not on the official equipment list of Kaga. I would also postulate that the people mentioned in the message are personal friends of the guy who sent the message."

I broke out the paperwork for another assessment and called Admiral Keenan and asked if he would grab my Captain and come to the intelligence spaces.

When they arrived I went through what we had and the conclusion that the attacks were going to be against westerners. I then laid the choices out to them.

"Why on earth would a task group commander allow such a message to be sent?" the Admiral asked.

"It was probably not an official transmitter," J.C. said. He then went on to explain about amateur radios and how they were used. "The guy probably thinks that he is so much smarter than westerners, especially Americans, that there is very little chance of them copying his message, and even so they would not be able to decrypt it."

"So what are they going to do?" the Admiral asked.

"I think they are going to attack Hawaii, Midway, Guam and the Philippines simultaneously. Two carriers each for Hawaii and the Philippines, and one each for Midway and Guam. I believe they are looking to totally destroy any opportunity that we might have to interfere with their plans in the South Pacific," I said.

"Write it up and we will go see the boss," the Admiral said.

I had all the information already sketched out and simply transcribed it to the proper format.

We had to wait for about five minutes to get in to see Admiral Stark. I handed over the message and he read it carefully. "So you think they will actually attack Hawaii?"

"There's no guarantee, but the use of the term Gaijin is only used to identify westerners," I said.

He picked up the phone, which was a direct line to the President and asked if he could spare a few minutes for some additional information relative to what he heard earlier from Admiral Kennan and Corey Ward.

The group was met by a car and driver and taken to the White House. This time the driver entered the grounds and dropped them off at the main entrance.

When they got into the Oval Office the President shook hands all around. He said to me, "We really have to stop meeting like this. People will talk."

The comment got the obligatory laughs from all of us.

I handed the message over and explained the circumstances under which it was acquired. "The control station for that circuit is in Tokyo and they change frequencies about every twelve hours. When they make the change over our operators search the likely band until they find them and it is then back to business as usual. In this case my guy found them right away and recognized the person sending the message by the way he sent code. It's kind of hard to explain without using the term witchcraft, but J.C. knows this guy's sending characteristics better than his own mother. He swears the sender is one of the operators off Kaga."

"If you couple that with the fact that it is probably not an official radio, and the C.O. doesn't know anything about the message being sent, then the conclusion makes sense. I was bothered by the use of so much firepower in a single task group from the start, but that was the way they worked-up so I accepted that. Now it appears that they will split into four task groups and attack the Philippines, Guam, Midway and Hawaii at the same time, assuming they all arrive in their operating areas undetected" I said.

"If the entire group was slated to attack the Philippines they should be there by now," the President said.

"Yes sir. Even at a lower speed for fuel conservation they should be there by now. If, as I now believe, they are going to attack multiple targets, the group scheduled to hit Hawaii, will have the longest voyage. The other groups will adjust their speed to arrive at a predetermined time, which will probably be two days from now. That will mean they have been at sea for seven days and the attack will occur between the 6th and 9th of December."

"Admiral," Roosevelt said to the CNO, "Get a message out to Admiral Kimmel and alert him of a possible attack and direct him to send surveillance aircraft to the most likely quadrant from which a Japanese attack would come. Make sure he deploys the carriers, probably in the direction of Midway until we find out for sure what the Japanese intentions are."

It was near 1600 when we got up to leave.

The President said, "Admiral, may I borrow Mr. Ward for a little more in-depth discussion. I will even feed him supper and see that he gets back to your area after I am finished with him."

"Yes sir. If you need anything else, let me know."

As soon as the others left he told one of his protective detail to tell Mrs. Roosevelt that they would be having a guest for dinner.

"I just finished my last scheduled appointment. Would you like a drink?"

"Yes sir, I would," I responded.

"You can pour. The bar is over there," he said pointing to a blank wall.

One of the Secret Service guys pressed the button that revealed the bar and asked, "What is your pleasure sir?"

He had already poured one for the President before I could respond. "Just bourbon with a bit of water and ice," I said.

"I would like to know what led you to the conclusions you reached concerning the two instances in one day," He asked.

"The only way I can explain it is that I have a little bit of knowledge about how radio's work. I can copy Morse code at about 20 to 25 words per minute. I do it as a hobby. Most of the operators in my section are good up to 35 or even 40 words per minute. It's kind of like a fraternity. Everyone wants to be considered the very best at what they do. I think I am the only supervisor who can copy code almost as well as they do, and they respect that. They even try to help me better understand the nuances at times. They will have me listen to some operator who has a quirky characteristic that helps to identify him when they next run across him."

"Then I have served a couple of tours of sea duty and know how the deep water navy works. I know a bit about gunnery, conning a ship, and how ships operate on long voyages. I know enough of the Japanese language to be effective unless absolute accuracy is required. And the final thing is that my operators trust me enough to alert me to little things that someone else might not notice. A conversation with the guy who actually copies the code is a lot more constructive than an operator's note in the log trying to explain black magic."

The President laughed. "I think you really mean that."

"Yes sir, I do. If J.C. came in here right now and explained to you how he knew the message he copied was sent by an operator he has never seen before he would have a hard time convincing you that something like a long C or a swinging Q proved that he was right."

"What about the two intelligence reports you generated today?"

"I just put the facts together as best I can. If the result is something that other people should know then I write it up. To me it is just common sense."

"You do realize that you will be recalled to active duty when we enter the war?"

"Yes sir, I figured as much," I said.

"What would you rather be doing, working in intelligence or conning a ship?"

"Without regard to my druthers, I think I can make a more valuable contribution to the war effort in intelligence," I said.

"I agree with that assessment, which is why I wanted to have a private talk with you. You may have heard that I use spies very liberally. I mean that in the sense that I send people I really trust to look into things that I feel others are not presenting in the full light of day. If something that I need to know about reflects adversely on the person writing the report, then the report will show the author in the best light, or in the better of less favorable circumstances. I need the very best information available to aid me in making the right decisions for the American people. The people don't always need to know the reason for decisions I make, but they need to know what the decisions are, and that they were made based on the best information available," he said.

"I can understand that, but I don't see what it has to do with me personally," I said.

"I am thinking about making you one of my spies. You are versatile, knowledgeable in the ways of the military, and not cowed by senior officers. If I send you someplace to confirm something or refute it, you will do your best to find out what I need to know without regard to the ultimate consequences. That is what Admiral Leahy is doing in France at the moment."

"Sir, I hope you are not putting me in the same class as Admiral Leahy," I said.

The President laughed. "Not at all. I am just trying to give you an idea about how I operate. Admiral Leahy is not what comes to mind when you think of an ambassador, but that is the position he is filling because it puts him in the place where he can do the most good for the country, specifically by keeping me informed of all the lesser known things about the war being waged in Europe now."

"There is a lot of opposition about us getting involved in a war on the continent. A lot of Americans of German extraction are sympathetic to their cause, and some high profile citizens have come out in support of the Germans. It's going to take a clear cut single action to get involved without splitting the American public into two camps. Admiral Leahy is attempting to keep me from making a fool of myself."

"I certainly don't travel in the same social circles as Admiral Leahy, and I don't know how I could be of use to you in that regard," I said.

"I think you underestimate your abilities. You had no problem writing up two incidents in one day that others would probably have overlooked. And just because there was a chance that you would look a fool for predicting something that might not happen, you didn't let that stop you from writing the reports. It's what is called the courage of your convictions."

"What if the Japanese do something entirely different from what I concluded they are doing?"

"Today is the sixth of December. If they have not been heard from by the tenth we will need to look for other reasons for their actions, but I believe your reasoning was sound and that they will certainly attack the Philippines, Midway, and probably Guam. I am not so sure they will tackle Hawaii at the same time, but in a perverted way I hope they do. If that happens it will be a deliberate act of war without any declaration and I can declare war on Japan with the blessings of the international community and with the support of the American people. I will, of course, deny ever having said that, but if they attack and we declare war on them, then Germany and Italy will declare war on us out of axis solidarity. We will then reciprocate and will have a free hand to become involved in any manner that is advantageous to the American Republic."

"The European allies can't hope to stop Hitler without our industrial support. That is the single most important thing we can contribute to the war in Europe I believe," I said.

"See what I mean about your intelligence. Most people your age would have said that the additional manpower was the most important factor, and they would have been wrong," Roosevelt said.

We talked for almost half an hour in the office, and had two drinks during the time.

Just after 1630 we were led to the second floor dining room. The President used the elevator. I had not noticed the entire time we were together in the oval office that he was in a wheel chair.

Eleanor, the First Lady, was a gracious hostess and a good conversationalist. The President had said grace, though a short one, and we had done the salad and the main course was being served when the President said, "Eleanor, what do you think of my latest spy?"

"I figured there was some reason for Mr. Ward's presence other than to provide the conversation while you eat," she said.

Roosevelt laughed. "There's a lot more to him than meets the eye. He is a watch supervisor for the navy's COMINT collectors. He wrote a report this morning about some coming Japanese actions that escaped the attention of others. He was brought to my office to explain the report to me. What he said made sense and I agreed with his reasoning. Then just about 1530 he wrote another report, expounding on the first and making what most people would consider a wild prediction. The Admiral in charge of the navy called and said he wanted to bring him and the report to see me. I was impressed enough to consider making him one of my personal spies."

"What was this wild prediction?" Eleanor asked, because she knew that her husband expected her to.

Roosevelt finished chewing his mouthful of food, took a sip of wine and said, "He thinks the Japanese are going to attack Hawaii within the next three days, along with the Philippines, Midway, and Guam."

Eleanor looked from one to the other. "Tell me this is a joke Franklin."

"No joke. The Japanese worked-up six aircraft carriers during the preceding six weeks, to the detriment of their low stocks of petroleum products. Corey reported the fact that one Japanese radio operator told another in Morse code that he would see him on the sunny beach in a week. The entire Japanese fleet then went to what they call radio silence, which they do when they want to keep something very secret. Corey predicted that the six carriers were going to surprise someone to the south of the Japanese islands. That report was delivered this morning. Before the day was out one of his operators copied a message from a circuit run by their Japanese propaganda machine that was sent by a person he recognized from the way he sent Morse code. Don't ask me how they can do that because I don't know. Corey tells me it is like black magic."

"How is that possible Mr. Ward?"

"I will explain if you will agree to call me Corey," I said.

"Okay Corey, the floor, or table is yours," she said with a chuckle.

"Our minds tend to file away certain things in order to have us recall them. When I look at you I see a not too young, attractive lady with little makeup, but styled hair. Those things are placed in my mental file cabinet. If I see you again tomorrow I look for those same characteristics to identify you. The more distinctive you are, the easier it is for me to recognize you. I listen to your voice and mentally compare it to other female voices. Over time I get used to the tempo of your walk and the list goes on."

"A Morse code operator works on the same circuits day after day. He comes across signals that he immediately recognize because of the call signs used. He can discard those right away because they don't fit his recognition pattern of what he is searching for. He knows that his guy uses a different call sign, or station identifier. He uses other mental clues to help with the identification process. Sending code is like speech. None of us use the same manner of speaking. Some pause between certain words, others emphasize important phrases, and so forth. The Morse code operator has the same characteristics, though not as many, and much more subtle."

"All letters and numbers in the alphabet have Morse code equivalents using only two elements, dots and dashes. A is dot dash. B is dash dot dot dot, and so on. Good operators can mentally file away the individual ways different operators send code. Something as simple as a microsecond pause between two elements of a letter can tell him who the operator on the other end of the circuit is. It is just a subconscious thing that radio operators do, and to try to explain to someone else it seems like magic."

"I think I understand what you are talking about, but how did this lead you to conclude that an attack is imminent?"

"The person who sent a personal message to some family members of his shipmates was identified by my operator as one who was on the Aircraft Carrier Kaga the last time he heard him. He made mention of the word Gaijin, which is Japanese for westerner, or specifically American westerner. The Kaga was still under radio silence, so we theorize that he was using an amateur radio that he built himself and his shipmates, especially the Captain and Admirals, were unaware that he was transmitting. The use of the term Gaijin would mean that the six aircraft carriers are going to attack American strongholds in the Pacific to prevent us from interfering with their push to the South

Pacific Ocean, from which they hope to replenish their oil and other natural resources."

"I find that simply amazing, that such inconsequential things can lead to a major assumption, or prediction, whatever the proper word is. When do you expect this attack to occur?"

"Within the next couple of days," I said. "Not later than the 9th of December."

"And what are we going to do about it Franklin?" Eleanor asked.

"I have done all I can do. We have no forces to resist them in any meaningful way. If they attack the Philippines, MacArthur has some planes, but most are not capable of standing up to the Japanese Zero's. Guam has very little, and Midway has a squadron of Marine F4F's. Hawaii has three aircraft carriers, about ten battleships, a bunch of cruisers and destroyers, but nothing to hold up against the Japanese arsenal. Even if they only attack Hawaii with two carriers, that is something over 300 planes,"

"So you are just hoping that you are wrong?" Eleanor said to me.

I didn't know how to answer that question and didn't want to put my foot in my mouth. I looked to the President for some indication about how he wanted me to answer the question but he was no help. He looked as if he was awaiting an answer as well.

I composed my thoughts before answering. "I don't know how to answer that because there are multiple answers. The president and I were discussing this in the Oval Office before coming up here. On the one hand, if my prediction is wrong, then someone else is going to get surprised, and the most likely recipients of the Japanese attack will be Australia and New Zealand, or maybe the British at Singapore and Hong Kong. If however, my hypothesis is correct and the Japanese attack the places I mentioned without provocation, then we have to retaliate, and that means a declaration of war on Japan. Japan will declare war on us, followed by Germany and Italy. We will then declare war on all of them and the free for all is underway. The really sad part of this is that we don't have enough evidence to convince the skeptics that an attack is imminent. I don't even have enough evidence to convince myself of that beyond any doubt. If we tell the world that the Japanese are going to attack Hawaii, Midway, Guam and the Philippines and they don't do it, then we look like fools."

"So what is the solution?" Eleanor asked.

"Pray that the casualties are light and that they don't completely annihilate our fleet at Pearl Harbor," I said.

"So, Eleanor, will Corey make a good spy for me?"

"One of the best I think," she said.

One of the Secret Service people dropped me off at the Navy Yard later in the evening.

Chapter 4

My section had the mid-watch that night and I couldn't see much point in going back home for the couple of hours sleep I might manage, so I went to the office in the secure area and sat at the desk normally used by what we called day workers, to distinguish them from the watch standers. They did most of the analysis of both our take and what came in from Hawaii.

I left the lights turned off and tried to get comfortable enough in the chair to fall asleep but sleep would not come.

I had too much on my mind. On the one hand, I was thrilled that I got to meet the President, and even have dinner with him, but the two reports were weighing heavily on my mind. What if J.C. and I had read too much into the couple of anomalies we found in the communications transcripts?

We could very well be wrong, but I would have bet my last dollar that the Japanese were going to surprise someone within the next 48 hours in a big way.

After a while I got up and went to one of the unoccupied Morse positions and put the headphones on. I just wanted something to do to keep my mind off more important things and started copying the fleet broadcast, which consists of coded messages sent out by our communications stations in different parts of the world.

The comm centers encrypt the messages, then type the messages on a machine that punches tape with the Morse letters, which can then be sent automatically over the broadcast circuit at a steady speed. They usually don't run the broadcast more than 20 to 25 words per minute. Sometimes the same message is run two or three times. They broadcast continually so ships at sea will be able to tune in the station at any time day or night.

The way our operation was set up was with two civilian supervisors and two Navy Chief Petty Officers as section chiefs. Since I didn't interface with the other sections that much we were not aware of one another's abilities.

When I sat down on the position and started taking coded groups the Radioman Chief who was the supervisor of the section on watch now came over and watched for a while.

I am not like J.C. I can't take code and talk at the same time.

I sensed that the Chief wanted a word with me so I stopped taking code and took the earphones off.

"Not bad for a civilian," the Chief said.

"I wasn't always a civilian," I said. "I went to the Academy and spent four years at sea on destroyers from '34 to '38," I said.

"Where did you learn to take code?"

"On my first ship. I would sit in the radio shack during my slack time and learn by trial and error. That was when the crypto room was separate from the transmitters and receivers. One of the guys made up a chart for me with the Morse equivalents and I studied it for a while. He then made up a sending key from an oscillator and I practiced whenever I had time. The CO made me the crypto officer and I spent even more time on the radios. By the time I left the ship I was pretty competent to about 25 words per minute. I copied the fleet broadcast a lot and even got officially certified as a Morse operator."

"I wanted to talk to you about the two assessments you put out today. Can you tell me what you keyed on?"

"The one in the morning hours was a result of some chatter between Japanese radio operators. They are usually pretty disciplined on the circuits but one operator on Kaga told the other on one of the other carriers that he would see him on the sunny beach in a week or so. It's kind of thin, based on that alone, but six carriers had been working up for over a month, even with dangerously low fuel supplies, so it was not hard to tie the comment together with past actions and predict that something big was coming. Admiral Keenan thought it was enough to inform CNO and he thought it was enough to inform President Roosevelt. I was taken to the White House to brief the President and managed to get through the explanation without embarrassing myself and the President bought the report."

"When I got back I had not even had time to eat a sandwich before my best operator came up and said he had something interesting. I told him to bring his copy and we would discuss it. The copy turned out to be a message off their propaganda network, you know the one I am talking about?"

"Yeah, Tokyo Rose's sidekick."

"Anyway, my guy told me that the message had been sent by one of the radiomen on Kaga, which has been under radio silence for a few days. I decoded the message and read the plain text copy. There was a reference to Gaijin. Do you know what that means?"

The chief shook his head no.

"That's the way they refer to westerners, especially Americans. Long noses is another term both the Japanese and Chinese use to refer to Caucasians."

"That was why I wrote the revised report. I know it is flimsy, but all the indicators point to what will happen in the next couple of days," I said.

"Well, I think that was a good piece of work, even if it turns out to be wrong," he said and went back to his desk.

I copied the fleet broadcast for about an hour and went to the cafeteria for some food before time to go back on watch.

The mid watch was very uneventful, except that I had trouble staying awake in the wee hours of the morning.

I would be off for the next two days, but I would probably sleep most of the current one.

It was Sunday morning, December 7th and I had a large breakfast and hit the sack for some much needed sleep. I got up just after noon to go to the bathroom and went back to bed again. That was going to mess up my sleep pattern for the next string of watches, but I was really wasted.

The ringing of my phone woke me up just before six in the evening. It was my boss telling me to come to work right now. He wouldn't even tell me what it was about. It took me less than 20 minutes to get to the office. The parking lot had more cars in it than I had ever seen at one time.

The first thing I noticed was that the guards at security checkpoints were now armed with rifles. "What's going on?" I asked the first sentry I encountered.

"The Japs attacked Hawaii and some other places in the Pacific this morning," he said.

"You mean this morning our time or the time in Hawaii?" I asked.

"I think it was their time. It just happened not long ago," the guard said.

The place was crawling with people, doing who knows what. Most were simply trying to make sense of what had happened, but it would be a few more hours before all the reports were collated to learn the extent of the damage and loss of life.

Admiral Keenan caught me as I was walking down the hallway and motioned me into his office.

"The President is going to gather all the brass for a briefing at the White House and he wants you there. How did the rest of your visit with him go yesterday?"

"Okay, I guess. I had dinner with the President and First Lady. He brought up the subject of the assessments I did to Eleanor and she asked some questions about the Japanese intentions. I at first thought she was talking to the President, but he was waiting for my answer, probably to see how I handled it. The question related to the second assessment and she had asked how I could determine what the Japanese actions might be, and what the assessment meant overall."

"The President and I had discussed the possibility of the Japanese attacking Hawaii in the Oval Office just before we went up for dinner. He wanted to see how I handled the question I think. I told her how I had arrived at the conclusion based on one of the carrier operators sending the message over the propaganda network and had to give her an example that put it in the proper perspective. She seemed to understand."

"The President then said, 'I'm thinking about making him one of my spies. Will he make a good one?'"

"Eleanor said, 'one of the best'."

"I was then driven back here by one of the Secret Service guys."

"I believe he wants you to brief the brass, just to let them get firmly fixed in their minds that we didn't know the Japanese were going to attack Pearl Harbor any sooner than that. The play is political, because a lot of people are going to say that we knew about the attack well in advance and allowed it to happen as a catalyst to get us involved in the war. While that statement might have been true if we had more notice, it didn't happen and he wants the public to know that we had absolutely no concrete evidence that the

Japanese were going after Pearl Harbor until yesterday, and even then the evidence was somewhat iffy," the Admiral said.

"Since all that is classified, how will he handle the press?" I asked.

"That might be the first question you ask him. I am sure he doesn't want the Japanese to know that we are reading their mail, but you are going to have to brief the brass with the absolute truth of the matter. I imagine the President will then admonish them to keep their mouths shut about how we got wind of the attack, even at such a late date."

"Do we have any damage assessments yet?"

"Just that they hit the battleships heavily and that most of the land based aircraft were either damaged or destroyed. We didn't have a lot in the way of fighter aircraft there and they probably caught them all on the ground. They most likely deliberately picked a Sunday morning for the attack knowing that we practically shut down on that day."

"That's a good piece of information for the brief if I have to give it," I said.

"At least the carriers were not in port. That would have been a disaster from which it would have been really hard to recover."

Admiral Keenan led me to CNO's office. He had several flag rank officers gathered in his office. He motioned us in and we found chairs at the conference table. I didn't know many of the officers present and Admiral Stark made the introductions.

"Mr. Ward is the supervisor of one of our COMINT sections. He and one of his operators came up with the information that resulted in the intelligence assessments issued yesterday. The President wants him to brief the flag officers later this evening. I was also directed to have him ordered to the White House and to process the paperwork for his recall to active duty. Mr. Ward is a reserve LCDR and will serve the President in whatever capacity the CINC desires. I assume all of you are by now familiar with the two assessments from yesterday."

Everyone nodded. One of the Admirals said, "I got the gist of the assessment in what it was predicting, but I didn't understand how the information was gathered."

"Maybe you had better answer that one Corey. It will be good practice for when you have to brief the entire cabinet," Admiral Stark said.

"I don't want burden you with a lot of BS, but COMINT is a form of silent warfare. We are constantly trying to figure out what the other side is doing based on the kind of communication he uses. We spend a lot of time copying what others put in the airwaves. A lot can be determined just by who is talking to whom, and the external chatter on a circuit. In the case of the Japanese, they use a numerical code that equates to the Katakana language. It is a fairly simple matter to decode it and many of the people trying to exploit the communications at first thought it was a ploy by the Japanese to lull us into a false sense of security. We have gotten enough information off their circuits to know that the code is for real. Why they don't use something more sophisticated is a matter of great speculation, but we can't look a gift horse in the mouth. They did a complete revision of the code almost a year ago now, but we were able to reconstruct it in a matter of a couple of months."

"Our COMINT operators are the cream of the crop. When this effort started the best Morse code operators were pulled from our own circuits and put to work against the other side. These guys are really good. Some can copy 40 words per minute or better. Some also have the uncanny ability to identify a particular person by the way he sends code over the circuits. That ability was what prompted the second assessment yesterday. One of my better operators was copying what we call the Japanese propaganda network, which is the way most Japanese sailors keep their friends and relatives aware that they are still alive. The messages are what we call family-grams. They are pretty short messages, some not more than 20 to 30 words, and just say something like, hello mom. I'm fine, see you soon. Love Yoshi, or whatever."

"Six Japanese carriers had worked up for deployment during the past six weeks. Five days ago they went to radio silence. We have not heard a peep out of them for that long. Then while my operator was copying the propaganda circuit for something to do, he recognized that one of the operators from the carrier Kaga was sending the message."

"I had not been back from briefing the President but a few minutes and he came to my desk and said he had something strange he wanted to show me. He could not read the message he was copying, but insisted he had correctly identified the operator who was sending the message. I decoded the message and read the Japanese characters. There was a reference to Gaijin in the message. Many of you know that Gaijin is the way the Japanese refer to American's in particular, and white people in general. My operator's confidence in the identity of the operator, the carrier work-ups and the radio silence of all the carriers pointed toward an attack against either us, the British or the Australians in the South Pacific. The only fly in the ointment, so to speak was that the C.O. or flag officer on the carrier would not allow such a message to go out."

"My operator informed me that most professional radio operators were members of the Amateur Radio Relay League and build their own radio components. He suggested that the operator was probably using his own radio that the officers on the ship didn't even know about. That's how the second assessment came about. I had to explain it to our people here and convince them that I had not been smoking funny cigarettes before briefing the President. I know the conclusion was not based on what could be considered proven methodology, but it happened, so the assessment was correct."

"Can you copy code?" one of the Admirals asked.

"Yes sir, but with nothing like the speed and professionalism of the dedicated operators. I copy about 25 words per minute, but the worst of the operators in my section can hit 35 to 40. It's a point of pride among them since they can't tell the rest of the world what they do," I said.

That brought a chuckle all around the table.

"I don't suppose you have a prediction as to what happens next," another of the flag officers said.

"I would expect them to withdraw back toward the western pacific. It would not surprise me if they attacked the Philippines in earnest next. This entire strategy was to weaken the U.S. to the point that we could not effectively hamper their efforts in the South Pacific to gain control of natural resources they desperately need, oil and petroleum products being the most important. They are trying to buy time to solidify their foothold in places like Indo-China, Burma and Siam. Another reason is probably to stop the flow of resources we are shipping to China via that route."

The CNO's telephone buzzed. It was the direct line to the President.

"Yes Mr. President," he said.

"Right away sir," he said and hung up the phone.

"That was the summons. We are to be there in an hour," Admiral Stark said. "Since we don't want to be late, let's meet downstairs in say, 15 minutes and we can take two cars."

We did as the Admiral suggested and arrived at the White House well in advance of the meeting time. The entrance to the grounds was swarming with reporters and it took some time to make our way past the gates.

When we moved inside Secret Service agents provided escorts to the briefing room. I was pulled aside by one of the President's personal detail and escorted to the Oval Office.

He rapped on the door and opened it without waiting for an answer.

The President was seated at his desk reading correspondence, probably messages from Hawaii. He pointed to the coffee pot and one of the detail poured coffee for both of us.

"Well, you now look like a genius to a lot of folks," he said by way of greeting.

"As you well know, that is far from the truth," I said.

He chuckled. "I am just glad we got the carriers out of there in time. Their loss would have been very difficult to overcome. The battleships and cruisers will be hard enough to replace, but they don't have the same implication for offensive warfare that carriers do. Carriers are the wave of the future for warfare at sea. It extends the defensive umbrella by hundreds of miles and the planes can strike from a great distance keeping the ship out of harm's way."

"I suppose that is true if you don't consider the submarine threat," I responded.

"Do you think a submarine can sink a carrier?"

"Yes sir, I do. It would take a pretty cunning skipper, but it can be done. The odds of the submarine escaping after the attack is an entirely different matter, but theoretically you would trade a submarine for a carrier any day, maybe even two or three. The Germans have started to send their submarines in packs against ships in the north Atlantic I have been told. They let the target get enough of a sniff to herd him into the path of a waiting accomplice and the tactic has apparently been working to perfection."

"Not to change the subject, but did Admiral Stark tell you that I want you to brief the brass here in a few minutes?"

"Yes sir. He even allowed me to practice on the navy brass. He also mentioned that you had instructed him to assign me to you and recall me to active duty. What am I going to be doing?"

"We will have to work that out as we go along, but basically you are going to be my sounding board until I can get the right people into positions where they can do some good. I asked the politicians to bump you up a grade. The scrambled eggs have a positive effect on a large number of people who might try to shunt you aside without them. There are going to be a large number of promotions in order to do the things that need to be done to bring our forces to a wartime footing. A lot of people will volunteer for service, but a lot will have to be drafted, some against their will, and the training will have to be quick and dirty. We need to get people involved in the war right away as a morale booster for those producing the equipment they will need."

"We had better head on down to the briefing room. I think most everyone will show up early anyway. There are going to be some civilians in the mix. Those in cabinet positions need to see the entire picture. I will caution everyone after the brief about keeping their mouths shut about where the information came from."

One of the Secret Service people went behind the desk and manipulated the wheelchair to head toward the door.

Roosevelt was so engaging that you forgot he was handicapped until he needed to move someplace.

As the President was wheeled into the briefing theater everyone stood at attention.

He waved everyone to their seats and took out his cigarettes and loaded one into the trademark holder. "You all know what happened a short while ago in Hawaii. I imagine you are all as short of information as I am. The sneak attack by the Japanese will have to be answered with force on our part. We can't even decide how to react until we know the extent of the damage, but there are a number of things we can do in preparation for what we know will be a large scale shooting war. I have been getting a lot of bad press lately about my handling of America's neutrality. Some even say I would do things to entice any of the belligerents to attack us. To some this will appear to be such an incident. Just to clear the matter up, I had no knowledge of today's attack until just over 24 hours ago. The gentleman with me is Corey Ward. He is a civilian assigned to the Navy Department as a communications intelligence watch supervisor. He is also a naval reserve Lieutenant Commander, who will be promoted either tomorrow or the next day and recalled to active duty. He will be assigned as my personal assistant. I have not done or said anything to influence the presentation he is about to make to you folks. This is the true story straight from the horse's mouth. It's all yours Corey."

"Good evening. What the President alluded to is a couple of intelligence assessments I put out yesterday, which is part of my charter as a section supervisor of a COMINT operation."

"I will caution you that what I am about to tell you is Top Secret. If the knowledge of how I came up with this information gets out it will set us back at least a couple of years trying to get back to where we are now. The Japanese use an obscure dialect of their language called Katakana. They transpose the ideographs to numbers and use them as a code, which it truly is not. We discovered what they were doing and figured they were trying to mislead us into thinking that was their primary code. We got enough valid information to confirm that they were actually using the code as a cypher. We have been exploiting this unexpected gift for more than six months. If they find out that we are reading their mail they will of course change the procedure, and we don't want that to happen."

"The two reports that I originated yesterday were based on COMINT intercepts and a bit of speculation. The first one actually was written on the evening watch the day before. It came about because two operators were chatting about sunny beaches, and that is not a euphuism for S.O.B's, on the circuit. Six Japanese aircraft carriers had been doing work-ups for the previous six weeks for a coming deployment. That is standard procedure for naval forces, especially things like aircraft operations and underway replenishments. At any rate, with the previous actions of the fleet units, and the fact that they were burning fuel at an alarming rate from stocks dangerously low, and the reference to sunny beaches, I concluded that they were going to attack some target to the south of the Japanese Islands. Now as you know, that covers a lot of territory. The most likely targets were Singapore, Hong Kong, the Philippines, and possibly some other islands down that way."

"The next day I was asked to brief the President, and I did that in the morning. I came back to my job site and stopped by the cafeteria and got a sandwich. I had just sat down at my desk when one of my best operators came to me and said he had something interesting. I told him to get it and bring it to the desk. What he had was a message off the Japanese civilian network they use for unofficial contact between sailors deployed and the home folks. The thing my operator told me had nothing to do with the message, but rather the fact that the message had been sent by an operator off one of the carriers we were trying to find. I decoded the message and found a lot of hello mom and pop, and how are the kids, but there was also a phrase in the message about gaijin, which is the way the Japanese refer to westerners."

"I have been studying Japanese for the past three or four years and while I am not fluent, I can interpret most of the things in the type messages we are interested in. I was amazed that a warship, obviously under radio silence, would allow such a message to be sent. My operator told me that the sender of the message was definitely one of the operators off the carrier Kaga."

"I told him that I didn't believe the C.O. or flag officer of the ship would allow such a thing to happen. He said that a majority of the better radio operators are members of the Amateur Radio Relay League, which is sort of a fraternity of communicators who are proficient at Morse code, and that they build their own equipment, which includes transmitters and receivers, and that those in command of the ship were not even aware that the message went out."

"Accepting his premise that the message had been sent as he suggested, it shed a little more light on what the Japanese might be up to. With the reference to Gaijin I figured the six carriers were going to hit U.S. bases in the pacific that could interfere with their moves in the South Pacific. That meant the Philippines, Guam, Midway, and Hawaii. Even though it was a lot of speculation I thought it warranted being sent out as a possible scenario. My boss, Admiral Keenan, agreed with me and when we briefed

Admiral Stark he also agreed. We then briefed the President. I had a hard time explaining how my operator could be so sure the message he copied was sent by an operator he had never seen. It is a hard thing to explain, but basically he knew who was sending the message by the way it was sent. I don't mean anything way out, just that one operator can identify another simply by listening to the way he sends Morse code. To most people it seems like witchcraft or black magic, but the reality is that experienced operators very seldom have to use call signs. Their correspondent on the other side of the circuit knows who they are talking to just as you would recognize someone's voice that you talk to regularly."

"Now all those things combined convinced me that I needed to write an intelligence assessment at least alerting people in those locations that they might be vulnerable to attack within two or three days. If I was wrong I might have a bit of egg on my face, but if I was right the advance notice could save a lot of lives, and possibly some valuable assets. I briefed the President late yesterday afternoon. He asked me when we would know for sure if they were going to attack or not."

"There was no hard and fast answer to that question, but based on how long they had been in radio silence, which was five days as of yesterday, they could have reached any of the targets I predicted they would strike, and I told the President this, also suggesting that there was no hard and fast evidence to support the assessment, other than the word of an insignificant COMINT operator who insists that he recognizes the person who sent the message."

"About all we could do was to notify the locations concerned to be alert for an attack by the Japanese within two days. That saved us three aircraft carriers which would have been anchored in Pearl Harbor with the rest of the fleet had they not been sent to sea to wait for developments."

"Now, while the things I did made me look like the good guy, you need to remember that we have units just like the one I work for in the Pacific, specifically at CINCPACFLT, and they didn't pick up on any of the things I just talked about, so the President had to take what I said on faith, at least enough to warn people about a possible attack. That was done yesterday afternoon."

The President picked up again. "Now, I must warn you all again of the classification of the information Corey just gave you. Not a word about it can get out, especially to the news people. For our part we will portray the event as a dastardly sneak attack on the Sabbath and without a declaration of war. I just wanted you folks to know what actually happened so that when you write your memoirs someplace down the road you will know the truth."

"What are our directions now sir?" an army general asked.

"Start preparing for war on all fronts. As mad as the American people are going to be, we are going to have to concentrate on Europe first. Things are not going so good on that front and the allies need our shipping to even feed the people. Our industrial output is going to have to be tripled at least, with half the labor force because of the troops we will need to get the job done. I say all this under the impression that Congress will declare war on Japan and that the Germans and Italians will stick with Japan and declare war on us, which in turn will allow us to declare war on them. Now I know this seems like a very low point in American history, which is absolutely true, but it will allow us to throw off the effects of the depression and put everyone back to work in a meaningful way. It will boost us off the floor and allow us to show the world our true capabilities. I am going to need at least two days to get things done. Congress has to take the first step with the authorization to declare war on Japan, which I believe is a foregone conclusion. We can then assess our losses and decide how we are going to fight the war."

One of the Army Generals asked if we were having any success with the German codes.

"I can't address that question sir. I know that my people aren't tasked to address that problem. I imagine the British and Russians, along with the Free French might be spending a lot more time than we are on the problem. However, I imagine now that we are about to jump into this war with both feet, we will devote a lot more effort to what is going on in Europe."

There was a lot more discussion about things I knew nothing about, but I listened and learned. I had never had any need to understand what the ground forces did, other than as it related directly to me, and in most of those instances it would be for gunfire support for an amphibious landing.

Now the conversations going on around me were about battalions, regiments, and armies, how they would be trained and how long it would take to train them; where they could be put to best use, and the logistics of the entire ball of wax. The President got my attention and motioned with his head for me to leave. I left the briefing with one of the Secret Service people and he told me the President would be out in just a moment.

When he came out we headed back to the Oval Office. "You handled that very well," he said. "You gave them the facts and then your suppositions, and most importantly you differentiated between them."

"I felt way out of my depth when they started talking about land warfare and building armies," I said.

"You know a lot more than you think. Didn't they teach tactics at the Naval Academy?"

"Yes sir, but they were tactics to use against an enemy at sea, or on the beach," I said.

"The principles are the same no matter where the battle takes place. You want to have more men, better equipped than your enemy, and you want your attack to be a surprise. Those are applicable to any battle, no matter where or what is being used to fight the battle."

"That's true at the most basic level, but devising a way to achieve those things is the hard part," I said.

"Those dying in the battle probably wouldn't agree with that assessment, but it is nevertheless true. We now have to start planning, both tactically and strategically, how we are going to engage the enemy. Keep in mind that we can't do this in a vacuum. We now have allies who will have to be consulted for most of our plans to use our forces. There are going to be times when we don't agree about how to approach a situation and those cases are going to need to be arbitrated by someone with a good head on their shoulders and an appreciation for what is possible and what is not possible. Just as soon as the chips fall into place with regard to the politics of this situation, I am going to send you to Europe to look things over. I want you to get a feel for how competent the big boys are. I am not talking about Churchill or Stalin, but the Generals and Admirals fighting the battles. Try to get a feel for their overall strategy and how realistic their plans are."

"Wouldn't Admiral Leahy be better suited to that task than me?" I asked.

"Oh, he will be doing the same thing you are. It's just that his perspective will be on overall strategy while yours will be geared more to the people actually doing the work."

"I suppose I am going to be spending the next few days studying Europe," I said.

The President laughed. "You will be spending a lot more time than the next few days on the problem."

"Get him a White House pass that is good anywhere, and let him keep his weapon. I don't think he will try to assassinate me," the President said to his senior agent.

To me he said, "I don't suppose you are independently wealthy?"

"Not with the salary I make," I said.

"I would like to have you close by, maybe in a hotel. If you can negotiate a good rate I will have the government pay for the room," he said.

I spent two hours the next morning getting a pass for the White House and another hour trying to arrange a room at the Willard Hotel, which was almost across the street from the White House. The rates were extravagant and I knew there was no way the government was going to foot the bill for a room there, even part time. I decided to look for lodging at one of the nearby bases. Or, I thought, I can try to convince the President that I am better off staying in my apartment, which is only about 15 minutes away.

Chapter 5

I was back at the White House by late morning and when the President got a break in his schedule he invited me into the office. "I am slated to give a speech tonight, or rather this evening, about the attack on Pearl Harbor. Congress has approved a declaration of war on Japan and that will provide the meat of the address. I want you to look over my speech to be sure I am not giving away too much. The announcement itself will not take very long, but the explanation about what it means to the nation will take quite a while. I met with Churchill this past summer to devise a strategy for supplying England until we inevitably entered the war. I don't want the speech to sound defeatist, but it must be realistic to prepare the people for the sacrifices that will need to be made and the back breaking work that it will take to win this war."

Allow me to pause at this juncture to explain a bit about how the President's schedule is managed, so as not to appear be overly enamored with my own importance in the overall scheme of the operation of our government, particularly as it relates to the President himself. Each service provides an aide to the President, who acts as the go between for his contact with officers of the different branches. The responsibilities include coordination with the Commanders of each branch for most of the day-to-day things that go on. If a medal is being presented by the President, for example, and the recipient is a member of the naval service, then the aide will notify all concerned as to time and place and procedures for the affair. If the President needs to see something that the navy has, then the aide will see to the requirement. Things like dinner invitations, seniority of individuals for seating arrangements, and a hundred other things keep the service aides busy.

What the President was going to use me for was outside the normal protocols and I had to grease the skids with the military aides to keep the peace. They each had desks of their own and had very little direct contact with the President.

"Did you find a hotel?" he asked.

"Sir, the prices are simple way out of my league and I only live 15 minutes away. I might be able to find a room at the Marine Barracks, which is even closer. I don't believe my staying in someplace like the Willard will send the message you want to deliver to the people anyway," I said, with what I thought as sound logic.

"Stay in your apartment for now. I will have a talk with some folks who might be able to assist with the problem. I want you to read this, and don't be bashful about making corrections. I did the rough draft and had the speech writer polish it up a bit. I did a run through and it is right at 30 minutes. Anything longer and I will lose the audience half way through and any shorter and people will say that I didn't give the matter enough due consideration," he said with a chuckle.

He pushed the speech to me across the desk. "Coffee?" he asked.

"Yes sir, thank you."

One of the detail poured the coffee as I stated reading. I only looked at the topic sentences the first time through. I then went back and read the speech in its entirety.

There was one paragraph where he tried to explain that we only learned about the attack the day before it was launched. I didn't think it needed to be in the speech, since it would key the newshounds to try to find out what we knew the day before. The speech was more political than military and was designed to get the American people behind the war effort.

I thought the phrase, 'a day that will live in infamy' was a stroke of genius and said as much. I explained that the paragraph dealing with when we knew what was not necessary to the speech. If the people view the falling bombs as the first indication we had that the Japanese were attacking it will keep them from asking a lot of questions that we would not answer anyway.

"That's a good point. Anything else?"

"I really like the day of infamy phrase," I said. "I also believe you could stress the fact that all Americans are in this together a bit stronger. Without a superhuman effort on the part of those in the industrial complex we cannot hope to succeed and it will give them pride in playing their part."

"I agree with that too. What we need is a catchy phrase for people to hang their hat on. Any suggestions?"

I gave the matter some thought. "Something like, 'we will show the world that Americans are the most productive people on this planet and when we are aroused no nation is our equal'. Maybe not those exact words, but something to inspire confidence that we will win this war and do it decisively."

"I like that too. Write it down and I will have the speech writer polish it."

"What time is the speech going to be broadcasted?"

"Six our time, which will make it the middle of the afternoon on the west coast. The networks have been announcing the time every 15 minutes so no one will miss it."

"Am I going to have an office, or continue to work out of the Navy Yard?"

"I would prefer to have you here when you are in town. Your promotion has been approved by congress so you can think about uniforms, though I don't want you to take that as an order to wear the uniform all the time. I think you will be much more effective around here in civvies. That way people will have to guess who you are and what your function is," he said.

He then turned to the head of his security detail and asked, "Is that office down the hall still vacant?"

"Not vacant, but only used for storage of extra desks and chairs. I think we can have the stuff pushed to one side of the room and make room for a working desk."

"Then do that. I have to brief some of the congressional leadership before the speech to let them know what to expect, so take the afternoon to do any personal errands that have stacked up," he said to me.

The office was almost full of extra office equipment. The Secret Service guy helped me move the desks to one side and we stacked the chairs on top of the desks to clear enough room for a single desk and two chairs, just in case I had company.

I didn't ask where the speech would be made from, but assumed it would be in the large conference room we had used for the briefing of the leaders about the assessment I did.

Once I got the desk situated the detail guy said he would have the administrators provide a typewriter and office supplies.

I left and went to my old office in the Navy Yard. I visited Admiral Keenan to find out what my status was.

"We've already replaced you as a section head. Your orders have been cut to recall you to active duty and assign you to the White House as an aide to the President. You won't need to worry about checking out here since you will still need your clearance and access to our spaces. I know you have probably heard this from a lot of other people, but the way you handled the situation with the assessments was really outstanding. I am going to put you in for a Navy Commendation Medal. The citation won't say much about what it is really for, but will look good on your record. I know that Admiral Stark is pleased with your work as well, and it doesn't hurt to have one of our own with the President's ear."

"I hope you understand that I can't serve two masters. As the Bible says, you will love one and hate the other, or words to that effect. My allegiance will shift to the President, but I will still provide any information that will make your job easier. My main function is still intelligence and I will be seeing a lot of you folks I am sure," I said.

"In one sense it is unusual for one as junior as you to find himself in the position you are in. On the other hand you will find out things that people would not think of mentioning to a flag officer."

"I think that is his take on the matter as well. He certainly will be getting enough information from the high ranking brass to make the decisions he will have to make. His words to me were that Admiral Leahy would provide input on those in the upper echelons and that I would be expected to evaluate those who would actually be doing the job."

"I don't have to tell you that is a lot of responsibility and to tread carefully in those waters," he said.

"No sir. I am very aware of the pitfalls."

"One of your first tests will come in just a short period of time. Have you heard of Bill Donovan?"

"I don't believe I have,'" I said.

"He is a friend of the President and will be offered the job of running the intelligence arm for the war effort. I don't know if they have decided what to call the outfit yet, but the idea is to have someplace where intelligence from all services is collated and then disseminated to those who need it."

"That makes sense to me," I said.

"While that is true, there is already a lot of animosity from some high ranking military officers who feel it is their prerogative to decide how to collect and disseminate intelligence within their own branches of service. What Donovan has going for him, in addition to being good friends with the President, is that he is filthy rich, and also has the Medal of Honor from WWI. He was, I believe, a Colonel at the close of the war. While he is now a civilian he is the Coordinator of Information for Roosevelt. He works out of New York but frequently visits the President. I am somewhat surprised that you have not encountered him yet. I imagine he will press for additional assets and power now that we are in the war."

"That's good to know. It will be interesting to see how the President handles my being around. He has me in an office down the hall from the Oval Office in a storage room. It is close enough that he can reach me at any time, and will give me a place to work on classified material. You know that he is giving a speech tonight at six eastern time don't you?"

"Yes that has been on the radio all day long. Anyone who misses that will have to have his head in the sand."

"He asked me to review his speech. I have no idea why, but he did the initial draft and then had the speech writer's work up a clean copy. It is one very powerful speech," I said.

"Why did he want you to review it?"

"According to him, to make sure he didn't divulge any information that would hamper our COMINT efforts. He had a statement that we knew about the attack the day before it happened and I convinced him to delete that paragraph. My thinking was that if the public thought the first we knew about the attack was when the bombs started falling it would be an easier pill to swallow, and if he had left that in we would have been hounded by the press until someone revealed how we knew and then our advantage over the Japanese would be lost. He understood what I was talking about and took that out. He asked if I had any more suggestions and I told him I thought he should stress the important role the civilians at home would be playing to supply the needs of the war machine. He bought that too and we tried to come up with a catchy phrase to boost the civilian pride. I really don't know why he asked my opinion, but I get the feeling that he is not nearly as secure in his thinking as he lets on. I have noticed he asks a lot of questions of people to make sure he understands what is being said. Inside I think he is as insecure as the rest of us. It's just that his decisions have a much greater impact than most of ours."

"The things you have done so far have really impressed him. Don't sell yourself short either. You came up with stuff that was available to others but nobody made the connection you did with the material. That puts you to the head of the line in his way of thinking, and I feel you deserve to be there. You have a good military grounding, a good head on your shoulders and you are not easily cowed by rank. Those are the attributes you need to do what I believe he wants you to do."

"I still feel way out of my league," I said.

"Just keep doing what you are doing and things will work out fine. You are going to be putting in some long hours though, so get used to that."

Chapter 6

I listened to the speech on the radio in my apartment. Even having read it through at least twice it still brought tears to my eyes hearing his delivery and the resolve in his words that Pearl Harbor would be avenged and America would stand against anyone who threatened her liberty and freedom.

I had taken my uniforms out of storage and checked to make sure they still fit. The trousers would need to be let out a couple of inches in the waist, but other than that things were fine. I would need new hats with the scrambled eggs and new piping on the jackets. I gathered all that needed to be altered and placed it in the sea bag to drop off the following morning.

I stopped by the uniform shop on the way in to the White House but it was not open at that hour. I would have to make another trip after they opened at 9:00 a.m. I had my new badge but I did not know all the Secret Service people, and they did not know me. I now wore my .45 in a shoulder holster and the guard stopped me at the entrance. He looked at the new pass and saw that it had just been issued the previous day. He called someone to verify that it was the real item before allowing me to enter the grounds.

When I walked by the Oval Office the Presidents detail head stopped me and said that the President had asked for me to come to the office when I arrived.

"Can I get a cup of coffee first, or will there be some in there?" I asked, pointing to the office.

He chuckled. "There's always coffee in there, and none of it more than an hour old. The man does like his coffee. Just as a note of caution, Bill Donovan is with him. You do know who Donovan is?"

"I got a bit of background on him yesterday from my Admiral. I think it was mostly true, though I could detect some resentment toward Mr. Donovan."

"There's a lot of that going around. I don't know who's right or who's wrong, but it is an interesting fight from where I sit. You on the other hand are going to be right in the middle of the fray. The one thing you cannot do is let Donovan get the idea that you are afraid of him. He is a trial lawyer and uses that tactic whenever he can to gauge reactions. Just be yourself and don't be afraid to tell him what you think. I don't think the President is going to have you working for him. With him maybe, but not for him. The President has indicated that you will be working directly for him and you are not subject to the orders of anyone below him in rank. Since he is the top dog, you answer only to him. That doesn't mean you can throw your weight around, but it does mean that he will back you 100 percent if you are in the right."

I was still in civilian clothing and wondered how that was going to go over with Donovan.

The agent knocked on the door frame and pushed the door open for me.

Roosevelt was sitting behind the desk in his wheelchair and Donovan was seated on the couch. Both had coffee and the detail guy poured me a cup as I shook hands with Donovan as the President made the introductions.

Donovan looked the part of a Wall Street tycoon. He was dressed in a tailored suit that probably cost more than I made in a year. His hair was neatly trimmed and he just oozed money. After we shook hands, the President said, "What did you think about the speech last evening?"

"It actually brought tears to my eyes, even after reading it at least twice beforehand."

The President chuckled. "I really appreciated your input. You picked up on a couple of very important points."

I got the impression the comment was for Donovan's benefit more than mine. I could see the questioning look in Donovan's eyes.

"Since you two have just met, let me tell you a bit about each other to make perfectly clear how I see each of your roles. Bill I have known for a long time, Corey. When it became obvious that we were going to get involved in the war in Europe we started putting the pieces in place to form an intelligence organization that would be responsible for all intelligence from all the services. I asked Bill to run that organization, which is now called the coordinator of information. That is not a very descriptive term, but Bill has been working on putting the pieces together for more than six months now. He works out of New York but that is going to have to change now that we are in the middle of the fray."

"Corey," the President said to Donovan, "Is the man responsible for the little bit of notice we did have about the Japanese attack. Corey was the supervisor of the COMINT section run by the Navy. You will have to ask him to explain how he arrived at the conclusions sometimes. It is fascinating. He briefed me twice before the day of the attack. The first brief just said that the Japanese were going to attack within three days some strategic targets in the Pacific. Some twelve hours later he wrote another report saying the Japanese were likely to attack the Philippines, Guam, Midway and Hawaii. That was the day before they launched the attacks. After the second brief I decided to have him stay for supper so I could pick his brain some about how he arrived at the conclusions he had drawn in the reports. We were discussing it at dinner and Eleanor asked how he could be sure about his information. He used everyday examples about how people interact to demonstrate how a Morse code operator can identify someone they have never seen or met before. He did a good job, because Eleanor understood exactly what he was talking about. It was at that time that I told her he was going to be one of my personal spies."

"You mean like Leahy?"

"Something on a much lesser scale than that. Corey is an academy graduate and has spent time at sea. He also took the time to learn Japanese and to copy Morse code almost as well as his operators do. He can get access to people who will be in on the planning of operations and get a feel for the likelihood of their success or failure. Leahy does that with the higher ups, but the ones who have to storm the beaches are the ones who really make or break any operation. You should know that as well as anyone."

"I get the impression that you are saying hands off to me," Donovan said.

"I'm glad we cleared that point up. He will be working directly for me and will not be subject to anyone else's orders. You may coordinate on things of mutual interest, and you may ask him for help in any of your endeavors, but you will not order his participation without my prior approval."

"You don't think the brass will ostracize him as the CINC'S errand boy?"

"I suppose they will, but I have every confidence that he can hold his own," the President said. "I just had him promoted to full Commander so he will have the scrambled eggs. Some people think that is important. He will be senior enough to have his say, but not so senior that those with stars will unduly worry about his opinions, which he will not express to them in any event, unless it bears directly on a situation that will cost lives."

"Will he continue to work out of the Navy Yard?"

"No. I have a little cubbyhole down the hallway where he can work when he is in town, but that will not be all that often. Eleanor made the comment that he was the only person in the entire government who seemed to know what was coming from the Japanese. There are a lot of people who prophesied a war with them, but most thought it would a good ways down the road. The first thing I want him to do is review our COMINT collection procedures and see how they can be improved upon. I know that you are concerned with that aspect of intelligence and I would expect the two of you to coordinate to come up with the best way to use our people."

"If that is going to be my first priority I would like to have one of the operators from my old section. He is probably the best Morse code operator we have anywhere in the navy. He can copy 40 words per minute and carry on a verbal conversation at the same time. His mind operates on an entirely different plane from the rest of us. If he hadn't recognized the operator from Kaga on the propaganda circuit we wouldn't have been any wiser about the attack. He, more than me, deserves the credit for what we came up with."

"What is his rank?" Donovan asked.

"He's a first class radioman with four years of service, but acts a lot older. All the other operators look up to him as the king of the hill," I said.

"If I might be so bold, a decoration and meritorious promotion to Chief Petty Officer will serve your purposes well if you take him along with you on your travels," Donovan said.

"I had planned to put him in for the Navy Commendation Medal, and the promotion will make it easier for us to hang around together if the President goes along with that," I said.

"I figured you would put him in for a medal, but now that it has come up, he will be invaluable to your efforts. I will ask Admiral Stark to promote him and detach him like we did with you. That still doesn't solve the problem about where to have you bunk while you are in town," the President said.

"What were you thinking, Franklin?" Donovan asked.

"I thought maybe the Willard, but Corey seems to think it will be more expensive than the government can afford."

"I have some contacts over there. I can probably get a break on the price, and if you really want to hide him you can say that he is assigned to me and funnel the cost of his lodging into my budget. I can then pay the bills without any questions about how the money is spent," Donovan said.

"That is a workable solution, as long as you remember who he really works for," the President said.

"I will contact them as soon as I leave here. I should have word for you this afternoon at the latest."

"If that is the way we decide to go, just get a two man room and J.C. and I can bunk together," I said.

"I'm glad I know how you meant that comment. Many people would have taken that the wrong way," Donovan said.

"Only those with dirty minds," the President said with a chuckle.

"I have to get some uniforms altered so I will stop by and have a talk with him. I believe he is on watch now, and I can kill two birds with one stone," I said.

"Now that the war is on, I am going to have to have some place nearby for training and as an intelligence center. I have been looking at the old Saint Elizabeth's sanitarium and it is ideally located. I don't know if it will give us enough room, but at least we can do most of the paperwork from there."

"Just out of curiosity, how many intercept operators does the army have?" I asked.

"I have no idea. They won't talk to me," Donovan said. "I am sure that General MacArthur has some but I don't know how many or how effective they are. I do know that we are going to have to put some procedure in effect to deal with the clearance and dissemination problem. The more people who know about a secret the more likely it is to leak, especially to someone specifically looking for just such information, as I am sure both the Germans and Japanese are," Donovan said.

"That is something that both of you need to consider, and the solution, or I should say the responsibility is not going to be delegated to any of the armed services. I really feel that is the area in which we now hold the advantage and I don't want to see it pissed away because of someone's ego," the President said.

"That seems to imply that you personally will make the decisions on who knows and who doesn't," Donovan said.

"If that is what it takes, then that is the way it will have to be. I simply will not have that kind of information passed around on reading boards because someone happens to wear stars. It is going to be disseminated on a strict need to know basis."

The President's personal detail were not cleared for the information, but they were, out of necessity, always around the President and were going to hear things. I thought that fact should be brought to the President's attention and said what I was thinking.

"You are absolutely correct Corey and I will have a word with all of them about the importance of this program. Now get out of here and let me get to work.

You," he said to me, "come see me when you get back so we can do some planning."

I drove to the Navy Yard and dropped my uniforms off to be altered.

"When do you need these?" the tailor asked.

"Yesterday would have been better but I will settle for close of business today. I also need to know what aiguillette is required for an aide to the President," I said.

"One of the most expensive ones. There's more gold on it than anything else in the inventory. I suggest you make sure you need it before you make the purchase. It will set you back about a month's pay."

"That's a good suggestion, and one I will follow. Can you have them done by this afternoon?"

"No problem. I will do the tailoring myself."

"Keep in mind my pauper status when you make up the bill."

He laughed. "It won't be much and they will be ready any time after an hour from now."

I went to the Intel spaces and stopped by to see Admiral Keenan.

"I got the word to transfer one of your operators to you. He is on watch now and hasn't been told. I thought you might want to do that."

"I also want to put him in for a Navy Commendation Medal. Will I need to work that up or will admin take care of it?"

"He's also going to be made a chief meritoriously. I suggest that we get all the paperwork for him and for your award and let the President make the presentations."

"I need to go tell J.C. what is happening. If you have a bit of free time I would like to get some information from you about my coming assignment."

"Stop back when you are finished."

I told J.C. what was going on. "I should have consulted you first but I figured you wouldn't turn down a promotion to Chief, even if you had to take on the Japanese single handedly."

"You're right about that, but I don't know how I am going to be able to help you," he replied.

"Who knows more about radio's than you?"

"Not many, I admit, but that is an entirely different ball game from setting up a navy network of intercept operators."

"You are going to have to expand your horizons. We are not just talking navy, but the entire war effort. You will do all right. I expect you could sit there now and rough out a plan that would take others days or even weeks to produce. You know communications and that is the knowledge I need to help me get through this. We will have a small office in the White House and will be quartered in the Willard Hotel, compliments of our government. The only drawback is that you can't write home about it and rub other's noses in the smelly stuff."

"You are going to be advanced to RMC and get a medal, probably tomorrow. You can go with me to the ships store and order chief's uniforms now."

"Really! Man that's great. I figured another two years, even with a war going on."

"I got promoted to Commander and that's way ahead of what I could otherwise have expected as well. We will be earning our keep though."

We stopped by the supervisor's desk, and told the new watch supervisor what was going on. We then swung by Admiral Kennan's office and he handed me two award citations and the promotion paperwork for each of us. "We will retain your records here with a notation that you both are on special assignment to the White House. Admiral

Stark thought that would be the easiest way to deal with the situation. The administrative people at the White House can provide the funding data and we will cut orders to wherever they tell us."

"Thanks a lot Admiral. I appreciate all you have done for me."

"I know a rising star when I see one. Just be careful in that minefield you are entering. Good luck to you too chief," he said, shaking hands.

"I sure like the sound of that word," J.C. said.

"Just do us proud in the future," the Admiral said.

We went to the exchange and picked up my uniforms. J.C. told the tailor he needed a complete set of Chief's uniforms for a radioman chief.

He took some measurements and said, "I think we can outfit you right off the racks. 33 waist and 31 length. Shirts size 15. You are going to need brown shoes as well. I can have it all ready in a day."

"How am I going to pay for all this?" J.C. asked. "I don't have that kind of money."

"The government gives you a clothing allowance along with the promotion. Of course it is not nearly enough to pay for all you need, but it helps. Take your orders to disbursing and they will give you the clothing allowance, and probably advanced pay to cover the difference. Let me total it up and you will know what you need," the tailor said.

After some figuring he said, "The bill is going to be just over four hundred dollars. They give you three hundred so you only need to come up with a hundred and change."

"I can write them a check for the difference and you can pay me back," I said.

We visited disbursing and got the clothing allowance for J.C. I asked about any allowance for officers promoted to field grade rank, not expecting that there would be any such provision. Much to my surprise I was told that there was a provision for anyone assigned as an aide to a flag officer for the extra things he would need.

"Does the President count as a flag officer?" I asked, trying for a bit of levity.

"Absolutely, and you get an additional ration allowance as well."

"Well both of us are going to be working directly for the President, so sign us up for all we are entitled to," I said.

The cost of the aiguillette was almost $50 and the additional rations allowance was nearly $30 per month.

Chapter 7

I took J.C. back to the White House with me. I had to sign him in. I had been assigned a parking space within the grounds which would not only make it easier to get around but would provide overnight parking so when we were at the hotel we wouldn't have to worry about the car.

We went to the Oval Office and had to wait until the President got finished with his appointment.

"The chief is going to need a pass like mine," I told one of the detail.

"Is that his service record you have?"

"No it's his promotion papers and a medal citation," I said.

"Give me the promotion papers and I can have Admin take care of it minus the picture. When you are finished here we can get the picture and the badge will be ready five minutes later," he said.

I passed the folder on to him and he headed for Admin.

A few minutes later the President finished with his appointment and we were shown into the office.

I introduced Chief Carter and the President shook hands.

"First let me say what a fine piece of work you two did over the last few days. Second, I suppose Corey, I should say Commander Ward, has given you some background about what you two will be doing."

"Yes sir, but not in detail. I know radio's and communications, but not a lot else about how the military operates, just so your expectations are not too high," J.C. said.

"I'm not worried, I trust Corey's judgement. If he thinks you can do the job then that is good enough for me."

"On another subject, Bill Donovan called and said that you could check into the hotel anytime. Just give them your names and they will show you to your rooms. I believe he actually got two rooms connecting in case one or the other of you needed privacy for any reason. He didn't tell me the cost, but the bills will be paid from his budget. That includes meals at the hotel restaurant but does not include booze."

"Are we going to keep the rooms while we are travelling?" I asked. "There may be times when we are away for significant periods."

"I would say yes. Otherwise you will be moving stuff to storage and back an inordinate number of times. He probably got a good rate by the month or something. Don't worry about it."

"I am going to have you go to Europe in the very near future. I want to wait until all the declarations of war are on the table and we know for sure who we will be dealing with. I will send a letter of introduction with you for Admiral Leahy. You can fill him in on all the particulars. I will basically tell him that you two are working for me directly so that he will be open and above board with you. I expect that I will be bringing him back here to make greater use of his military mind in the near future," he continued.

"I am going to do some preliminary research here in the area before we go to Europe. How will I handle getting access to the high ranking people I will need to talk with?" I asked.

"I will issue each of you a letter on White House stationery designating you as my personal representatives and certifying your clearance for anything of any classification. And while we are on the subject of security, have you given any thought to how to address the program that you will be putting in place?"

"We need a codename specifically for each section of the program. The efforts against the Japanese might be called magic, or witch craft. The program against the Germans probably already has a name supplied by the British, but if they don't, then something like starlight or salamander. The Italians we can deal with separately based on their role in the war. The intercept operators and analysts are going to need to have the proper clearances but I don't see anyone below flag rank even having knowledge of the existence of the program unless they have a specific need to know. I would suggest that you be the arbitrator in those instances with maybe Donovan handling the paperwork and giving you his recommendations for those to be given access."

"I like that approach. It will provide a central location for keeping track of who's involved and still give me the responsibility for the decisions as to who has access."

"Stop by here first thing in the morning and we will do the presentations and promotions. I will have letters of introduction for both of you by morning. If you have any trouble getting an appointment with any of the military brass have them call me," he said.

We got J.C.'s picture taken and got him his badge. As we left the White House I told J.C. "If you have a car I suggest you find someplace to leave it. Nobody has said anything yet, but I think a rationing program will be instituted very soon for items associated with the military needs. I know for sure that gas and probably rubber will be the first things considered. Parking is another problem if we have two cars. I have a parking spot and we can use my car for any needs either of us have."

"What should I do about my apartment?" J.C. asked.

"The President just told us that we have permanent rooms in the hotel, so there's no sense in paying for an apartment that you will not be using," I said. "I am going to let my place go just as soon as I get my personal stuff moved out. I rented the place furnished so I don't have to worry about furniture."

"Same with me. If you will drop me back at the Navy Yard I will pick up my car and go get my stuff."

"Let's check in at the hotel first so we will know where to take our luggage when we come back," I said.

Since the Willard was just a short distance we walked there from the White house.

As we walked I told J.C., "You want to check out a pistol from the Navy Yard. I suggest a shoulder holster like mine. I don't know that we will be in a situation to need them, but I do know that we will be transporting classified material from one place to another and the regulations require that we be armed, so rather than checking out a weapon every time we need one it will be more convenient to carry them all the time."

When we walked into the hotel we got a few curious glances. J.C. was still in his dress blues and I was in civvies with a sport coat hiding the .45.

We went to the desk and I gave our names to the desk clerk and was told to wait while he checked with the manager.

In a short while the manager came out and grabbed two keys and told us to follow him.

He led us to the elevator and pressed the button for the third floor. The rooms were at the end of the corridor.

"Mr. Donovan suggested a room with two beds but I told him I would let him have two single rooms for the same price, so you each have your own room for any private matters that you might encounter. Mr. Donovan is taking care of all expenses so if there is anything at all you need just call the desk."

"Neither of us drinks heavily, but we do take an occasional drink and if we happen to be entertaining guests there might be a need for some whiskey," I said.

"The bars in both rooms are stocked with the usual ingredients for popular drinks. If you find you need additional materials just call room service. There will be no charge for the alcohol unless you have some large group and require additional drinks. Mr. Donovan requested a private phone for you Mister Ward. He also intimated that the President might visit occasionally and that we exercise sound judgment with regard to whom he was visiting."

"I think he might have told you that to get into a better position for bartering. I can't imagine why the President would visit me. That usually works out that he sends a summons and the summoned appears when he orders," I said.

The manager smiled. "Still, one working directly for the President deserves to have his private time as comfortable as it can be. Mr. Donovan did tell me that you answer only to the President, and one in that position might have occasion to put in a good word for our humble establishment if the opportunity arises."

J.C. burst out laughing. "I'm only a chief, and that only happened today, but I think I am going to like the perks."

"I didn't ask what you gentlemen will be doing for the President, but if you will be working with Mr. Donovan then I can guess that you have something to do with intelligence, and I know enough not to ask questions. If you need anything at all, don't hesitate to ask."

The rooms were not what you would call suites but they were large enough to accommodate a couch, a coffee table and a couple of overstuffed arm chairs.

I dropped J.C. off to get his car and went on to my place to pack up my few belongings. By the end of the day both of us had our complete wardrobe in our rooms.

We had supper in the hotel and sat around my room talking about an approach to the problem the President had saddled us with.

"What do you know about the European war?" J.C. asked.

"Very little, other than what I read in the paper and that doesn't paint a rosy picture for the allies," I said.

"I am referring to the silent war," he said.

"You mean COMINT?"

"Yes. I have been an amateur radio operator since I was in my teens and I followed what was going on in the nether world. The crypto system the Germans, and probably the Italians, are using goes back to just after the First World War. I forget the name of the guy who came up with it, but it was the first system that I know about that was what you would call a true cryptographic cypher. It was developed commercially and took several tries before the designers got it to a point that governments were interested in it. If I am boring you, just say so."

"I'm all ears," I said.

"Well once it came into widespread use, and by that I mean that enough people were using it to warrant looking for ways to break it, a couple of Polish mathematicians started to work on ways to break the codes sent on the machine. I think that happened in 1932 or 33. The Poles were very afraid of the Russians and the Germans, both of whom used the system. The machine is called ENIGMA. The first versions used three sets of rotors mounted on a single spindle. The three wheels all had the 26 letters of the English alphabet plus, in later versions, the numbers one through nine."

"The machine has notches on the cypher wheels so that they can be moved to the proper setting as the key. The machine has a series of plugs and a display of lights which would light up when the machine was in use and the letter punched on the typewriter keys would light up the appropriate light. This was so the operator would know that he had made the proper entry. The plug setting was usually good for a month, so all the messages for that month would use the same plug setting."

"When the system first came into widespread use the key would be transmitted as a three letter group and repeated as the second group of letters. This would tell the recipient how to set up the machine to decrypt the message, which was just the reverse of the encryption process."

"The number of variables in a cryptosystem dictate how secure the system will be. If you use straight substitution, letter for letter and have a good data base to work from the code can be broken pretty fast. I am talking about as few as four or five messages. In that system the frequency of the same letters appearing in the message leads to analysis of the frequency of the letters that appear. E being the most used letter is pretty easy to find. Then you just go down the list of letters and soon you have enough to put the message together and find out what the other letters represent. Having said that, decrypting a single message using that system is very difficult because you don't have enough of a base to work from."

"The poles had one of the machines and took it apart to see how many variables there would be, then employed mathematics to arrive at that number. I think I remember that with just the three wheels and the plugs there were well over half a million variables. Later, as more wheels were added to the unit, the task became something like millions."

"The Poles who worked on exploiting the system kept the secret until, I believe, 1937. When they became convinced that either the Russians or the Germans had designs on the country they did what most anyone in their position would do. They informed the British and French that they had broken the code and said that they would supply each of them with one of the machines and a copy of their work."

"That last part is not common knowledge. I learned about it from a British radioman while I was in port in England in 1939. I had talked to him on the radio, Morse code, and we arranged to have a drink together in Portsmouth. He had a few more than I did, but we were both into amateur radio and he gave me the gist of what I just related to you. He also told me that the British COMINT effort was headquartered at GC&CS which stands for Government Code and Cypher School. He had orders to go there in just over a month."

"I think what that means is that the British are reading some of the German military traffic, but I have no idea how much. If we go to Europe we are going to have to talk to them, and I am not sure how to do that without telling them that one of their radiomen ran off at the mouth two years ago," J.C. said.

"You say the machine is called ENIGMA?"

"You got it. I am also pretty sure that there are multiple variants of it."

"I wonder if any of our guys know about that."

"I don't believe they do. I haven't heard anyone mention it, and based on what we know about the Japanese if they did they would surely have made a comparison."

"I wonder how much the President knows."

"That might be a question to ask either him or Donovan," J.C. said.

"I think we should pose that same question to whoever is in charge of COMINT operations for our different branches of service. I don't believe we need to give them what you just gave me, but it will be interesting to see if any of them know about the history of the ENIGMA machine."

"You don't think Donovan would have our rooms here bugged do you?"

"I hadn't thought about it, but I think he is capable of doing that if he feels it will enhance his position with the President."

J.C. went to the telephones and took them apart to see if anything was there that shouldn't be. "The phones are okay, unless someone can bug them at the trunk line."

He made the rounds in both our rooms, taking pictures down, taking lamps apart, and removing cushions from the chairs and couch. He even looked under the beds.

"I don't see them if they are there. Just the same I think we might treat the rooms as if someone else is listening," he said.

"That's for sure."

"Roosevelt met with Churchill this past June. I wonder if Churchill might have mentioned the ENIGMA problem to him."

"It wouldn't hurt to ask."

"What are you going to do about your car?"

"There are several people in our old watch section who could use a car. I think I might try to sell it to them as a community asset, each paying a third or fourth of the asking price. I don't believe it is worth more than about $300. That wouldn't hurt them too badly, and would provide transportation for them."

"Your benevolence humbles me," I said.

"Repeat that in English."

"It simply means that you are a good guy," I said.

We both drove to the Navy Yard and went up to our old stomping grounds.

As we neared Admiral Keenan's office I told J.C. "You go do your thing and stop back here when you are finished."

The Admiral's door was open and the secretary motioned for me to go on in. I knocked on the door frame and walked into his office.

"So how are things going so far?"

"Okay, I suppose. J.C. and I are ensconced in the Willard Hotel at government expense. I have a parking spot at the White House and J.C. is now trying to unload his car to some in the watch section. We will only need one, and I have a feeling that we will not be spending a lot of time in this area. The President is going to tell us what he has in mind in the morning."

"Is there anything you need from me?"

"I would like to know what you know about a crypto system called ENIGMA," I said.

"I don't know that I have ever heard of it," he replied.

"It was invented just after WWI and has been in use by various governments and companies since about 1928 or 29. It is an electromechanical system that has three alphabet wheels mounted on a single spindle. The initial setting is usually sent with the message so the receiving unit will know how to set the machine up to break the message. With the plug board that comes with it that provides 26X26X26X26 variables for each letter encrypted. That provides about half a million variants."

"Why are you so full of such information?" he asked.

"Because that is the system the Germans are using and I was told that the Poles learned how to defeat the system around 1933 and passed that information on to the French and British in 1939. They also provided each of them one of the code machines."

"How did you learn this?"

"J.C. told me. He was on a destroyer in Europe in 1939 and he struck up a friendship with one of the British radiomen. They had a few drinks and since both were members of the Amateur Radio Relay League they talked about radios while consuming a few beers. The British seaman told J.C. about the machine, which was commercially available since 1928 or so. It has been in widespread use since them. The Poles realized that they were next on either Stalin's or Hitler's invasion list and passed the information and the machines on to the British and French."

"And you conclude that the British are reading Hitler's mail?"

"If they aren't then they are not as smart as I have been giving them credit for," I said.

"What are you going to do with the information?"

"I'm going to ask the President if Churchill happened to mention that little tidbit to him last June when they met. His answer will determine what I have to do after that."

"You reason that since we are now into the war phase that we should have access to their intelligence?"

"Yes sir, and we are going to set up pretty strict procedures for access to the Japanese decrypts. I imagine there will be a quid pro quo for accessing their data."

"Who is going to control access to those programs?" the Admiral asked.

"Bill Donovan is going to maintain the records, but the President will be the only one who can approve access to the intercepts. I have been tasked to come up with the procedures for accomplishing that, and I think he wants to see that before I start my travels to Europe."

"The only three locations I know about for the actual copying of their COMMS is here, the Philippines and Hawaii. We have about 50 people on our list and I imagine Hawaii has about the same number, though it could be higher now considering the circumstances. We have a Commander by the name of Wenger who has been the mouthpiece for extolling the virtues of COMINT since the early thirties. He was primarily responsible for our being as prepared as we are for what is to come. MacArthur probably has some operators dedicated to the task on Corregidor, though I don't know this for sure. I do know that he is provided with the intercepts from Hawaii by courier at least twice a week. If you follow that line of reasoning, then he must have people dedicated to the task. There is a special code used for passing the time critical stuff via Morse code. The code name for the information is MAGIC."

I simply had to laugh.

"What's so funny?" the Admiral asked, somehow not amused by my levity.

"The President asked me what we would call this information and I told him either witchcraft or magic. I did not know that was what we called it already."

"We don't put the code word on any of the information we pass to him at present. We are probably going to need to do that to keep track of messages."

J.C. knocked on the door frame and walked into the office. He came to attention and the Admiral waved him to a chair.

"The Commander here was just telling me about your amazing storehouse of knowledge," he said, in an oblique way telling me to use J.C.'s rank, not his initials.

He colored a bit at the remark. "Sir, it isn't like the ENIGMA is secret. It has been on the commercial market for about 20 years. Many of the amateur radio operators talk about it routinely and speculate about the odds of someone breaking it."

"I apologize if I embarrassed you Chief. That was not my intention, but rather an affirmation that the Commander made a good decision to bring you into this."

"If you will pardon the French, sir, that machine is really a bitch to deal with. I am talking about it being so cumbersome that the operators sometimes get confused themselves. Others don't want to spend all the time to set the machine up and take shortcuts. I think that is where most of the success is going to come from in exploiting that system. It is my understanding that the Germans use it for all their sensitive traffic. There are probably multiple keys for each branch of service, and probably, by now, a lot of variants, so it will not be a simple matter of breaking one rendition and applying that to everything else."

"I appreciate the lesson. I am sure that the information will come in handy somewhere in the not too distant future."

"Who is the current commander of Marine Corps signals?" I asked.

"That would be Col. Keller Rockey, and no I did not give his last name first. His last name is Rockey. His office is at Eighth and I, where the Commandant hangs his hat."

"I am going to try to get an appointment to talk to him tomorrow. Would it be better for me to make the appointment or have someone like you grease the skids?"

"I think you should see how seriously the brass takes your appointment as a mouthpiece for the Commander in Chief. That will be a good indication of how much opposition you will face."

"Then I guess that is what I will do."

The Chief and I went back to the White House.

The Secret Service guy motioned me over. "He told me to catch you if you came back in today. He is with Secretary Knox now, and I think he wants to introduce you two." He knocked on the door and opened it.

We went inside and Frank Knox stood to shake hands.

"The President has been telling me about you and what he has planned. Do you have any reservations about the tasking?"

"No sir, only that it is a lot of responsibility for one not used to wielding that kind of power."

"What do you plan to do first?"

"I believe the President has indicated that he wants us to go to Europe and assess the situation there. I define my role, based on the guidance that the President has provided, as looking at the nuts and bolts and trying to streamline the things we do or are planning to do."

"Can you give me an example?"

"Yes sir. I was going to ask this question anyway. Mr. President, when you met with Mr. Churchill in June did he mention anything about ENIGMA?"

"What's that?"

"That is the code machine that the Germans use for all their encrypted message traffic."

"How do you know this?" he asked.

"Because the machine has been available on the commercial market since the early 20's. Since the Chief here is more familiar with it than I am, let him explain it."

J.C. went through much the same lecture he had given me.

"The problem is not the machine so much as it is the flexibility of it. Just by changing the settings the same machine can be used for all branches of the military as well as other government agencies. The Polish scientists broke the code in 1933 by reverse engineering the ENIGMA machine, and passed that on to the British and French when it became inevitable that they would be invaded by either Russia or Germany."

He went through the mechanics and the number of possible variants.

"Mr. Churchill neglected to mention that little tidbit to me, just as I forgot to mention that we were reading what the Japanese sent on their circuits. I imagine we could interest them in an exchange of methods," he said.

"There is a code name for the Japanese intercepts, and believe it or not, it is MAGIC," I said.

"And you did not know that when we had our little discussion?"

"No sir. Admiral Keenan told me this afternoon."

Secretary Knox asked, "What do you plan to do first?"

"Get some education. I want to talk to the people in charge of COMINT within all branches of the military, and probably the diplomatic community as well to see where we stand now, then try to build a strawman of where we need to be. I will then try that out on the President and with his blessing, brief the senior of the parties concerned. One thing I already know we will need is a school to train our intercept operators. The bureaucracy is not going to stand for us taking the cream of the crop of their communicators, and we need the cream of the crop," I said.

"That is a good point. I know that the President has told you that you have a free hand, but do not neglect to keep people like myself informed. I do not expect that you will divulge your reasoning or even the choices, but you will find the brass more inclined to cooperate if you make them think they had an input into the decision making process."

"I will put that to the test tomorrow. I need to talk to all the services to determine what they have as a baseline for what will be needed. I had planned to call General

Holcomb tomorrow to set up an appointment with Col. Rockey, his signals guru."

"I don't believe you will have any opposition from him. He was at the brief you did about the assessment, but if you need to bandy my name about you can tell him that you discussed it with me and I agree. I really believe the letter the President is going to provide will open most doors. The amount of cooperation is another matter entirely, but they will at least have to talk to you."

The President took the two letters out of his in box and handed them to me. "Those are the originals. I have copies on file here."

"What kind of time line do I have for the trip to Europe?" I asked.

"I would like to see you do that no later than next Monday. The declarations of war will come out within the next couple of days and I want that done before you leave for Europe. I want you to touch base with Admiral Leahy first and get his take on the other heavyweights over there."

"Is he going to be in London, or will we have to go someplace else?" I asked.

"I will send him a message and ask him to be there and give him your names. You can explain what your mission involves."

When we left the White House that afternoon we were both awed by the complexity of what we had been tasked to do.

"When we finish with the Marine Corps tomorrow you can start making arrangements to get us to London. Get the funding data from the White House Admin section and take it to the Navy Yard. Have them cut orders authorizing the highest priority for flights, the authority to go anywhere and do anything, and certify our clearance as the highest we have."

"What about money?"

"Have them authorize advanced pay. We are going to need to bunk someplace and a hotel is probably the best option. Food will eat up a good bit, so plan for two weeks away. We can always draw additional funds from any disbursing office."

The next morning we went to our little cubby hole of an office, which at least had a door and a coffee pot. A telephone was on both desks. I had not used mine and I picked it up and listened for a dial tone. Instead I got an operator. "What can I do for you Commander?"

"I need to talk to General Holcomb of the Marine Corps."

"I will ring you when I have him on the line," she said.

I hung up the phone and less than a minute later it rang.

I picked it up and General Holcomb was on the line.

"Sir, this is Commander Ward. I briefed you and others here at the White House last week. I wonder if I might stop by for a visit when you have a hole in your schedule."

"You mean like today?"

"Yes sir."

"The only time I have free is the lunch hour. Could I offer you some lunch to discuss whatever we need to talk about?"

"Yes sir. I will have Chief Carter with me. I also need to speak with Col. Rockey if possible."

"I take it this is official Presidential business?"

"Yes sir, very much so."

"Okay, be here at 1130."

"I think we are going to need uniforms for this trip," I said.

"That will help me to realize that I am really a CPO. My mind hasn't caught up with that yet," J.C. said.

97

I got the White House operator on the line again and told her that we would not be available until after lunch if anyone should inquire.

Chapter 8

We then went to the Willard and changed into uniforms and had a cup of coffee waiting for the clock to move around to 1100.

We were a bit early and sat in the lounge area waiting for General Holcomb to get free. He saw us a few minutes early and told his aide to order lunch for all of us.

Once we were seated at the conference table in his office he said, "Okay, what can I do for you?"

"The President has tasked us to put together a plan for exploiting communications of both Japan and Germany. We already have a small group at the Navy Yard that does that, plus an unknown number in Hawaii. I haven't spoken with the Army yet, so I have no idea what they are doing. The reason I want to talk with Col. Rockey is to find out what the Marine Corps has along those lines and figure out how to put this all together to form a centralized collection effort so our operators aren't concentrating all their efforts on the same thing."

"I don't know that we have any people dedicated to doing what you suggest, but the President obviously thinks it has merit if he has tasked you to come up with a plan," General Holcomb said.

"Are you familiar with any of the European operations?"

"Specifically what?"

"Their COMINT efforts," I replied.

"No. I think our primary focus is going to be on the Pacific and that is where I have my people directing most of their attention."

"Chief, give the Commandant the scoop on ENIGMA."

"You are talking about the German crypto system?"

"Yes sir, but that is something of a misnomer. Go ahead, Chief, just like you laid it out for the President."

J.C. told General Holcomb how the crypto system had come into being and how it had progressed to the point that it was the single most important cryptosystem in the German inventory.

J.C. didn't mention that the British had broken some of the codes. I guess he wanted to leave that to me as the final nail in the presentation.

"The thing is that the British are reading some of Germany's message traffic. They have not deigned to inform us of that fact, just as we have not informed them of the fact that we are reading the Japanese's coded traffic."

"The President feels that both those facts are probably the most important thing we have going for us at this time, and he does not want any chance of that information getting back to either the Germans or Japanese. He wants a structured COMINT effort with very tight security and trained operators to copy the circuits that are of most interest to us. That puts me in the position of having the cart before the horse. I need to know the volume of traffic we will need to exploit before I can determine the number of operators to do the job. On the other hand, I can't determine the number of operators until I know the volume of traffic we need to copy. I thought the best approach would be to determine what we have right now and extrapolate to a degree in order to set a training pipeline to get the required operators."

The steward brought the food and I shut up until he had served the food and left the room.

General Holcomb said a quick grace and we dug into the food.

"How long have the limey's been reading the German mail?"

"At least since 1939. I can understand them keeping a tight lid on that effort, and we must do the same for the Japanese. The source is just too valuable to even take the slightest chance that it will be compromised. The President is going to have Bill Donovan... You do know who Bill Donovan is?"

General Holcomb nodded affirmative.

"Donovan is going to keep the security files on everyone privy to the program and the President is going to exercise sole responsibility for the decisions as to who is briefed and who is not. I would expect that except for the people doing the actual work, the list will be made up almost entirely of Flag Rank officers."

"What about the German stuff?"

"I am going to have to iron the wrinkles out of that starting next Monday. We already have flight arrangements to London. Admiral Leahy will try to help me out over there but the President's thought is to offer a quid pro quo for the Japanese intercepts."

"I can see how the concept should work, but I am not sure you are going to have the horsepower to put it in motion."

"That's not my decision to make. I am going to study the problem and give the President a recommendation as to how to do what he wants done. If he buys the approach he will order that it be implemented through the service chief's if necessary."

"I hope to be able to point out the advantages of working together, and here I am talking about our own service components, to accomplish a common goal."

"How will that work?"

"The army will concentrate on army traffic, the Navy on naval traffic, and the Marines on whatever seems to best fit their tasking at the time. I know I am not telling you anything new, but the Germans are going to get the bulk of our attention to begin with. The amphibious landings that I know you and your people are already planning play second fiddle until we can establish a foothold in either Southern Europe or North Africa. I expect there will be some amphibious landings in the European theater before pushing the Japanese back to their home islands."

"Who and how will you determine which is army traffic and which is navy traffic?"

"You ball Chief," I said.

"The short answer is that they use different procedures. We can also tell from the type of traffic they send. Call signs are used to identify them one to another, and the type of chatter also comes into play. A good operator can differentiate almost immediately. We will need to set up a central location for decoding the traffic and doing what we call traffic analysis. That term covers everything that happens on a circuit except for the actual messages they send. We have to keep track of things like frequency changes, and new people on a net. The list is pretty long. But the bottom line is that our analysts can tell pretty much which net is which as they look at the traffic. They make notes and provide these back to the operators as an aid in helping him to do his job."

"Where are the operators going to come from?"

"We already have a cadre of experienced operators like myself who were pulled from the fleet. Being an intercept operator is a lot different from being a regular radio operator. If a regular operator misses something, or copies something he is not sure about he simply asks the operator on the other end of the circuit to repeat. An intercept operator can't do that. He has to learn to copy through static and overrides by other communications and even guess at what was sent if he feels confident that the character is one of maybe two or three. He then underlines the character so the analyst will know that he is not 100 percent sure about the letter. A good operator also copies behind the letters streaming constantly across the air waves. I usually copy three or four characters behind so if the sending operator makes an error and stops to correct it I still have clean copy of the actual message when he finishes. We are going to have to set up our own facilities for training the operators, and I have no idea where those will be."

"Let me call Col. Rockey and have him join us here," General Holcomb said. He used the intercom and told his secretary to ask Col. Rockey to join him.

It was not five minutes later that Col. Rockey knocked on the door.

He came in and reported in the prescribed manner.

General Holcomb then introduced us and said, "You have the floor Commander."

"I have been tasked by the CINC to come up with the requirements for COMINT operators for the war effort. I am here to find out what you currently have and what you think your needs will be for the next three, four or five years. First question is, do you currently expend any effort trying to exploit enemy communications?"

"Do you mean officially or informally?"

"Either or both. I need to know what capability you have and what you believe you will need to carry out the tasking that is surely to come the Marine Corps' way. We then have to figure out where we will find the people to train and where and how they will be deployed. I asked Secretary Knox who to talk to in the Marine Corps to get that information and he gave me your name. I then called General Holcomb and outlined my tasking to him. If this sounds as if I am bumbling around in the dark then you have me pegged," I said.

"Who are you doing this for?"

I took out my letter from the White House and showed it to the Colonel.

He handed it back and I showed it to General Holcomb.

"In answer to the first question, my charter is to provide the people and equipment to carry out the functions of all forms of communication for the Corps in whatever theater we find ourselves. We have standing orders that lay out equipment and manpower requirements for any of 20 or 30 scenarios. Those include squads operating independently on reconnaissance missions to companies, battalions, and divisions operating in a combat environment. I have the responsibility for all the crypto equipment and communicators for those purposes. We have no formal tasking for communications intelligence collection but we do educate our operators on the need for security and circuit discipline."

"Since sometime in the early thirties we have had some people involved in COMINT. I don't know the extent, or how many of our people are involved, but I do know that some were trained here in the District as early as 1930. What they do is always hush-hush, but some of the senior enlisted operators have talked about them being able to read the old Japanese code. I think they changed to a different one some half a dozen years ago. I don't know what the status of the effort is. Seems that those who get any training as intercept operators are shipped to the Pacific. The Marines do not have any tasking for intercept operations but helps the navy out instead.

Chief Carter said, "Assume you have just conducted a landing on a hostile beach. You have established a beachhead and need to evaluate the intensity of the enemy facing you. What do you think would give you the best indication of their strength?"

"I suppose sending out reconnaissance units at different locations along the skirmish line."

"If you had a COMINT unit that had been concentrating on short range communications from the beach even before you made the landing do you think this would provide any advantage to you?"

"If they could tell me what we were facing, obviously."

"That's the kind of thing we are talking about here. A good COMINT operator can give you some indication as to the size and complexity of what you will be facing long before you hit the beach, based on the communications of the enemy force. It will not always be cut and dried, but some information is better than none. Those are the kinds of things we need to quantify before we can come up with any plan that makes sense. You can look at it as reverse engineering. The things that you would want to protect, the enemy will likely want to protect. And the things you want to know are the things he would want to know. It isn't scientific but will give us some baseline data to work with. We have to do this across the entire spectrum of all our forces, so if you don't want the Marine Corps to come crying later about not having enough support then you should be very diligent in outlining what your needs are."

"Those things should be the prerogative of General Holcomb," he said.

"I'm sure General Holcomb doesn't have your knowledge of communications and procedures, but you are correct that it is the prerogative of the General. However, if you don't provide the information that he needs to make that decision then he is less likely to include things that do not come to mind when he is making those decisions. He needs the raw material to articulate the actual needs of the entire Marine Corps. I am not trying to embarrass you, but something like this needs input from the individual trooper all the way up the line. If I don't have those things then I cannot give the President a complete picture of the needs of all our forces. My task is to come up with a plan for our entire armed forces. Look at this as a wish list. If there is information that would make storming a beach easier, put it in the list. We can always pare the list, but we can't add anything we don't know you need," I said.

"How long do I have to make the list?"

"At least ten days, maybe longer. We are going to London on Monday and I have no idea how long that trip will take. I will give you a call when I get back if that meets General Holcomb's approval."

"I think we can work with that. You really want all the little things that it would be nice to know?"

"Yes sir. As I said, I can always pare the list, but I can't add something that might be important that isn't on the list. Remember, we are going to develop manpower requirements for this program when it is implemented and they will come from your branch of service based on your needs," I said.

"Okay. Leave it at that and give us a call when you get back. Now get out of here and let me get back to work. By the way Commander, that was a first class brief you gave to the Security Council. I can see why the President is using you the way he is. Good luck on your trip. And thank you Chief Carter for the information about ENIGMA."

We were back at the White House by 1300 and I decided to try to get to the Army brass that afternoon, or at least set up an appointment for tomorrow morning.

I picked up the phone and asked the operator to get me General Marshall's office. Gen. Marshall was a four star, and was Chief of Staff of the Army. That meant that he exercised control of all army assets anywhere in the world.

The Ditty Chasers

As with the Navy situation with Admiral Leahy, the army had a similar problem with General MacArthur, a five star, outranking the Chief of Staff who issued the orders.

Now those might seem to be insignificant side notes to the uninitiated, but to the military, and to a degree, the President, they presented real challenges to keeping the peace between the various operations that went on throughout the military. Military rank structure is taken on faith by those in the profession of arms to be engraved in stone. A junior does not issue orders to a senior and that is a sharp knife to juggle. What the President wanted had to be conveyed through the Army COS, General Marshall, who was a four star as a suggestion.

It was not as much a problem for CNO with Admiral Leahy since he was not filling a military role, but MacArthur was old school and took his rank and the prerogatives that accompanied the rank very seriously. He was not above telling the COS that his planning was inadequate, or that he was way off base if he did not agree with what was 'suggested'.

Since I had gotten to General Holcomb I decided to use the same tactic with General Marshall. He might shunt me off to one of his subordinates, but I would be able to get the information I needed either way.

When the phone rang a minute later I picked it up and identified myself.

I had the senior aide of General Marshall on the line, who was a very senior Colonel.

I introduced myself and said, "I need to confer with someone from the army who is familiar with all communications and intelligence needs. I have been assigned a task by the President that requires me to do so. I figure this office could point me in the right direction, and since I will be discussing army policy I feel that General

Marshall needs to know what I am doing so there are no misunderstanding."

"What exactly are you up to?"

"I can't discuss it over the phone, but if you can give me a few minutes of your time I will lay it out for you and you can suggest the best method to do what I have to do," I said.

"Where are you stationed?"

"I actually have an office in the White House, but I don't think I will be spending a lot of time there. I work directly for the President and this task concerns an assignment he has given me."

"May I speak with General Marshall and get back to you?"

"Certainly. Just call the White House switchboard and they will connect you."

The call back came within ten minutes.

"The General will see you this afternoon if you can be here by 1530," he said.

"That's at Myers?" I asked.

"Yes, of course."

"I will be there with a party of one at 1530," I said and hung up before he could ask about the other party.

Chapter 9

I really hadn't expected General Marshall to personally see us, but that is the way it happened. Fortunately I had made a good impression on him as well as General Holcomb when I did the brief for the Security Council.

I took out the letter and handed it to him.

He glanced at it and handed it to his aide.

"Okay, you have my attention. What is it you need?"

"The President has tasked me to determine the COMINT needs of our forces, then design a plan for acquiring the bodies and training them to do the job. In order to work that out I need to know what we have in place now as a baseline. I know the Navy has approximately 100 people dedicated to the Japanese problem, and the Marine Corps has a few. I asked General Holcomb to make a list of his intelligence requirements, listing even the mundane, so we could figure out how to get what is needed. Just as an aside, have you heard of ENIGMA?"

"You mean the German code machine?"

"Yes sir, but it is really a Polish code machine. If you have a few minutes Chief Carter will give you a bit of its history."

He looked at the Chief and made a come on gesture with his hands.

For what seemed the fifth or sixth time J.C. went through the explanation, again leaving the fact that the British and French had the machines and the codes.

General Marshall was impressed and told J.C. that he thought he was the right man to look into our own efforts.

"The clincher is that the British and French both have the machine and the results from Polish mathematicians in attacking the system and have had it since 1939. The President told me that Churchill did not mention that fact to him when they met in June of this year in Newfoundland. He had not mentioned to Churchill that we had broken the Japanese code either, so we might have some bargaining chips to even the playing field a bit."

"I find all that very interesting, but how are you going to decide how to set up units to do what needs to be done?"

"I will talk to your signals officer to find out what your people are doing now and identify any loopholes in the plan, then ask for an intelligence wish list. All the things that you need to know about the potential enemy will be prioritized in some way and we will determine how many trained operators we need to fulfill those requirements. We then have to set up a training program to get the people capable of copying the circuits to acquire the information."

"Once the President approves the plan and I can validate the requirements, we will start a training pipeline to do those things. We can probably get an early start on the training even before we decide what the operators will be doing. It takes about six months to train an operator and some of that training can be taking place while we iron the wrinkles out of the collection plans."

"The army doesn't have any official COMINT collectors but some of our radio operators copy other communications to take up slack time. If I had to bet, I would wager a large sum of money that MacArthur has an effort going on in the Philippines."

"I feel sure that is correct. There is a COMINT unit composed of navy operators on Corregidor, and Hawaii sends copies of their intercepts to them weekly, or as often as they can get a seat for a courier on one of the planes going that way."

"You probably know this already, but Europe is going to be our first priority. That is based on tactics and politics.

The Japanese can't do us much more harm than they have already. The Philippines are going to fall because the Japanese need someplace to use as a choke point for sea borne traffic into the South Pacific Ocean, where they will probably very soon attack Singapore and Hong Kong. They need the resources and that is the only way they can be assured of moving their shipping without a lot of risk."

"Your reasoning makes sense. Is this the President's plan?"

"No sir, but it is based on things I have either heard in discussion, or been asked directly for input. My only direction from the President is to determine our COMINT needs and set up a program to achieve those things across the board. He will then decide to implement it, change it, or veto it."

"What are we going to do about Europe, since we will be going there first? I mean, we have no intelligence capability about the Germans and Italians at all."

"We are going to have to coordinate our efforts with the British, whether they like it or not. We simply must have access to all intelligence in planning to retake all the territory the Germans have already gobbled up. This is going to be one of those things where operations will be jointly planned, and that can't be done in ignorance of the enemy. If you were asked to start planning for an invasion of Southern Europe, or North Africa right now I imagine you could pull an operations plan off the shelf that was written sometime in the recent past. You would then go over it item by item and determine your intelligence requirements. Many of those questions can be answered by the British allies, and since their troops will be in the same danger as yours they will likely provide any intelligence they have. The only exception would be using something that they would have no way of knowing except through exploitation of German codes."

"Okay. I will have the information you requested compiled. When do you need it?"

"Ten days to two weeks. We have to go to London next Monday and will be gone for that long. I will call when I get back."

As we headed back to the White House I said, "Things are going too smoothly to my way of thinking. You think it might be because the Flag Officers don't believe we can do what we were tasked to do?"

"I think that might be part of it. But it is more likely that the people we are talking to simply don't understand how important COMINT is and what can be accomplished without making direct contact with the enemy. I think the navy has embraced the concept because knowing the location and intentions of units at sea plays a more important role in tactics than they would for land operations."

"You can bet your bottom dollar that the British are devoting a lot of time and effort to COMINT," I said.

"I don't believe they disseminate their success very widely. I'll give you odds that they won't be willing to talk to us unless Leahy puts in a good word for us. Even then I would expect someone very high ranking to make the decision," J.C. said.

"We have a couple of days before we leave. I don't think we are going to get any more useful information from anyone. Both the army and Marine Corps will provide what I asked for, but I don't believe any of them really think we can provide anything of value to their operations. I think we should start to develop a plan based on our own knowledge about how the process works."

"In what regard?"

"Things like order of battle, special functions performed by specialized units, that sort of thing. If we approach it from the perspective of the analyst we can identify the things that routine communications reveal. Things like how many people on their nets, who controls the net, where they are likely located, what routine reports they send and how often. Even things like the precedence of their message traffic will be useful."

"Kind of reverse engineer the requirements?" J.C. asked.

"Yes. We know how we assign operators to the Japanese navy circuits, so we can do the same thing for army units. Another thing we need to address is linguistic requirements. Most of the chatter and decrypted messages have to be translated and without the linguistic capability we will just be spinning our wheels."

"That's another of those things we don't need a plan for to start the process. We can probably start looking for people fluent in German and Japanese right away. Let's do that tomorrow. I think the Bureau of personnel for each service will have the information we need about people who already speak those languages. We can then interview them and make our own determinations."

"We also need to determine where the intercept sites should be located to be most effective."

"I didn't realize the magnitude of this assignment when he laid it on us. We are going to need our own small staff to put it all together."

"Donovan will probably be glad to lend you the people from his group to help devise the plan. He seems to think that COMINT should be under him anyway."

"He's going to have a hard enough time keeping Hoover and the FBI out of his hair to be overly worried about anything we might do," I said.

We went back to the White House and parked the car. I checked in with the Secret Service and asked if the President wanted anything from us before we called it a day.

He told us to come in and asked for a brief of the day's activities.

"We visited General Holcomb and had lunch with him. He called his signals officer, Col. Rockey in and we explained what we needed. Rockey indicated that the Marine Corps only has a few COMINT operators to his knowledge and they are working with the navy in the Pacific. I asked him to put together a wish list of intelligence he would need for an invasion and for different levels of forces. General Holcomb seemed to understand what I needed and said it would be ready when we returned from London."

"General Marshall indicated that the army didn't have anything significant going on in that area but thought that MacArthur might be doing something in the Philippines on his own. I have about concluded that we are going to have to list the things we would like to know about an enemy and write our plan based on finding out those things. We are going to need a lot of operators and linguists to man the effort. I thought we might get a start on training operators and linguists right away since they will not be tied to anything specific other than Morse code and the languages."

"Do you have any idea of the number of people we are talking about for a service wide effort?" the President asked.

"I know a bit about the background of the navy's efforts. They have been at it since around 1930. The effort was started by a Chief Radioman who realized that the Japanese were using the Katakana code and he got enough Japanese language training from the Japanese wife of a shipmate to gain enough knowledge to start to make sense of the code. This somehow got to the Commander of the Asiatic fleet and he requested formal training of intercept operators. During the next few years they trained some 150 to 200 intercept operators on the roof of the Navy Yard building. It took almost a year to train the operators because they were taught enough Japanese to read some of the decrypted communications. Most of what they learned is from what we call traffic analysis, the method I used to determine the Japanese were going to attack us."

"I believe they have used two or maybe three iterations of the code. I know they had a special code for senior officers, but we received so little traffic using that code that we didn't stand a chance of breaking it. There was a guy by the name of Joe Wenger who was very influential in convincing the Commander of the Asiatic Fleet of the worth of COMINT. The history is very sketchy because there were no formal records of any of this and most of it is hearsay."

"The navy is the only service with a program now, and it is very modest compared to the amount of communications sent by the Japanese. There are about 100 people involved in the work right now, so based on that, and the fact that the Japanese are only one part of the equation, I could see somewhere in the neighborhood of 2,000 operators and another 200 to 300 linguists and analysts," I said.

"Will that be enough to make a significance difference?"

"I don't know how to answer that question. A lot depends on how much longer we are able to read the Japanese traffic. Even if we continue to be able to do that an operator can only copy one circuit at a time and we have to find them and learn their habits and frequencies when they shift. It will take months to build the data base so we are sure about who is talking to whom. We essentially will need to build an order of battle from only their communications. The navy's efforts have only been concerned with the Japanese navy. Since Europe comes first we will have time to devote to other Japanese circuits before we start storming the beaches in the Pacific."

"When you get back from Europe you can start putting the pieces together," the President said.

Chapter 10

J.C. got the funding data from the White House Admin department and went to the Navy Yard to get our orders cut. There wasn't much to do during the weekend before we were to catch the flight on Monday so we went to the Navy Yard and worked a bit on the ideas we had come up with so far.

The navy had a leg up, so to speak, on the other service branches. Someone with a bit of vision relating to wireless communications in our navy had started the effort around 1930. The navy established a section under the CNO as the office responsible for that function. They had a designation, which was OP-20G, though they probably didn't have much in the way of assets.

That was a time when the depression was at its height and there was not much money in anyone's budget, much less for something that was not well defined.

I heard that the first of the operators worked on the roof of the headquarters building at the Navy Yard. They didn't have a title and somehow became known as the 'on the roof gang'. As it became clearer that the U.S. was going to get involved in the war, especially after the Germans invaded Poland in 1939, and shortly thereafter they started pounding the British Isles, the COMINT effort started to gather a bit of steam.

The efforts associated with the Japanese and the intelligence that it yielded convinced others in high ranking positions that the information gained from the Japanese intercepts would prove invaluable in the event of war.

The situation in the Far East had deteriorated, at least from the U.S. viewpoint, when the Japanese started to suborn the Chinese and Koreans. Everyone who had any knowledge at all about that area realized that the Japanese were going to need natural resources, and the logical places were from Eastern Russia and in the South Pacific.

During the period when the major powers had a presence in China, the Japanese had paid lip service to the fiction that every country represented had a voice in how the Chinese were governed. The British, Americans, Italians and Japanese were the major players in that arena. The U.S. had a handful of marines and the Yangtze River fleet of gunboats, though their forces were centered in and around Shanghai. In reality the force could not do much more than try to keep American citizens who happened to be in China safe.

The British had more forces than the U.S. because of their heavier presence in the Far East, but they were inadequately equipped to do much to counter any moves made by the Japanese.

The Italians were Japan's allies, so the handwriting was on the wall as far as allied forces were concerned.

The U.S. had pulled the Fourth Marines out just before Pearl Harbor and sent them to the Philippines.

The United States was supplying the Chinese with material support, but the route they had to take to deliver it was long and arduous. A rag-tag outfit that had been assembled with pilots who were willing to go to China to fly the planes that were being supplied by the U.S. was having some success and the Japanese were intent on blocking the supply routes coming from the south through Burma and Indo-China. That was the main reason the Japanese had attacked those sectors.

By chocking off the supply lines through the South China Sea they essentially cut off the movement of war materials used against them in Southern China.

"You know, one aspect of the problem we haven't looked at is triangulation," J.C. said.

"You mean locating them using azimuths from different locations?" I asked.

"Yes. That tactic should work pretty well in the Pacific. There are enough islands that we should be able to locate small operating units with the sole intent of keeping track of Japanese Navy and airplane movements. It wouldn't take more than a ten or twelve man unit to operate a direction finding station. If we could set them up from the Aleutian Islands, some other places in the Hawaii chain, and maybe even in Australia, it should give us a good picture of their movements. A communications circuit will have to be set up to support the function, but the entire operation could be handled with less than 100 operators. They won't need any specialized training and the net control could alert all the locations of the frequency and identity of the target signal. They then simply tune to the frequency, and once they are sure of the identity of the target they get the bearing to the signal and report it back to the control station. The control station will need more people because they will be plotting all the targets. It would probably be worthwhile to locate the control station with a regular intercept station so the operators can notify them when a signal of interest is heard."

"That is one thing we definitely want to do," I said. "Do we need specialized antennas for that?"

"If we want to do it right, the answer has to be yes, but we could make do with steerable antennae. The bearing would not be as accurate, but in general terms it is better to know what area a ship or plane is in than to not know anything at all. With enough separation of the DF units it will at least let us know if the target is someone we have to worry about right away."

"Rough something up on that so we don't forget to include it in the plan," I said.

We spent about five hours working on various aspects of what we thought would be required.

Sunday we stayed around the hotel and packed for the trip. I stopped by and talked to the manager and told him that we would be out of town for as much as two weeks so he would know that the rooms would not need attention daily.

We both kept our .45's, though they were packed in our suitcases.

Early Monday morning we got a lift from the Secret Service to NAS Anacostia, where we boarded a flight to Newfoundland. From there we flew to Iceland, and the last hop from Iceland to Scotland. We then contacted the U.S. liaison officer and managed to get to London, all in two days. (The last phrase was meant to be sarcastic, but I found out later that it was actually pretty good time for the trip.)

Both of us were amazed at the destruction all over the country, but in London particularly. There was rubble all over the city. Buildings burned out, walls falling in all directions and pathways made through the rubble to access building doorways.

We asked directions to the military headquarters and eventually found what we were looking for. We were both in uniform, the only ones we had brought, and each had two sets of civvies in the suitcases. The weather was cold and damp, a condition I found to be typical for London at that time of year. It was still over a week to Christmas, but decorations could be seen in the form of wreath's and plastic Santa's.

Once we found the military headquarters and gained access the M.P. at reception told us that Admiral Leahy had left a note for us and had to scramble around in the desk drawer to come up with the envelope.

The note simply asked that we meet him at his hotel and provided the address.

When we finally made contact with Admiral Leahy he suggested we talk in his room. J.C. and I both handed him the letter from the President.

"I received a message saying you would explain all the little details. I have no idea what the President ordered you to do, so fill me in as best you can," he said.

"I am a reserve naval officer. I graduated from the academy in 1934 and after my active duty I went to work for the government at the navy yard as a section supervisor for one of the COMINT sections. I studied Japanese on my own and became very familiar with the language, though by no means fluent. The Chief here was one of my best operators. I suppose you know that we are able to read a lot of the Japanese message traffic. Anyway, the Japanese had spent almost six weeks doing work-ups for six carriers. We were very interested in them and devoted a lot of manpower to copying the circuits they used."

"J.C. here copied a message where the operators were chattering about meeting in a week on 'sunny beaches'. With all that was going on I thought it made reference to where they planned to be in a week."

"Just after that the entire fleet went to radio silence. I thought what we had was enough to alert operational commanders to be prepared for an attack. I thought the target would be the Philippines and said as much. My boss, a two star Admiral took me to the CNO to explain what the assessment meant. The CNO thought it was worth the President's attention so I briefed him."

"The same day J.C. copied a message sent on the civilian propaganda circuit to Tokyo. He got my attention and told me that the message had been sent by a radioman on the Kaga. He had been copying the Japanese navy circuits and recognized the way the operator sent code. Since Kaga was under radio silence it didn't make sense, but the Chief insisted that he was right about the operator. I broke the message and it had a reference to dealing the Gaijin a crippling blow. Since Gaijin is the word the Japanese use to refer to westerners, Americans in particular, I went along with his thinking that it was his operator. The thing was that I could not imagine the Flag officer on the carrier authorizing the communicators to send such a routine message while under radio silence."

"J.C. told me that many of the senior radio operators are members of the international Amateur Radio Relay League. They build their own transmitters and receivers and he thought that the radio used was not on the ships equipment list and that the officers probably didn't even know about it."

"The bottom line is that I issued another intelligence assessment saying that the Japanese were going to attack the Philippines, Guam, Midway and Hawaii within the next 72 hours. I was taken to the White House again to brief President Roosevelt. He bought my line of reasoning, even though there was no concrete evidence that what I suggested was going to happen. He directed CNO to get the carriers out of Pearl. The very next day the Japanese did exactly what I predicted."

"After I briefed the President the second time he told CNO to go on back to work and that he would make sure I got back to the Navy Yard, that he wanted to talk to me a little more in-depth. We spent about an hour talking in his office and he invited me to dinner with him and Eleanor."

"He brought up the assessment to her and she asked how I could be sure about what I had predicted. This was before the fact and I placed a lot of credence in J.C.'s insistence that the message was sent by the carrier Kaga. I had to explain how he could be sure he was correct and used some everyday examples of recognition and extrapolated that to Morse code. She seemed to understand and asked what we were going to do about it. The President explained that we had already done all we could do by alerting the concerned locations of a possible Japanese attack."

"Before the meal was finished he told Eleanor he had decided to make me one of his spies and asked her opinion. She said she thought it was a wise decision, but I had no idea what he was talking about. He then used you as an example of how he could get unbiased information that he could absolutely trust and said he wanted me to do a similar job at a lower level."

"I briefed the Security Council just after the attack, more I think, to establish the fact that we had no hard and fast evidence of the attack than for any strategic purpose."

"He made space for an office down the hall from the Oval Office and Bill Donovan arranged rooms for us in the Willard. When he told me he wanted me to design a COMINT program including all the services I asked for J.C., who had been an operator in my section. He had him promoted to Chief and recalled me to active duty and made me a full Commander."

"I met Donovan, Secretary Knox, and all the military heavies. He made clear to Donovan that the two of us were not subject to his orders although we would be working together in some cases. I asked him if Churchill had mentioned anything about their ENIGMA operation to him during their meeting last summer. He said that he had not. I suggested that we would share our Japanese successes if the British would share what they have on the Germans. He agreed that we should do that since we are going to be involved in the European war much sooner than we will address the Japanese problem."

"That's about where we are now."

Leahy asked J.C., "You can tell an individual operator on a Morse code circuit from others?"

"If I work with the circuit for a while it is pretty simple. All of us have little characteristics that show up when we are sending code at 30 to 40 words a minute. I don't consciously do anything to aid the process but it happens. Some of our better operators can do that and some can't. It's just something that happens."

"I have been around the navy for a very long time and I never heard anyone say that."

"Many times I am not even conscious that I am doing it, and I think most operators are that way. You don't talk about how people speak, though the voice timbre, speech cadence, and regional accent are all mentally programmed when you engage them in conversation. Morse code is the same."

"Are you familiar with the ENIGMA machine?" I asked.

"I only know that's how they refer to it within their intelligence circles but that's where my knowledge stops. I know that the British are devoting a lot of manpower, and woman power, to the job. I think a lot of women learned to copy Morse code and do that from home. There's a place called Bletchley Park where they have a lot of people trying to decode the messages."

"J.C. can give you a short history lesson if you are interested," I said.

He nodded and J.C. went into his ENIGMA lesson.

"I never realized that the machine had been around that long," Leahy said.

"When used properly, unless you have the key to the cypher, it is a real job to decode the messages," J.C. said.

"So what can I do for you here?" Leahy asked.

"Get us to someone in the British COMINT field. It needs to be someone who will take us seriously and who has the horsepower to negotiate our COMINT cooperation," I said.

"I could probably get an audience with Churchill, but I don't know how seriously he will take you, even with the letter from Franklin," he said.

"A tour of Bletchley Park would be nice if it can be arranged. I know that the British are engaged heavily in the Far East and if we can come to some arrangement to provide them with the Japanese decrypts it will surely be beneficial to them."

"Let me work on that and I should know something by tomorrow. If Churchill will not see us then we will go down the chain of command until we find someone who will listen. If that doesn't work we can ask President Roosevelt to send a message via the British Embassy in Washington to Churchill asking him to see us. I really don't think it will come to that, but that is the plan."

"Shall we come back tomorrow and see where we stand?" I asked.

"Leave your number at the hotel and I will call you later this evening. I don't suppose you have any plans for dinner?"

"No sir. We are at your orders," I said.

We left his room and went in search of one of our own.

"Why don't we just stay at the hotel where Leahy is?" J.C. asked.

"I don't know. If they have room it is worth a try."

We stopped by the desk and inquired about vacancies.

"Just something with two beds, or a bed and a couch that makes into a bed will do just fine," I said.

"There's a military hotel that is set up for transient military members that would be much cheaper. I can direct you to it if you wish."

"The thing is that Admiral Leahy is staying here and he is trying to set up some meetings for us. It would be a lot more convenient if we stayed here. How steep are the rates?"

"I can let you have a room for £12. That's about $25 American."

"Let's do that, at least for a couple of nights. We only have dollars though."

"That's fine. We don't take Deutschmarks, but dollars are as good as gold."

I signed us in and called Admiral Leahy on the internal line and told him that we were staying there.

"I was going to suggest that but didn't know your schedule or your financial status," he said.

"I think the government will reimburse us. If not then we will chalk it up to experience," I said.

"Be sure you read the instructions in the room about possible air raids. They are very conscientious about those."

Leahy had called and invited us to dinner. We were in the dining room when the air raid sirens sounded.

People immediately got up from tables and started making their way to the designated shelters. Most were underground and there was no panic or crowding. It was almost as if it was a nightly happening, which it probably was.

Leahy led us down the street to the shelter and we went inside. It was crowded but people moved to give room without a second thought. In the back someone had started to strum on a guitar and people started signing. It was like an outdoor concert, except we were twenty feet underground.

The Ditty Chasers

Within a few minutes we started to hear the sound of aircraft and soon thereafter the sound of bombs exploding. The British had already been enduring this for two years and seemed to accept the inconvenience as a part of life.

We vaguely heard the sound of gunfire, probably from the fighters who had gone up to intercept the German bombers, or it could just as easily have been the German gunners trying to keep the British planes at bay.

Twenty minutes and it was over. The siren sounded again and people started leaving the shelter.

None of the bombs had sounded very close to our location but it is hard to judge distance when underground. I had felt the ground shake a bit underneath my feet while in the shelter.

Once outside we could see fires at several locations within a mile of where we were.

So that's what it felt like to have bombs falling on you, I thought.

We made our way back to the hotel and to the same table we had deserted when the siren sounded. The waiter even apologized for the inconvenience.

We finished the meal and went back to Admiral Leahy's room.

He offered a libation and we both accepted.

"I have scotch, bourbon, vodka and gin," he said.

"Bourbon for me," I said, and J.C. seconded the motion.

Once we were seated with drinks Leahy said, "What have you come up with regarding a COMINT effort on our part?"

"The navy is the only service that has any ongoing efforts to speak of. Some marines, I think about 30 went through the school they had a few years ago and are integrated with the navy people copying the Japanese circuits. The Army has some people working the problem but it's all extracurricular. They don't have a training program of any substance."

"How large will the effort need to be in order to make a difference?" Leahy asked.

"I told the President that 2,000 operators and 200 to 300 analysts was a ball park figure, but I have already changed my mind about that. J.C. mentioned that the single most important thing we could provide on a continuing basis would be the position of Japanese shipping. He thinks with stations in the Aleutians, along the Hawaii chain, Australia, and any other islands we can secure will give us enough signal bearings to get a good feel for the location of ships at sea, and airplanes for that matter. I imagine we could include army units if we have enough movable platforms to triangulate the bearings. He says it wouldn't take more than ten or twelve people to operate the stations since they won't be trying to exploit any of the signals, only take bearings to their location and report back to the control station. The nerve center of that effort would need to be located with a larger station to identify the signals of interest."

"How many people does the navy have trained right now?"

"The original training program that operated from about 1929 to 1933 trained around 200 people. Some others have been pulled from the communications operators of the navy. I think we have about 100 to 120 working COMINT at the Navy Yard. I think Hawaii has about the same number. With a four section watch that gives us the capability to man 25 positions around the clock. There are additional operators in the Philippines with MacArthur but I have no numbers. The shortage now is with analysts and linguists. I plan to get something in place right away after we get back to start those training pipelines."

"How long before you get any people actually on line to do the work?"

"The linguists will take at least six months and another three months for the analysis part. Operators we can turn out in four to six months. They will get additional on the job training once they get to their stations. I figure a year before we can expect to see any tangible results above and beyond what we are doing now."

J.C. said, "The direction finding part is a snap. We can pull people out of the radioman training pipeline and start to use them right away. We will get some opposition from their previous sponsors but our priority will override those objections."

"Where do you envision intercept stations being located?"

"We have D.C. and Hawaii now, and to a lesser extent, the Philippines. I could see something in or near San Francisco, San Diego, and possibly something in Central America to give us a cut from that direction. As we start to take the islands back from the Japanese we can set up additional units on those islands. At the rate we are currently manning our stations the navy alone will need in the neighborhood of 1000 people. When you add the army and Marine Corps to the equation the number triples at least. Then we have to worry about instructors for the training."

"May I give you some advice?"

"Of course."

"Always ask for more than you need. People all along the chop chain will try to reduce the numbers, for no other reason than that they don't understand what you are trying to do and there are a hundred other programs and needs that have to be met with not enough resources. It's not a good way to do business but is a fact of life, especially with the military. Commanders want the largest force they can muster for each mission, and don't see the contribution people dedicated strictly to COMINT can make. Once they learn the true value the war will be so far along that they don't want to admit an error in judgement, so they just keep quiet."

"I already realized that to a certain extent, but I don't want to make the demands so great that it will truly make a difference in the success or failure of an invasion. I know the value of COMINT and hope to convince others in high ranking positions of the value without a lot of animosity. There is going to be a lot of that because the President is going to keep the success under wraps, only allowing the highest ranking officers to see the take and what the organization can really do. If the majority of our officers realized the true extent to which COMINT plays a role they would back the program at least on an equal footing with the physical needs of their battle plans. On the other hand, if the word got back to the Japanese about the extent to which we are reading their traffic the source would dry up completely."

"I see your reasoning and agree. It is essential that the leaders, and here I am talking about Roosevelt and Churchill in particular, understand the importance of the program."

"From the fact that Churchill didn't even tell Roosevelt that they were reading some of the German traffic I think they both realize the importance of knowing the enemy's intentions."

"Churchill is the person that you have to convince that your proposed COMINT plan will work. He knows how much effort goes into his own signals group and the results of those efforts. He also realizes the importance of keeping the information absolutely secret. He won't even allow his people to use any of the decrypted German traffic unless there is some way to independently gain the information."

"Britain is hanging on by their fingernails now and the Germans are launching air raids almost every night. The German traffic provides targeting information at times, but until they cross the coastline he won't allow RAF pilots to engage them. They could probably lessen the damage that the Germans do, but they would wonder how we got the information to meet them before they reached their targets. I certainly don't envy him the responsibility for those decisions."

"Just out of curiosity, has Bill Donovan approached the British about combined clandestine operations?"

"I don't know the answer to that, but I do know Donovan and he will make his pitch at the earliest opportunity. I imagine he will do much as you are doing with the COMINT program. He will have to draw his people from the services and he has no successes to strengthen his argument. I think he will operate primarily in Europe. It will be difficult to disguise white faces in the Asiatic countries. A Caucasian spy would last about a day after being dropped in the target area. It just won't work," Leahy said.

"The new name of the outfit he is running will be the Office of Strategic Services, or OSS. He has been working on the plan for six months from New York but will soon have offices in Washington. He mentioned to the President that the Saint Elizabeth's sanitarium grounds would be a good fit for his use. I don't know if he just thought of that after Pearl Harbor, or if he had designs on the location beforehand."

"I believe he and his people can do a lot of good in the war over here, but I don't know that the British will welcome his people with open arms. They have been sending people into enemy territory for more than two years and rightfully believe they have a handle on how to do it. If Donovan's people come in and start trying to take over the management of their program they will be politely ignored when it comes to intelligence and resources. The same thing can be said to a lesser degree about your COMINT program. I believe your successes with the Japanese problem will go a long way toward convincing him that we are not Johnny-come-lately's to the silent war."

"Just for the record, the program I am trying to structure will be totally separate from Donovan's operational role. The only thing we will have to do with his operations is maybe brief some of his teams on intelligence matters. None of the people in my group will be allowed anywhere near enemy fortifications. If there is even the remotest chance that they might be captured they don't go. That is going to be one of the strongest tenets of the effort. Some will not like it, but I think I can convince the President that it absolutely has to be that way," I said.

J.C. had not said much to that point and I could tell he was running something through his mind. I said, "Okay, J.C., what's on your mind?"

"I was just wondering if it would be a good idea to let Churchill know that his ENIGMA success has been known to us since 1939, or would that make him mad enough to shoot the messenger?"

"What do you mean?" Leahy said.

"When J.C. gave you his history lesson about ENIGMA he didn't include everything he knows. Please don't mention this to anyone else, but J.C. has personally known that the British were breaking ENIGMA messages since 1939."

"How did this come about?"

"I don't know if I should tell you sir. I have never told anyone else about this but Commander Ward, and the knowledge has the potential to get people into trouble."

"How did you learn about their success?" the Admiral said, a bit sternly.

"I told you about how I became interested in code machines through the Amateur Radio Relay League. That was the main reason I joined the navy. I served two years aboard a destroyer and we visited Portsmouth, just about the time the British jumped into the war with both feet. I struck up a friendship with a British sailor on one of their ships and we got together for a few beers when we arrived in port. The topic of conversation was radios."

"He was about my age, maybe a couple of years older. I had been very interested in the ENIGMA machine since I first learned about it in the early thirties when I was in high school. I read all the information I could get my hands on and had visions of being the one to break the code for the machine. As I grew older I toned down my research knowing that there was no way I could even set up a lab to work on the thing. The British radioman was enthused to find someone with a mutual interest in something that had consumed his formative years about as much as it had mine."

"He had a few more beers than I did and told me that he was being transferred to GC&CS to work on the ENIGMA intercepts, and that they had gotten the machines and decoding schematics from the poles just recently and he was excited to be a part of the program. He realized that he had talked too much and swore me to silence about the conversation. I never mentioned it to anyone until Commander Ward and I got tagged to put our own COMINT program together."

"I wondered if mentioning that we knew about their success with ENIGMA from 1939 and had kept our mouths shut might sway him to get onboard with our effort. I won't tell him how I got the information, but I can quote names of the Poles who gave him the machine and the benefit of the work they had been doing since 1933."

"That might be your ace in the hole. Try to convince him with the merits of the program and if all else fails you can lay that on him. I don't know him well, but from what contact I have had he seems to be very reasonable and he is one smart cookie," Leahy said.

We broke up the conversation and went back to our room. I pulled rank and told J.C. that the couch was his.

Chapter 11

We had breakfast at the hotel the next morning. The fare was not like what we eat at home, but was close enough to allay complaints. The sausage was about the same, and the potatoes were more like what we called home fries. The spread for the toast was more like marmalade and was not nearly as sweet as the jams and jellies with which we were familiar. The preferred drink of the British was tea, but we convinced them to provide coffee for us.

Admiral Leahy came into the dining room and joined us for the meal. We had dressed in civilian clothing and he was as well.

"I got in touch with Churchill's office and managed to get an appointment for this afternoon. We are on the schedule for 1400. I have a car and driver and we can all make the trip together if you want."

We talked about general things at the table. How the British were holding up; how the supply effort on our part had been working; the hardship on the British population and the fact that a lot of women were now doing what had traditionally been men's jobs. Things like industrial plants, and most of the administrative stuff for the military. They served as air raid wardens and many of them worked in the government code and cypher school to keep British communications up and running.

Admiral Leahy strolled around the city with us, commenting on different areas and how the air raid shelters were set up. It was an enjoyable morning, but I think we pushed Admiral Leahy to his limit keeping up with our young legs. I didn't pay it much mind until we stopped for a break in a park and he commented about how out of shape he was.

I apologized and told him that we were so engrossed in the scenery that his advanced aged wasn't considered. I said it as a joke and J.C. was the one to crack up first. The Admiral belatedly realized that I was joking and took it in good spirits.

"I can see why the President wanted you in his corner. You are really quite personable and have a good sense of humor."

"I just hope I can convince them to cut us in on their COMINT take. Very few people, and I am talking about combat leaders, realize the benefit to having the bits and pieces that come from the effort. Reading the messages aside, we can tell a lot from the way they communicate and even get a lot of useful information from the chatter between operators."

"You are probably right. I never gave the concept much thought until I learned that the British were breaking the ENIGMA messages. I know for sure that you will not have to convince Churchill of the value of the intercepts," Leahy said.

We slowed the pace on the way back to the hotel. It was safe enough walking around the city in the daytime. The Germans didn't risk their bombers when they could be seen from a distance. The British didn't have a lot of fighters, but they had pilots with more courage than brains and they had been very successful in dealing with the threat in the daytime hours.

Admiral Leahy didn't say as much, but I got the feeling that he wanted to nap a bit before the meeting. We all went to our rooms with the agreement to meet in the lobby at 1330.

The Admiral looked a bit better when we met and the car was waiting for us.

I had no idea where Churchill's office was and frankly was somewhat surprised that he was in a nondescript building that was only three stories tall and had maybe 20,000 square feet of usable space. The entry was well guarded and we were vetted thoroughly before being allowed entry. A messenger had been sent down from Churchill's office and led us to the top floor.

We weren't kept waiting. The secretary apparently buzzed Churchill when we walked into the outer office, because he came to the door and invited us in.

After the introductions were made he asked, "And what can I do for our benevolent cousins?"

I handed him the letter from President Roosevelt and told him that my companion had one as well.

He read it and handed it back. "Don't tell me you are here as an advanced party with a troop regiment this early on?"

"No sir. We are in the COMINT business. I managed to get some insight into the Japanese attack on our Pacific bases beforehand but we had nothing to put up against them. The information was based on Communications intercepts and was not concrete enough to get everyone excited. We did put three carriers to sea that were at Pearl beforehand on the chance that the information was reliable, which saved them."

"What kind of information did you provide?"

"They had worked up six carrier groups the month before the attack and from the Morse code traffic we knew their composition and that they were planning something big. A slip up by a radio operator indicated that they were going to invade someone to the south of the home islands and the Philippines seemed the logical target since they could then choke off traffic to the south pacific. I brought that to the attention of my boss, who informed his boss, who informed the President. I briefed him and he agreed with my take on the situation. The next day we found one of the radiomen off one of the carriers sending a message to the propaganda network. The intercept operator recognized the man sending the Morse code and brought it to my attention. I decoded the message and it was pretty innocuous. There was one sentence that related to dealing a heavy blow to the Gaijin. Since the nearest Gaijin were in the Philippines, on Guam and Midway, and on Oahu, I reasoned that they were coming after us before further invasions in the South Pacific. The President also agreed with my analysis on that one. The next day Pearl Harbor was attacked, along with the other islands I had identified."

"When you say you decoded the message, does that mean you have the code keys?"

"No sir. The Japanese don't use codes the way we do. They don't lend themselves to transliteration from the pictographs they use in their language. They use an obscure version of the Japanese language called Katakana. They developed something over 1,000 four element groups to represent different ideographs in the language. We have been exploiting their communications since around 1932. They have changed a couple of times during that period, but our analysts and linguists managed to get the new code in pretty short order."

"That's the first I have heard of that. I wonder why President Roosevelt didn't mention that to me last June."

That opened the door for me and I stepped right in. "Probably for the same reason you didn't mention to him that you were reading the German codes."

"What makes you think we are breaking the German codes?"

"History for the most part. You do realize that the ENIGMA machine has been on the commercial market since the mid to late twenties?"

"I seem to remember hearing something about that."

"The fact is that the first versions of the machine were so bad that it took them almost five years to come up with a version that the commercial people would even consider. As more people started using the system the Amateur Radio Relay League, what we call Ham operators took an interest in the system. Every amateur worth his salt had dreams of breaking that code. Some had better luck than others, but with Russia and Germany both using the system, a couple of Poles started working on the project full time. They had some success and when it became apparent that they were going to be invaded they provided the machine and their work to a couple of governments opposing the Nazi's."

I stopped there to see what his reaction was going to be.

"Do you have any idea who these couple of countries are?"

"Yes sir, I do."

"And how long have you known about it?"

"Since 1939, but the secret is still safe. Only four people in our government know about it, and the President is one of the four. I asked him if you had offered the take from ENIGMA at the June meeting and he said you hadn't mentioned it. I can readily see why you didn't. We were not part of the war effort, I am talking about the shooting war, and it would have been foolish on your part to divulge that information to an ally, even one as close to you as America is."

"So what is it you want?"

"I want to start providing your people with information about the Japanese and what they are up to. I imagine they will be attacking Hong Kong and Singapore on their way to Australia and possibly New Zealand very soon."

"How do you propose to do that?"

"I haven't quite got that worked out yet, but should have something set up within a month."

"Why do you use the personal pronoun?"

"Because the President has tasked me and my partner here," I pointed to J.C., "to set up a COMINT program for all our service components in which we will have missions pretty much the same, but each service will look at their own counterparts. The navy will concentrate on communications from enemy naval units, Army for Army units, and air and Marine Corps units on whatever beach they are due to hit next. It doesn't make sense to have other allied countries copying the same circuits when we can cover more ground and get more intelligence as a joint venture."

"And how would you disseminate this information?"

"In much the same way you do now. Operational commanders above flag rank will be provided sanitized data based on how sensitive the data is, and what impact we project it will have on whatever operational plan is being undertaken. The list of recipients will be small and the President will personally approve who has access and who doesn't. Everyone who is given access will be thoroughly briefed on the sensitivity of the information and we will set up a separate circuit strictly for use in passing the data. The encryption system will be designed especially for that purpose."

"How much of the Japanese traffic are you able to read?"

"Most everything we copy. The roadblock is getting trained operators to copy the Morse code. They have one high level code we haven't been able to break, but it is designed for high ranking officers to talk one to another. It is used so seldom that we don't have a good data base as yet."

"Why is someone of your rank tasked with this job?"

"I suppose because I was the one to predict what the Japanese were going to do, and because the President made me one of his spies."

Admiral Leahy had a broad smile on his face. "Maybe I had better explain that. Franklin does not always trust the information he gets when he orders someone to do something or other. He has the habit of using people like the Commander, and myself for that matter to ensure that he gets the straight scoop. He is reluctant to act on any task unless one of his 'spies' tells him that the information he has gotten is correct. That's why a fleet Admiral is an ambassador to a country in the hands of the enemy."

"What specifically has he tasked you to do?" Churchill asked.

"To design and implement a COMINT program across the board within our defense system that will complement the other intelligence necessary to the conduct of offensive operations."

"How are you going to decide on the manning?"

"That's one of the things I had hoped to get from your people. I can make a guess on the needs based on my own experience over the last several years, but I need to refine the kinds of information needed to arrive at the right number of operators and analysts for the task. You have been concentrating on the German problem for quite some time, so your number of operators will give me a benchmark to start the process."

"Who in the American effort would you imagine to receive the ENIGMA intercepts?"

"That's up to you and my boss to work out. I personally would limit the knowledge to operational commanders above a certain rank. That would also need to be based on the importance of the command tasking. I know that the President has said that he alone will control access to our COMINT product. That would indicate that he attaches the same importance to our success with the Japanese codes as you do to the ENIGMA product."

"Does your effort have any relationship to the newly formed OSS?"

"The only relationship is that Bill Donovan, who heads the OSS will be the keeper of access files. I may need to coordinate with him as to his intelligence needs for his mission, but I do not work for him, and the President made that abundantly clear to both of us."

Churchill smiled, his first since I started the brief.

"Do you have any indication as to when U.S. troops will start to arrive and in what strength?"

"Not a clue sir. That is not within my charter but I wouldn't expect that they will arrive next week, or even next month for that matter. All I can tell you about that is that there has been a sudden influx of military recruits. The very minimum of time to train them, even marginally, is three to five months. Airborne troops will take even longer, and tankers as well. The command structure will, of necessity, have to be in place before they start arriving, and I expect that you will have other visitors in short order to start setting that up."

"I pray I am not out of order in revealing this to you, but my special warfare people do not want Donovan's people to have a finger in their pie."

"Then perhaps they should bake another pie. We are involved in the war fully now, and if our side wants information they are first going through our chain of command. If the operation is a joint venture then Donovan is going to want representation equal to that provided by other allied countries. I am out of my depth here, but his mission, like mine, is to do what is good for the country, and his people will be trained for the same purpose as your special warfare people. He will take it as a snub if you exclude him. My suggestion would be to invite a small number, whatever you can get your people to accept, and have them train with and accompany your people on their missions until both parties are satisfied that the other is not totally incompetent."

"Well, that wasn't very diplomatic, but then you are not a diplomat," Leahy said.

"You think his idea is a good one?" Churchill asked.

"Yes I do, but only because I know both Donovan and Roosevelt personally. What Commander Ward says is very true. Donovan is stubborn, and also very competent. He received the Medal of Honor from WWI, so there is no doubting his courage. He is also a very prominent attorney and has the ego to go with the title. What Corey suggested makes sense to me. You will be able to exert some amount of control but you will need to have a heart to heart with your special warfare commander to make him aware of the sensitivity of the matter. Keep in mind that Donovan, while not one of the President's spies, is a very close friend of Roosevelt."

"I will take that under advisement. As to the COMINT collaboration, I agree in principle, but we will need to spell out the specifics so that we each know what is expected of the other. How long before you will have your program up and running?"

"We have about 150 navy operators working full time on the Japanese problem now. That will grow considerably over the next year. Currently we only operate out of Hawaii and from Washington. Chief Carter here suggested a series of direction finding sites would aid in keeping track of naval and air units. We can start that off with sites in the western U.S., Central America, Hawaii, Australia, and add to the net as we take back the Islands the Japanese have occupied. With three or four lines of bearing on the same signal we can get a pretty good idea about where they are located. That is especially helpful to the navy. We will disseminate this as regular intelligence so we won't need to make special arrangements for everyone in the fleet. As to the full complement, I would say about six months to a year to get enough people trained to make a difference."

"Okay, when you have a plan formulated come back and see me and we will set up procedures. The answer as to sharing the intelligence is of course, yes. Now what else?"

"Would it be possible to have someone cleared for ULTRA give us a tour of Bletchley Park? I want to see what approach they are taking to exploit follow on versions of the ENIGMA machine," I said.

"That can be arranged. How long are you in town?"

"Ever how long it takes," I responded.

"It has been a real pleasure meeting you. Even though America is an ally, some of your folks can be downright unreasonable. I will have someone pick you up in the morning around 0800 at your hotel."

"Thank you very much sir, and it was my pleasure meeting you."

Leahy added his thanks and we were escorted back outside where the car was waiting to return us to our hotel.

144

Chapter 12

We were picked up at the hotel the next morning and taken to Bletchley Park. Just looking at the place was an utter disappointment. The buildings were hurriedly erected for the mission and not for aesthetics. In other words the place was even uglier than the Navy Yard. The buildings were various sizes and some joined by covered walkways, others by enclosed passages.

I didn't notice a lot of antennas and surmised that the prime purpose was exploitation of the message intercepts. I didn't ask any questions in the car. We had a Navy Commander escorting us but I didn't know the status of the driver. Since the Commander didn't approach the subject I took my lead from him.

It was obvious that the facility had grown a lot during the previous few months. Some of the buildings didn't even have paint but were raw lumber. The one thing the facility did have was a plethora of guards, both stationary and roving.

Our identification was checked at the main gate before we were granted entry to the grounds, then again when we got out of the car, and a third time before we entered the administrative building.

There another person in civilian clothing met us and took us to the operations center. No one wore uniforms, other than the guards.

The man who met us was affable and asked what in particular interested us.

J.C. said he would like to see the inside of an ENIGMA machine. We were then taken to a laboratory where they had one torn apart.

"This one has two thinner wheels to replace the one thicker one," Chief Carter said. "Is that to provide more variables?"

"Absolutely. Let me get Mr. Turing. He is our resident wizard."

He picked up a phone and said a few words and within a matter of minutes a rather pale and skinny man of perhaps 30 years came into the Lab.

"Yes sir, what can I do for you?" he asked.

"These two gentlemen are Americans who work in their COMINT program. They have had a session with the Prime Minister and he wanted to have them see how we handle the decrypts of German codes. They have a fundamental knowledge of the ENIGMA machine but wanted to see the interworking's to get a feel for the complexity of what we are trying to accomplish."

He nodded, and said, "You understand the basic principle that the more variables you have the harder it is to break the code?"

We both nodded.

"I have been working on a system to step through the settings in sequence until we arrive at the proper setting for the message we are interested in decrypting. We are working on a machine, which we call a bombe, to rapidly go through the sequence until we identify the first element. We then repeat the process to arrive at the next element, and so on. It would take an analyst 50 to 100 times as long to perform the function manually. Our problem now is to try to speed the machine process up to shorten the decryption process."

He went to an ENIGMA on one of the work benches that was lying in parts and explained how the machine worked, which we knew, but wanted to make sure we understood the process correctly since we had no hands on experience with the machine.

"How do you get the intercepts to work with?" J.C. asked.

"That's the beauty of the set-up. We have ladies all over the country trained to copy Morse code. We don't tell them what they are copying, but give them a frequency and schedule times. We have our own efforts in out of the way places, again mostly with female operators. The men are doing the fighting, so we had to take what was available. Some of them are quite good. I also imagine some of the housewives can guess at the purpose of their assignments, but they never ask questions unless they are related to the job," Turing said.

We toured the different sections and got briefed by section heads. One asked the reason for the briefing.

"We are now in the war on all fronts and we don't want to duplicate anything you folks are doing with our COMINT efforts. We are setting up a full-fledged program just as soon as we can train the operators and linguists. We have a handful of analysts and about 100 operators now but that is going to increase to whatever level we need to get the job done. I have been tasked to come up with a COMINT plan for the entire defense department. How do you differentiate between German navy, Luftwaffe, and Army circuits?"

"Mostly through the procedures they use. We also have a lot of traffic analysts who concentrate on keeping track of their schedules, frequencies and call signs. Are you familiar with the term?"

"Very much so. That was my job until the President saddled me with this one. Do you folks do anything with triangulation, or direction finding?"

"We would dearly love to have such a capability, especially as it relates to their navy. About the most we can do is get a general idea of the direction by steerable antennas, and that is not nearly good enough to react to."

"We are going to try to develop a DF network in the Pacific if it is feasible. I suppose we will need to do some research on antennas to find the most logical choice, but I believe the choices of sites in the larger ocean area will lend itself to more success than such close quarters as you have here."

"You might want to look at what the air force are using. They employ a steerable antenna for navigation purposes. I don't see why that wouldn't work for a fixed site as well. If you come up with something that works let us know."

"How often do the Germans change their key codes?" J.C. asked.

"Usually monthly. The different services components don't operate on the same schedule and that sometimes causes confusion among their operators. Operator chatter often aids in breaking the monthly code sooner rather than later. It's a never ending battle trying to get the strategic stuff."

"Do you know how many versions of the machine the Germans are using?"

"We actually have two machines that came off German submarines, along with their code books. One was on U-110, which we acquired in May, and another off U-570, which we only recently came by."

"How do you get your product to the end users?" I asked.

"We have a dedicated circuit and our own codes. The list of people granted access to ULTRA material is very short, and where possible the information is hand-carried. We have courier runs to the Admiralty, and Downing Street several times each day."

We spent the better part of the morning at the site and were driven back to London in the early afternoon.

"I thought that went well," J.C. said on the way to our room.

We had a long skull session with Admiral Leahy that evening.

"You did a good job at the meeting with Churchill. I especially like the way you got into the ENIGMA discussion. Most people are somewhat reticent to engage him fully. I think that is a characteristic of most strong leaders. He has a lot on his shoulders and it is a heavy burden," Leahy said.

"I just hope I have the same result when I start asking for large numbers of people to man the circuits."

"The President trusts you, and if you say you need 3,000 people he will see that you get them. Secretary Knox is a good man to have in your corner as well. I imagine I will be coming back before too much longer. I am not doing much good here now that the Germans pretty much have France under their thumb."

"I guess we will start trying to make our way back home tomorrow."

Even with the highest priority it took us two days to make it back to Washington.

Chapter 13

We got back into Washington late in the evening. We were both pretty worn out so we hit the sack early and didn't even go down for breakfast until after 0800.

While we were waiting for the food I asked J.C., "Do you think we have enough information to start to formulate a plan?"

"The job is so daunting that whatever number we choose will not be enough to do the job properly. I believe we should get the requirements from the Army and Marine Corps and work the navy stuff from our own experience. Once we get some idea about how close we are to some form of implementation we will run it by everyone before we present it to the President. One thing we need to do right away is start to get operators and linguists into the training pipeline."

"I think we should draft a message to all the services and tell them to start screening for linguists. We can levy them for operators at the same time. I believe the best bet will be to get instructors from experienced radio operators. We also have to decide where to train them," I said.

"Let's check in with the White House and then go to the Navy Yard and look at some maps. I want to identify locations for DF stations. We also need to touch base with the technical people to see what will work in the way of antennas," J.C. said.

We were in uniform and made the short walk to the White House. The head of the personal detail gave us a wave and said, "Hang around. I know he wants to see you."

The current appointment lasted another ten minutes and we stayed out of sight until we got the nod to go into the office.

"I hear your visit to England went quite well. Admiral Leahy sent me a message extolling your virtues. Tell me about it."

"The Chief and I talked about how to handle the situation if they were reluctant to share the ENIGMA take and decided that he would need to be told that we knew about the effort since 1939. The Prime Minister actually opened the door for me to inject the fact without it seeming like a threat or rebuke. Mr. Churchill was pretty frank and open with us. He related that his special warfare people, or spies if you prefer, would not look kindly on any attempt by Bill Donovan to intrude on their turf. The way he worded it was that they would object to having other fingers in their pie. I told him at that point that if that was the way they felt that they should consider baking another pie."

"We talked a bit about it and I suggested that some of Donovan's people be assigned to work with the British until they were satisfied that American's could hold their own. I also pointed out that there was no other option than to share because other allied forces were going to be involved in the planning and execution of the operational plans. I may have overstepped my authority with relation to Donovan, but I saw it as an opportunity to at least get a foot in the door without having the British dictate how the war was going to be run. I think that if Donovan sends 15 to 20 of his best troops to work with the British Special forces they will welcome the help and it will allay the suspicions of the British that our people are incompetent."

"Admiral Leahy told me about the pie thing. He thought that your answer was ingenious, as do I. He also said that Churchill seemed to be impressed with your carriage and grasp on the extreme importance of secrecy with regard to both their intercepts and ours. He said you were even invited back to brief him when our program gets on track. I guess Eleanor was right. You are going to be one of my best spies."

"The Chief and I have been discussing the various aspects of what we need to do. I think we should take the input from the Army and Marine Corps and use our personal knowledge of how the system works to arrive at a number that will at least let us know if we need more, or what we trained was overkill. The British use a lot of the womenfolk to copy the German messages. They don't tell them what they are copying, but you can bet your bottom dollar that they have guessed. My first inclination is to let the British keep on doing what they are doing. The decryption process is very slow, and all the German services use different codes. A guy by the name of Turing is trying to develop a way to get the codes broken faster with a machine that compares the different possibilities until they find the first element, then they start to work on the second and so on until they have the code setting for the month. They have probably in the neighborhood of 200 to 300 people working on the decryption process alone."

"You are saying to let them handle the German problem and we will deal with the Japanese?"

"Not entirely. I think we still want a hand in the process so we can learn about the machine and the cypher systems. Maybe half a dozen of our best cryptanalysts to work at Bletchley Park. I would also envision the army operating at a site somewhere in England or Scotland to concentrate on the German army communications."

"How long before you have a recommendation?"

"I have one already. Send out a message through the Chiefs of all the services to screen records for operators and linguists. We will find instructors by the time they locate enough to start the first class. To keep from having a redundant effort I suggest we do all the training at one location. We will find instructors from all the service components and put them together. The first few weeks will be devoted almost entirely to learning how to copy Morse code. All will have to be screened for security clearances. The FBI can be given the names and the task assigned as a priority. By the time we get them to the point that they start learning just what they are training to do, we should be able to weed out the bad apples. We are going to need someplace secure to conduct the training as well."

"Have you started to look yet?"

"No sir. It would be nice to have our own base for security purposes but I don't know how feasible that would be. I think I am just going to each of the services and ask for recommendations about using facilities already in place. We will use pre-recorded tapes for training purposes. Later in the training cycle we will want them to copy actual signals off the air and for this we will need antennas. The navy has some sites already operational for high frequency direction finding. The Chief thought we should set up similar stations to do nothing but take DF bearing. I didn't know that we already had stations operational. Other than the one on the strand at Coronado, California we probably have one on Hawaii. That will need to be refined further, but if we can set something up in Central America, maybe Australia and somewhere in the Aleutians we should have pretty good geometry for locating Japanese shipping, and to a lesser extent, aircraft."

"Draft the message for locating potential operators and linguists and I will have it sent by all the services. List yourself as the point of contact and let all the service heads know what is happening and why. You might also have each service branch try to find a suitable location for the training," the President said.

J.C. and I spent most of the day working on the plan.

"If the navy has a HFDF site in California that might be a good location to train the navy operators. I don't know about barracks space and the other logistical aspects, but we certainly cannot ask for a new base. We are going to have to tie in with someone else and the site near San Diego seems the best fit. Mare Island is where they train the radio operators, so we could tie in with them and send the first group there while we work on someplace secure to get into what our guys will actually be doing," J.C. said.

"I believe the best way to do it is to lay out the requirements and allow each service component to train their own people based on a curriculum that we will produce. That way they will be more likely to support the plan that we come up with," I said.

"What we really need to do to start the ball rolling is come up with some numbers. We know the Navy has about 200 people in the program now, and that is only two stations. A site in Australia is a must, and we do not currently have much else in the Pacific. I believe the Philippines are going to fall and unless we want to look toward China there are no other choices."

"How much of the Japanese navy traffic do you think we are missing now?" I asked.

"It's hard to say. I don't know who works up the schedule for the stuff we copied here, but I do know that we didn't have any dedicated search operators. What needs the most attention is our traffic analysis. We don't have any continuity now, and that is going to be a must if we want to do this right. We are also going to need a better system for communicating among our own stations, just to get the technical data out in a timely manner."

"That shouldn't be all that hard to do. We need our own codes and sending and receiving equipment. If we locate with operational bases we can use their antennas.

154

The Ditty Chasers

There has to be a central clearing house for looking at everything and feeding our operators the technical data. That should be here in the area," I said.

"I would suggest an inter-service manning scheme. Each to be devoted to their own branch of service. I could see at least 50 people from each branch of service to do the analysis. We are going to need history files on all the circuits we copy and that is going to be time consuming. I don't see the need for the linguists to be trained in traffic analysis. They will devote their time to translating the message traffic."

We started to put things on paper as we talked about them. At the end of the day we still didn't have anything but some numerical guesses. This was going to have to be one of those things that changes as we learn more about how well we are satisfying the need.

"Let's levy each branch of the service for 400 operators and 50 analysts each for starters. As the plan comes on line we can reevaluate and adjust the numbers based on how valuable the information is," J.C. said.

"What about the Pacific DF net?"

"We need to find someone who knows about it and see what they have anywhere other than California," I said.

"I can work on that after we get the initial message out."

I started to rough out the message based on what we had talked about. The body of the message read:

1. *Each service is directed to identify and assign 50 personnel from among new enlistees who have an aptitude for copying Morse code. Use of standard radio operator's assignment criteria is to apply. Any personnel who have arrest records are not to be included as the assignment will require a Top Secret*

clearance. Further, it is expected that 50 additional personnel meeting the same criteria will be required at six month intervals for a two year period.

2. *Any enlistee who is fluent in a second language, other than Spanish and French, will be identified along with the second language and names and current duty stations included.*

3. *It is anticipated that these personnel will be identified during the enlistment process. Background checks will be performed prior to their completing basic training.*

4. *Training will be accomplished for Morse code operators at army and navy facilities currently providing that training for the respective services. Marine Corps personnel will be trained at naval facilities.*

5. *Individuals identified pursuant to para. 2 will be interviewed individually during the basic training cycle by Cdr. Ward.*

6. *POC is CDR Corey Ward. Message address is CNO OP-20.*

"We will make the rounds again to let folks know what is planned. I think Donovan might assist us in finding linguists since he will need them as badly as we do. I also want to let him know about the meeting with Churchill, although the President will probably already have done that."

I called the White House operator and asked if she had any way to get in touch. She made the connection and called me back.

"Sir, I need to talk to you if you tell me where to come," I said.

"You are obviously at the White House now. Why don't I just meet you there in about half an hour?" he replied.

"I will be here," I said.

I let the President's detail know that Donovan would be in the area and asked them to let the President know.

J.C. and I had rearranged the furniture in our office a little better to free up enough room for a second desk and an additional chair. It still looked like a storage room but served its purpose.

One of the Secret Service people led Donovan to our office and said, "The President wants to see all of you when you are finished."

Donovan shook hands and sat in one of the straight-backed chairs we had available.

"While we were in London Admiral Leahy got us an appointment to talk with Churchill. During the discussion the subject of your organization came up. I didn't bring it up, he did. He agreed in principle to share COMINT with us and gave us a tour of Bletchley Park, where they do most of their analysis of intercepts. He stated that he didn't think his people wanted American fingers in their pie. I saw that as an opportunity to put in a good word for your organization and suggested that your people would of necessity have to work with them to some extent to support the allied effort. I further suggested that he consider assigning some number of your people to work with his special branch operations people. He agreed that was a good approach. I emphasized that I had no authority to speak for you on the subject. I hope I didn't do something that goes against your plans for the organization."

"The President showed me Admiral Leahy's message and they both agree that you only seized the opportunity for input when it presented itself. I have already been working with William Stephenson from their special operations branch and we are going to pattern our organization along the same lines as the British. Stephenson and I have not talked about the integration of our assets for regular missions, probably for the very reason Churchill mentioned. I have no animosity toward you for helping my cause. I will seize upon the opportunity to get some people assigned to London to work directly with them."

"While we are on the subject, do you know of any likely place in the area where we can establish a facility to process the intercepts that will be coming in when we get our COMINT program set up?"

"I am looking at an area in the Maryland countryside to establish a training facility for my undercover operators. I don't know how large an area you will need, but it might be possible to set something up for you if this works out all right. It will also provide security of the perimeter area."

I showed him the message I had roughed up.

"I'm going to show that to General's Holcomb, Marshall, and Admiral Stark before it is sent."

Donovan read the draft and made the same comment I had heard earlier about asking for more than would actually be needed.

"I am going to stress to all services that this is only the initial levy for troops and that a lot more will be needed when we can find a place for them to work," I said.

"Another area you might want to look at is Camp Meade, just up the road in Southern Maryland. They have a lot of acreage and I thought about trying to get some to set up my training facility. In the end I decided that my mission would be better served with my own real estate, but it would seem to me to be an ideal location for what you need to do."

We talked for a few more minutes and headed to the Oval Office.

We went in and got coffee as the President lit another of his cigarettes in the holder.

Being a non-smoker my curiosity got the best of me. I said, "Why do you use the holder for the cigarettes?"

"Number one, it keeps the tobacco out of my mouth. And number two, it has a cellulose filter inside it which filters the smoke. I don't know what good it does, but my doctor ordered it and it sort of became a trademark. Do you know that you are the first person to ask that question, other than Eleanor of course," he replied.

"How goes the message?"

"I have it roughed up," I said and handed it to him.

He read it and handed it back. "I think the army trains their radio operators at Fort Monmouth, New Jersey. They might have enough room for your group there. If it requires building additional barracks and classrooms we can get that done on a priority basis."

"The navy trains at Mare Island, near San Francisco. They also have a facility on the Coronado strand near San Diego. I think that is where the advanced school should be. Once the individual services teach them to copy code we can do the sensitive part of the training there. Again, we will probably have to expand the base to some degree. Chief Carter is going to address that issue just as soon as we get the message out," I said.

"You plan to train the Army and Marine Corps troops along with the Navy at Coronado?" he asked.

"Yes sir. It will cut down on the need for instructors and will be beneficial in teaching the operators to distinguish between different circuits," I replied.

"You will probably want someone to look into the logistics with the large influx of people," Donovan said.

"Chief Carter is going to look into that this week. He needs to evaluate their HFDF capabilities so we can incorporate that into the plan. We should have some idea of the numbers by the time he gets back. I don't know much about contracting, but we will need a high priority to have barracks built for them. We will also have to look into mess hall facilities."

"Once you determine your needs just turn it over to the Navy and have them handle the contracting. Give them a date that you need the facility and they will handle the rest of it. Give them an earlier date than what you actually need to be on the safe side," Donovan said.

We talked for another 15 minutes until the President's next appointment arrived, then went back to our little cubbyhole.

Chapter 14

"Are you going home for Christmas?" J.C. asked.

"Probably not. I don't have much family left and I don't know how I would spend the time. Rationing is going to have to kick in pretty soon. My guess would be at the beginning of the New Year and I imagine tickets on trains and planes will be restricted to some degree. Hopefully I will be able to get some work done. You can take some time if you want. Fold it in with the travel to the west coast and it will be cheaper for you," I said.

"I just want a couple of days to impress the young ladies with my new Chief's uniform," he said with a laugh.

"You are pretty young to be a chief," I said.

J.C. had orders cut the next morning and was on the way by that afternoon. I made the rounds again with the military commanders and discussed the message that they would get formally very soon.

General's Holcomb and Marshall provided the list I had asked for to try to get a handle on the tasking that would comprise our early efforts to launch the COMINT program. I explained that the training pipeline would only be able to handle 100 to 200 people at a time and for that reason the levies for manpower were staggered.

"This will also give us time to refine the tasking with the first group and build on that as the additional people are trained."

The linguists would need to be vetted by someone who spoke the languages, but the positive side of that task was that they could be determined through a check of records, and that could be done rather quickly by each of the service branches.

The Christmas holidays proved to be a good time for me to spend some time becoming better acquainted with navy operations. I spent some time in my old work spaces and still more time in the personnel section of the navy department. I wanted to get a good handle on exactly how many people we had working the Japanese problem at that point in time.

I learned that there was a total of 238 people cleared for Magic intercepts at three locations, here in Washington, at CICNCPACLFT in Hawaii, and in the Philippines, under General MacArthur. Of that number only a handful were not directly involved in either copying the messages or decoding and translating them.

It was hard to determine exactly how many staff officers were privy to the intercepts. The intelligence sections within the Army and Navy structure were the only ones with a handle on exactly who was cleared. That was going to have to be addressed very soon.

The Japanese had put a lot of troops ashore in the Philippines, especially on the islands of Luzon and Mindanao. Luzon, of course, was the major island within the chain and most of the U.S. and Filipino troops were garrisoned there. The ports of Subic Bay and Manila Bay were the best suited to seaborne commerce and both were heavily targeted by the Japanese during the initial attacks on the 7th of December. The Japanese navy bombarded both locations heavily from surface ships and aircraft from the carrier.

They received very scant resistance and within a couple of weeks had a large contingent of ground troops ashore.

I was worried by the possibility that some of the intercept operators stationed there might fall into the hands of the Japanese and that was an unacceptable situation. I had no doubt that the Philippines would be in the hands of the Japanese within a very short period of time.

I visited Admiral Stark and expressed concern about the possibility and he agreed that we could not allow any of the group to fall into Japanese hands.

"The problem is that the operation is under General MacArthur. He is a five star and is the senior person in all the military forces. He would not take kindly to someone back here telling him how to use his troops. We can only hope that he has the foresight to get that group out of harm's way at the earliest opportunity. I might be able to order CINCPACFLT to make a submarine available to evacuate them. We are probably going to have to find enough assets to evacuate MacArthur and his staff before much longer. There's no way he can hold out against what the Japanese are going to throw at him. You might want to bring this up to the President. It is too important to allow ego to enter the decision making process."

"Yes sir, those were my thoughts, and I will do that very soon," I said.

I managed to get an appointment to talk to the Army G-2, who was a Brigadier General. I discovered that the army had already started to train Japanese linguists. They had sixty students currently undergoing language training at the Presidio of San Francisco. Most of these were second generation Japanese Americans who had learned at least some of the language from parents and other relatives but they had been educated in U.S. schools and most did not use the Japanese language enough to be considered fluent. There were two Caucasians among the group and the program was slated to run for 24 weeks.

I was happy to learn this, and asked if the program could be expanded to include Navy and Marine Corps personnel.

"I don't see how we will be able to do that with the limited space we have. I agree that the training should be inter-service and since we already have a program up and running it makes sense to use it as the starting point. My people routinely screen records for people with second languages, so your message requesting that has already been done."

"How do you determine that the people who profess to have language skills actually do have them?" I asked.

"That's one of the weaknesses of the program at the present time. The people in the current classes were interviewed by a fluent Japanese language speaker. I don't know how you will handle the other languages," he said.

"Would you be willing to have someone look into the possibility of finding a location where there is enough room to teach several languages at the same time. I envision as many as 200 to 400 students simultaneously," I said.

"I will do that just as soon as the holiday period is over."

So far I was pleased to find that we weren't as far behind the power curve as I had thought. If the Army would handle the language training I should have a school set up to teach traffic analysis and cryptanalysis by the time the first students graduated from the language school.

With the President's concurrence I set up a small group within the navy COMINT program to handle the administrative aspects of the effort. Things like security clearance questionnaires and background investigations would have to be conducted. I visited the FBI and explained that I needed to have a large number of people vetted for top secret clearances on a priority basis.

The President had mentioned to Hoover that the requirement would be forthcoming and he had already designated a senior agent to handle the case load.

The President had been tied up with a meeting of the allies' representatives, which included 26 countries. On the first of January they passed a resolution not to negotiate separately with any of the axis powers. The solidarity was considered a very important element of the wartime strategy.

On the 2nd of January we got the word that Japanese forces had entered Manila, in the Philippines.

J.C. returned on the 2nd and I brought him up to date on what had happened during his absence. "I am very concerned about the intercept operators in the Philippines. I would like to think that General MacArthur has enough sense to evacuate them, but there are no guarantees that he attaches the same significance to their safety that we do. I am going to ask the President to remind him," I said.

"You can never assume that someone else is going to look at a problem the same way you do. There's an old saying that to assume makes an ass out of u and me," J.C. replied.

I had not spent much time in the presence of the President during J.C.'s absence. I was too tied up trying to find out where we stood with the other aspects of the program.

"What did you find out on the west coast?"

"The area on the Coronado strand is a good location. We will need barracks and probably a new mess hall. The classrooms can be built fairly quickly. We can task the navy to provide security for the area. A fenced compound will work I think. There's enough open space for erecting antennas and that can be done while the other construction is going on."

"So you think we should train all the operators there?" I asked.

"It makes more sense to do that than to set up separate facilities to do the same job."

"I agree whole heartedly. The army already has a language training program that they started in November. They have 60 students, mostly second generation Japanese/Americans. I talked to them about including other languages and handling all the service branches. It looks like that is the best way to go."

"Then the only major stumbling block is where the analysis facility is going to be located and how it will be staffed," J.C. said.

"Don't forget that we also have to set up our own codes and communications procedures," I said.

"That shouldn't be all that hard. We can have either the army or navy generate special code books for our use. The actual messages can be sent and received by regular radio operators. They won't be able to see what the messages say because they will be encrypted in a second code. They will simply comply with special handling procedures to get the messages to whoever it concerns and our people will have to break the message in our secure spaces."

"What about the HFDF problem?"

"They have stations in San Francisco, at Coronado, and on Oahu. They don't have any procedure manuals or coordinated effort. I think that can be handled by adding a couple of more stations, specifically somewhere in central or South America, and someplace in the Aleutian Islands. The program needs to be formalized and run by dedicated operators, but I think it will work like I told you earlier."

We spent almost the entire month of January pulling all the pieces of the plan together. The area at Camp Meade, Maryland looked like the best location for an analysis center and I drafted a message for the President's signature to have the army prepare the physical facilities. The message asked for the facilities to be completed within six months. Until then we continued to use the facilities at the navy yard.

We found a small island in the Aleutian chain, Adak, to locate a DF station and a small garrison of troops and several artillery pieces were planned in case the Japanese got frisky in that area.

Panama seemed to be the best location for the southernmost DF station and the Ambassador was told to find a location.

There were at least a thousand things to be done and there didn't seem to be enough hours in the day.

The service branches designated the number of people I had asked for and they would comprise the first training class after their recruit training was completed. It looked like the specialized training would commence around September, 1942.

J.C. and I still spent time in the navy's intelligence spaces to try to keep abreast of what the Japanese were doing.

The navy had been tasked to construct the barracks and training facilities in California and we had helped the engineers with the design of the school building.

The army located an area at Camp Savage in Minnesota to establish the language school, so that was on track.

Each of the services designated a fairly senior officer to handle the tasking as we developed it. Everyone knew that the President was behind the effort and there was no foot dragging. I was frankly amazed at the degree of cooperation we received.

We still did a lot of traveling to look at each facility early in the process to make sure the plan was going to work.

The antennas for the DF stations had to be designed. I had no idea how to do any of that but explained to them what was needed in terms of accuracy and reliability.

Within sixty days we had the station in Panama up and running. We sent twelve operators under a Chief Petty Officer and integrated them into the communications net.

The station on Oahu was designated as the net control and sent short messages to all the stations with frequency and call sign for each target. Bearings were then sent back to the control station where dedicated plotters applied the data. The system was not accurate enough to base an attack plan on, but it gave a good indication as to where in the ocean the target was located within a 100 to 200 mile radius.

That sounds like a mighty large area, but with the size of the world's oceans, especially the Pacific, it helped mightily in tracking Japanese shipping. We were interested not only in warships, but in merchantmen carrying vital supplies to Japan.

Arrangements were made with the British to exchange high priority intercept information via special circuits. The U.S. provided the code books which were delivered monthly to the person handling the coding and decoding of messages.

We had barely gotten the procedure set up when we got a message from Bletchley Park that the Germans switched naval codes on the first of February. It was probably only a routine change, but everyone held their breath that the action was not exacerbated by some action on the British part that revealed that they were breaking the code.

It set the effort back somewhat but was deemed to be a routine change of codes.

The British troops in the Far East, especially Singapore, were sent sanitized versions of intelligence as to the Japanese movements and intentions. Something as simple as a location of military units at given times could be encoded in regular codes and would be very helpful to military commanders.

The Japanese in the Philippines had forced the U.S. and Filipino troops back toward the Bataan Peninsula and were pressing for an early victory. MacArthur started retreating on the 7th of January and the battle raged for over a month.

Allied forces were eventually pushed all the way to Fortress Corregidor, a military outpost at the tip of the peninsula, where they had very little food and ammunition.

I learned that a submarine had been dispatched to pick up the COMINT operators sometime in February.

On March 11th MacArthur and his immediate staff were evacuated from Corregidor to Australia, where he was designated Commander-in-Chief of Southwestern Pacific Operating Area, or SWPOA, as it came to be called.

It was going to be a long war.

Chapter 15

It wasn't long before an event took place that proved once and for all how important COMINT was to military operations in a manner that all the senior officers could see.

In late April of 1942 the COMINT group on Hawaii copied and decoded a message relating to Japanese plans to invade Port Moresby, in New Guinea, and Tulagi in the Solomon Islands during the first week of May.

Once the initial discovery was made, special attention was paid to the circuit from which the information came. Soon the U.S. knew the dates the invasions were planned, and the major Japanese warships to be involved.

The Japanese had two carriers and a light cruiser, plus the amphibious task group and replenishment ships in the convoy.

The U.S. didn't have a lot of ships to oppose the planned landings but sent USS Yorktown and USS Lexington, both aircraft carriers, along with Australian and an American cruisers to challenge the landings.

On the 3rd and 4th of May the Japanese landed troops on the Island of Tulagi, at the tail end of the Solomon chain, and quickly took control of the island.

The invasion of Port Moresby was to take place two days later but aircraft from Yorktown located the Japanese task group and a battle ensued in which none of the opposing ships sighted each other. The battle was conducted strictly by aircraft from the respective groups.

Admiral Fletcher commanded the allied group and Admiral Inoue the Japanese group.

The battle on the 4th and 5th of May saw several ships from the Japanese task force sunk by planes from USS Yorktown, though none of the Aircraft Carriers were damaged badly.

The 7th and 8th of May saw almost constant combat between planes from both forces. During that time span the Japanese carrier Shokaku was heavily damaged while the U.S. carriers Yorktown and Lexington were badly damaged. Lexington sank and Yorktown was out of action as well.

Tactically, the allied force came out on the short end of the stick, but strategically a winner because Admiral Inoue called off the invasion of Port Moresby.

All the military commanders followed the action from message traffic and it was clearly established that COMINT had been a deciding factor in locating and determining the intentions of the Japanese.

While this was going on plans were being made to get some offensive action on our part underway in the Pacific theater. When the Japanese landed troops on Tulagi, in the Solomon Islands as part of their effort to control the South Pacific Ocean, they had constructed a seaplane base. From there they could reach Australia as well as other allied installations in the area.

Allied commanders wanted to eliminate that threat and a plea was made to take some action in the Pacific in addition to supporting the European theater of operations. Those championing that cause included the Commandant of the Marine Corps and the Commander in Chief, Pacific, Admiral Nimitz.

They saw the repatriation of Tulagi as a valid, even essential target to relieve the stranglehold the Japanese had on the South Pacific. Both made a strong case to the military leadership for an operation in the area to hamper the Japanese ability to reach high value targets in Australia and other major sites in the area.

One of the major problems was the boundaries separating the Pacific Command from the Southwest Pacific Area, (General MacArthur).

In order to keep the operation under CINCPAC the boundaries were shifted for the respective areas of responsibility enough to bring the Solomon Islands, at least most of them, under Admiral Nimitz. That way the operation could be planned without regard to MacArthur's direct input.

The original battle plan was to retake Tulagi, thereby eliminating the seaplane threat, Florida Island, and the Island of Guadalcanal.

Then, in the month of May, while we were still trying to get some operators trained to increase the effort to exploit communications, still another pivotal battle was on the horizon.

The intercept station on Hawaii had a partially decoded Japanese message indicating that the Japanese were planning a major invasion. The message was not complete and there was a large amount of concern on the part of the U.S. commanders as to the target.

Joseph Rochefort was the OIC of the COMINT unit and was an accomplished cryptanalyst. The possible location of the planned invasion was either Midway Island or one of the Aleutians. The higher ranking members of the staff leaned toward the Aleutian scenario, while Rochefort was pretty sure that Midway was to be the target.

Nothing came from intercepts during the next few days to confirm either of the locations, which were designated by two letter digraphs, and the target date was getting nearer and nearer.

Rochefort and his analysts came up with a possible way to determine for sure which location was the true one. He convinced CINCPACFLT to have Midway send a message in plain language on U.S. Navy circuits which detailed a major casualty to the desalination plant, the only way to get fresh water on the tiny Atoll.

The Japanese copied the message and took the bait. Later the same day the Japanese command sent a message to the task group commander instructing him to make sure he had desalination equipment among his stores.

That provided proof that Midway was the planned invasion site.

The invasion was supposed to take place starting on June 3rd. The U.S. had ample time to prepare an ambush for the Japanese, whose intention was to demoralize the Americans by taking Midway Island, from which they could again bomb Pearl Harbor. Midway was nearly 1,300 nautical miles from Pearl Harbor, but within striking distance of long range bombers. Again, strategically, the plan didn't make a lot of sense to the American hierarchy.

The Japanese task force was comprised of three of the carriers which had conducted the December 7th attack; Akagi, Kaga, Soryu and a fifth, Hiryu.

The battle took place on June 4th and 5th, and resulted in one of the most one sided naval actions of the war, though that wasn't known at the time. The Japanese lost all four of their Aircraft Carriers on June 4th and 5th, while USS Yorktown was damaged and later sank on the 7th of June. More than 3,000 Japanese were killed and roughly 300 Americans died in the action.

Just after the Battle of Midway, as the action would become known historically, our first class of intercept operators commenced their final segment of the training program, which dealt with identifying and copying Japanese communications. The first language class, mostly Japanese Americans had graduated and were sent to duty stations to put the ability to use. Most went to operational commanders of large combat forces, almost entirely in the Pacific.

The second levy for potential intercept operators was quickly fulfilled by each service component and the training pipeline was doing the job.

Had the battles of Coral Sea and Midway not been fought it might not have made a lot of difference to the development of our COMINT program, since it had the blessing of the President, but the Generals and Admirals who knew the whole story of both battles were now absolutely convinced of the value of a productive COMINT effort.

J.C. and I had synthesized the intelligence wish lists of each service and come up with what we called Intelligence Requirements lists. These would be folded into the training curriculum for the prospective operators in the final phase of their training.

To complicate matters further, an allied reconnaissance plane had noted the Japanese building an airfield at Lunga Point on Guadalcanal. This happened in early July. All the theater commanders quickly recognized the significance of the Japanese plan. From Guadalcanal, bombers could be launched with the ability to reach many of the strategic targets in the South Pacific area.

This added a measure of urgency to the need to neutralize the Japanese efforts before they got the airfield operational.

Guadalcanal, which had been sort of an afterthought during the operational planning stage now became the focus of the first U.S. offensive operation of the war.

Meanwhile, the COMINT job was simply too large for two of us to deal with all the details, so, with the President's blessing, we asked each service component to designate a small group to ramrod the COMINT program for their respective services. Among other things, they were tasked to identify possible locations for establishing listening posts based on their commanders projected needs.

Strangely enough, Bill Donovan had not raised a stink about wanting the COMINT program under his umbrella. Many, including myself, had thought he would make a play to have that happen. He had been recalled to active duty as a Colonel, his rank at the time of his previous release from active duty after WWI.

The FBI had turned out to be more of a problem than the OSS. The clearance vetting process was strictly adhered to and they wanted to reject more than half of the people they investigated, mostly for minor violations as teen agers, and at times based on ethnicity. I had to ask the President to have a talk with Hoover about the problem and even had to sit in on a conversation with the gentleman to explain the problem.

"In any society the large majority of the population are not going to be squeaky clean. If we rejected all the people your agents want to deny clearances for such minor offenses we will not have much to work with. Things like shoplifting as a teen ager or drinking under age are not grounds for rejection from the program. While it would be nice to have 100 percent of the people we use near perfect, it is not going to happen. The intent of the vetting program is to weed out obvious bad apples," I said.

"My people are simply following the guidelines set up to detect subversive elements," Hoover said.

The President came to my defense. "What the Commander is saying is that the program he is setting up is a very high priority and unless we allow the little stuff to pass we will not be able to get the project off the ground. Have your people get together with Commander Ward and refine the list of disqualifying actions, subject to your approval of course, to eliminate some of the minor offenses as disqualifying," the President said.

Hoover told me to get together with his lead agent assigned to vet the potential operators and do as the President suggested.

I was surprised one morning to run into Admiral Leahy at the White House in late May.

The President had mentioned that he was being recalled from his Ambassador to Vichy France position to become his personal Chief of Staff.

He was very cordial and wondered if I had an opportunity to visit Churchill again.

"No sir. I have been so tied up trying to get our COMINT program up and running that the opportunity hasn't presented itself yet. I suppose you know that Donovan is on a pretty even footing with the British special operations personnel now. He even has a regional director assigned in London," I said.

He laughed. "Bill Donovan usually finds a way to accomplish what he wants in the end."

"I was very sorry to hear of the death of your wife sir. Do you think it might have been different if American doctors had done the surgery?"

"I really don't know, and since the surgery could not wait it became a moot point. She died from an embolism, which could have happened here just as easily as in Europe."

"If there's anything I can do for you, give a shout," I said.

"I am fully aware that the navy already had a COMINT program going but you have done an admirable job of getting everyone else on board. Of course the COMINT contribution to the most recent naval battles didn't hurt your cause any," he said with a chuckle.

"I was frankly not sure I would get the support of some of the higher ranking officers, but that hasn't been a problem. They are even giving us a high priority for construction of facilities for training and analyses," I said.

"As I said, the COMINT contribution to the two latest battles in the Pacific make the best case for the need."

"I believe the overall program will be at full strength within six months. Each service will designate someone to run the programs and the analysis center will be staffed by all services with the command of that function rotating amongst the different services. It's going to be at Camp Meade, Maryland, by the way."

"What will you do then?"

"Whatever the President tells me to do. I suspect that he will assign the Chief and myself to you for day to day functions," I said.

There had been some major changes to the command structure since Pearl Harbor.

Admiral Kimmel, who was CINCPACFLT at the time, had been replaced by Admiral Chester Nimitz at the end of December. The move presented Admiral Kimmel as the scapegoat, which was politically necessary, but still unfair to the man as an individual.

Admiral Stark, the CNO, had been replaced by Admiral Ernest King in March. I liked Admiral Stark and hated to see him go, but again, the move was more political than a reflection of his military prowess.

As with my case, the two major battles in the Pacific had reflected well on the replacements.

The strategy of the major players in the war was also something for me to think about, though I was not involved in the action except in a very peripheral way.

The Japanese stressed aircraft carriers for their naval operations. They needed the air power to accomplish the air support for beach landings and to project power a great distance.

The Germans stressed submarine warfare because that was the best method to sink ships bound for Europe from America, which was crucial, especially during the early part of the war. They turned out an average of two submarines per month, which was a necessity to make up for their losses.

Japan also continued to build carriers, but their production of these ships could not hope to keep pace with what the U.S. was building. First, the population was not large enough, and second, they lacked the raw materials.

Britain and the Soviet Union were playing catch-up to combat Germany's naval power.

Neither needed to project power, rather they were more interested in defending their respective countries.

I saw and heard enough around the White House to know that the U.S. was gearing up to produce ships, especially landing craft, at an unbelievable pace.

While both of the sea battles, Coral Sea and Midway, had been major turning points in the navy balance of power to favor the Americans, the British were not faring as well in the Pacific.

The Japanese had attacked Singapore and systematically decimated the British and ethnic defenders. The same fate befell Malaya and the Dutch East Indies.

The British and other allied forces simply didn't have the logistic ability to combat the Japanese. Add to that the fact that the Japanese attacked through dense jungle terrain while the British were looking in the opposite direction didn't help the allies' situation at all. The captured POW's were shipped to Japan and became slave laborers in the Japanese mines and rice paddies, though that did not come to light until later.

The same fate befell the U.S. and Filipino forces who surrendered at Corregidor and endured the Bataan death march.

I had never met General MacArthur and only knew of him by reputation. That he was a believer in COMINT became obvious when one of the first things he did was request more COMINT support in his role as SWPOA Commander.

He had Australians trained as intercept operators and was the recipient of some of the latest operators trained under the program we had set up.

Another thing MacArthur did that incensed the OSS Director was refuse to even talk to any OSS representative Donovan sent to see him.

The President had Admiral Leahy, myself and Chief Carter in for a chat shortly after the battle of Midway.

"I want to send you back to London to speak with Churchill again. Basically to ensure that communications and procedures are in place to protect both our efforts to exploit Axis communications," he said.

"I might have problems getting an audience without someone like the Admiral here to run interference," I responded.

"I think he will see you if he knows you are in town. I also want you to see if you can get some idea about how Bill's people actually get along with the British. The clandestine war is going to be very important as the war rages on, and I want to be sure I am getting the truth about how things are going," the President continued.

"I believe our COMINT program is on track and everyone is onboard with the right objectives. It's now just a matter of getting more operators qualified to copy the circuits," I said.

"Then plan on going back to London next week. I will make a list of the things I want you to do as they come to mind between now and then."

Frank Knox had mentioned my assignment to Admiral King when he relieved Admiral Stack in March but I had yet to meet him personally. Secretary Knox was in and out enough that I encountered him occasionally at the White House and he asked if I had met Admiral King yet.

"No sir. Haven't had the pleasure yet, but I am going to spend some time with the COMINT unit so I might possibly see him later in the week," I said.

"Make a point of introducing yourself and tell him a bit about your assignment. The President has told me that he is sending you back to London. Admiral King might have some additional guidance for you," he said.

Chief Carter and I spent the remainder of the week at the Navy Yard, primarily with the COMINT section. The number of operators had increased, as had the number of positions for their use. The analysis section had also increased and I spent some time with them trying to design a template for the kind of things an analyst should look for.

The obvious thing was reading the messages the Japanese sent, but nearly as great in importance was the technical aspects of the intercepted communications. Things like call sign rotas, frequency schedules, unit locations, and order of battle were important to the operators to help them ensure that they were copying the proper circuits.

I was beginning to feel like the odd man out. All the services were onboard with the COMINT effort and others were running the program on a day to day basis. I wanted to get back to intelligence duties but I knew that wasn't likely to happen. The President would find some use for me, even if the mission was outside my area of expertise.

I stopped by my old boss, Admiral Keenan's office, and mentioned that I had not met Admiral King and that Secretary Knox had suggested I stop by to make my manners.

He accompanied me to the CNO's office and the two of us went into the office after the secretary informed Admiral King of our presence.

Admiral King came around the desk and shook hands.

"I've heard a lot about you," Admiral King said, "From no less than Frank Knox, and I have been following the progress of the COMINT effort. I figured you would get around to coming to see me before long."

On the surface the comment sounded like a rebuke, but he was smiling when he said it, so I simply pled ignorance of procedures.

"It has been a formidable task, but the cooperation from all the services has been extraordinary," I said.

"Is there anything in particular we need to talk about?" King asked.

"I have just gotten orders from the President to visit London again, probably next week. I wonder if there is anything I can do for you while I am there?" I said.

"Who in particular are you going to see?"

"Prime Minister Churchill, then Alan Turing at Bletchley Park. I imagine the President will want me to visit General Eisenhower if he has found a place to hang his hat by now."

"Why is it that the President has a very junior Navy Commander hobnobbing with such illustrious company?"

I took out my letter orders and handed them to Admiral King.

"I really don't know, except that he seems to trust my judgement, and wants information from the lower ranks as well as the heavy hitters," I said.

"It couldn't be because you were the only one to figure out what the Japanese were up to, could it?"

"I suppose that has a lot to do with it, but I think his primary reason is that he knows I won't lie to him, even if I know the information is not what he wants to hear. He uses others in more or less the same capacity. Even Admiral Leahy was made Ambassador to France for that express purpose. Don't misunderstand me; I am not even hinting at putting myself in the same category as Admiral Leahy, but when I approached Prime Minister Churchill about cooperation on the COMINT front he agreed and asked that I come back and talk to him again when the program was up and running. We are at that point now and the President suggested I go to London again with a list of things he needs to know. Since I am still a member of the navy I thought you might have some guidance for me as to what questions to ask."

"Secretary Knox has been singing your praises almost every time we get together. I know the arrangement is a bit unusual for you, but Mr. Knox described you as unflappable with a sharp mind and even indicated that you can hold your own with Bill Donovan. Not many people can do that. I was not being flippant when I asked why you were keeping such esteemed company. I know that most high ranking military people in particular, and bureaucrats in general have a tendency to equate influence to rank. I genuinely wanted to know why you were chosen for the positon you are now in," the Admiral said.

"The most truthful answer is that the President is only human. The first time I met him I thought that he was a very insecure man. I don't mean that in a derogatory way, just that I realized during our meeting that he is only human and has the same doubts and fears as everyone else. The only difference is that his decisions carry a lot more weight, and responsibility than others. He tended to question the little things to try to extract every detail about the subject."

I continued, "When I did the second assessment on the same day predicting the Japanese attacks he seemed to be impressed with the methodology for determining what was going to happen. He invited me for dinner with his wife and during the meal he was telling Mrs. Roosevelt about my prediction for what the Japanese were planning. She wanted to know how I could be so sure. I told her that one of my best operators had recognized the Japanese operator sending the Morse code. I had to explain, and managed to make her understand how it was possible. The President then told her he was going to make me one of his spies, which I later came to learn was exactly what I have become."

"So what exactly do you do?"

"Whatever he tells me to. He wants to know and understand what is going on below flag rank level. Admirals and Generals plan most operations, at least that is the common fiction. In reality, most of the planning is done by O-5's and below. A lot of input is required from the enlisted ranks as well. The President wants to know what the people at those levels think about operations that are planned. I am not talking about anything earthshattering, just a general feel for whether or not the operation will be successful. The letter orders usually gets me an audience with the higher ranking officers as well. I have some military background and can relate to many of the situations that come up. The last time I talked to Mr. Churchill he invited me back, and that is the purpose of the coming visit, at least on the surface. In reality I think Churchill is trying to use me in the same manner as the President is doing. He wants a personal messenger that he can trust."

"How do you get along with Donovan?"

"Very well. The President explained the working relationship between the two of us very explicitly at our first meeting. We both would be working directly for him, though there might be times when cooperation would work to our mutual benefit. I suspected that Donovan would bide his time and wait for me to fail at something before trying to bring COMINT under his charter. One of the things that is going to be tough to deal with is the massive amount of communications necessary to keep the program running on a day to day basis. The analysts are going to be generating messages to the various facilities on a daily basis about things such as call signs, frequencies, and schedules for the circuits our people will be copying. That is going to place a heavy burden on the normal communications channels. I suspect we are going to have to set up our own separate circuits but I haven't gotten that far along with the thought process," I said.

"I know about the contributions of COMINT to both the recent naval battles in the Pacific, and like most senior officers who know about it feel the same way. But can we expect that level of support to continue?"

"I don't know the answer to that question. One of the reasons we have been so successful thus far is because the Japanese, either through pride, or because the languages are so dissimilar, believe their communications are secure. Not many people know, but after the Coral Sea battle we intercepted a message asking Admiral Inoue if there was any possibility that his operation had been compromised before the fact. He answered that he was very confident that the operation was not compromised, and that the Americans had just been lucky to have opposing naval units there at the time of the operation. We held our breath until we were sure that they weren't going to change procedures again," I commented.

"And what about the Battle of Midway?"

"We didn't copy anything relating to that after the fact, other than damage reports. We did confirm the naval ships that were either sunk or disabled during the battle. If they had changed the codes after that it would have still been the proper action to oppose them there. The carriers alone will set them back months, if not years, attempting to replace them. Churchill doesn't allow any of the ULTRA information to be put to use unless there is some other way to have gained the information that the Germans would know about. He doesn't allow the RAF to engage the Luftwaffe until they are over England for fear of compromising the fact that they are reading some of the German traffic. That's a burden of responsibility I would not like to have."

"You do know that General Eisenhower is now in London?"

"Yes sir. I will obviously have information to pass to him from the President. I know he is going to want to know how his people and the British get along. I suspect also that the subject of providing COMINT to the Chinese will be an issue that is discussed somewhere during the visit. The loss of Singapore, and the ongoing battles in Malaya and the East Indies have been a bitter pill for the British to swallow. The Chinese have a very large number of people with which to oppose the Japanese, but without training and equipment they will be next to useless. They are, however the only opposition to the Japanese in their country," I said.

"I have to agree with Secretary Knox. You are unflappable, and seem to have a grasp on the long term objectives of our involvement in this war. While I in no way want to infringe on your mission for the President, I would like to know how our navy is doing in the European theater at the grass roots level when you return. We are planning, at least the European theater commander is planning, to land troops in North Africa to try to clear the Germans out before moving onto the European land mass. I expect the planning is going on right now. We will see the Operations Order because we will be providing a lot of the sea power for the landings when they take place, but I want to know how the skippers and sailors are reacting to the coming battles," Admiral King said.

"I don't know how much contact I will have with those folks. London is a long way from any of their major seaports, but I might have contact with some of the personnel planning the landings," I said.

"Whatever you can learn that might be helpful will be appreciated," he said.

"You are aware that we have an amphibious landing scheduled for the near future in the Solomon Islands, are you not?" he continued.

"I have heard that it is in the planning stages but have not had any involvement. When the Japanese canceled the landings at Port Moresby in New Guinea I think everyone in the upper echelons thought they would shift their interests to other areas. That hasn't happened yet. We got some indications through COMINT that a large force was active someplace in the South Pacific but have not been able to pin down the location yet."

"The President had the lines of responsibility redrawn in order to allow Admiral Nimitz in the Pacific to conduct the operation as opposed to leaving the task to General MacArthur. We feel that shutting down the seaplane base on Tulagi is vital in order to protect Australia. The landing force is already enroute to New Zealand to do the rehearsal. The actual invasion should take place within the next six weeks," Admiral King said.

"I know that the President was not too keen on the amphibious landings in the Pacific until we get a toehold in North Africa."

"We, that is all the service commanders, ganged up on him. He was still reluctant but finally agreed to allow the operation."

"I hope it is successful. I might get to see some of that up close during my trip to the Pacific, which is not too far in the future," I said.

After I left Admiral King's office I swung by the COMINT section and rejoined Chief Carter. We then headed back to our little cubbyhole at the White House.

We met Donovan in the hallway near the Oval Office. He was apparently waiting for the President to finish his current appointment.

"Just the man I was hoping to see," he said.

"Well you don't have your .45 out, so I don't suppose it can be too bad," I replied, smiling.

"I understand you will be going back to London soon," he said.

"The President said next week, but I haven't laid on any travel arrangements yet."

"Any indication as to when you will visit the Pacific theater?"

"I perceive that to be a loaded question?" I said.

He laughed. "It is. I haven't been able to get anywhere with MacArthur about helping him out with his clandestine operations. I was hoping that a personal representative of the President might be able to help my cause if you ever have reason to travel to Australia," he said.

"The President hasn't mentioned that as a possible scenario yet," I said.

"That's because I haven't made my case to him yet to have you make the trip."

"Can we discuss this before you make your pitch to define exactly what it is you want me to do?"

"Why not hang around until he is free and maybe we can all discuss it at the same time?"

"Let me drop my briefcase off and I will be right back."

Chapter 16

I dropped the briefcase off and J.C. and I talked about what had just happened.

"I wonder if this is a ploy on Donovan's part to pull you and me into his organization," I asked.

"I don't think so. I think it is more to make sure he has a hand in the war in the Pacific. I can see the drawbacks about putting people into oriental countries to try to blend in with the populations, but the other part of his charter is clandestine operations, and they can certainly do that without worrying about blending in with the local people," J.C. said.

"Well, we will find out soon enough," I said.

We made our way back to the Oval Office and were shown in where Donovan and the President were already seated and drinking coffee.

The Secret Service agent poured us a cup without asking.

"What have you been up to today?" the President asked.

"Visiting with Admiral King. That was the first time we had met face to face. Secretary Knox has been talking to him about my position. I think mainly he wanted to see if his Commander in Chief was playing with a full deck," I said without thinking about how the comment would be taken.

To my relief the President laughed. "It's better to keep them guessing. Did he have any gems of wisdom for you?"

"I told him that you were sending me back to London and asked if there was anything I might do for him over there. He asked if I might be able to give him a feel for the attitude of the lower level sailors. I frankly don't know how to do that without spending some time with the fleet, and that might not be easy to do."

"I have started a list of things to do for you, but I feel Bill wants to talk about other matters, so we will defer that until later," the President said.

Donovan laughed. "You can read me like a book. I wanted to talk about the Pacific Theater of Operations, and since these two," he motioned to J.C. and myself, "figure prominently into the thinking we could all discuss the problem."

"What specifically is on your mind?"

"As you know I have not been able to make any progress with General MacArthur relative to using my people in his area. He hasn't refused to work with my people but manages to shunt them aside to others under him, where they sit around hoping to get an audience with the great one," Donovan said.

"Is that what you call him?"

"Well, he is also known as 'Dugout Doug', and other less flattering names. The point is that he doesn't seem to think my people can contribute anything to his part of the war. While I can understand that white faces won't blend in well with the Asian population that is far from all we do. My thoughts were to use my people in situations where they train guerrilla forces to oppose the Japanese, either in enemy territory or in areas where we expect them to attack. He won't even give my people the courtesy of an audience so they can relate our capabilities."

"I can't give him a direct order to use your people, and you know that. He is the theater commander and gets his guidance from the Army Chief of Staff, to whom he is senior, so what we want done is suggested to him. It's not the best way to run a military organization, but he is obviously the best man for the job and to relieve him would be folly. Even if I sent a personal message the communicators and others would see it and the word would get out within 24 hours, either intentionally or by accident. I hate to think of the effect something like that would have on the civilian morale."

"I am aware of that sir, and that's where Commander Ward comes into the picture. MacArthur is a staunch supporter of the COMINT program, and since Commander Ward is the architect of the effort he would have reason to visit Australia. If he should do so and manage to get an audience with General MacArthur he might mention some of the other capabilities of my people, and even inject two or three specific locations where the training of indigenous troops would make sense," Donovan said.

"Do you already have specific locations in mind, or will that come later?" I asked.

"The Philippines in particular. There are several islands with Japanese troops occupying them. Luzon is simply the largest, both in area and population, but Mindanao, Mindoro, Cebu and Samar come to mind as locations where we could do a lot of good. If we had a small contingent on a couple of the other islands we could help train the local troops and possibly arrange for shipments of military supplies to them by submarine or air drops. I haven't gotten into that part of it yet, but if I knew where we could get troops I believe we can do a lot of good."

He continued, "Another use of my people would be as spotters on some of the other islands along the flight paths of Japanese airplanes. I know there are what the Australians call Coastwatcher's on some of the small islands, especially in the Solomon's. If we could fold some people into that program we could also contribute to the war effort."

"I have heard that there's a pretty good network of such people under the Australians already. Playing the devil's advocate, what could your people do that the Australians are not already doing?"

"Deliver some reliable radios for one thing. That's the biggest headache from what I have been able to learn. Aircraft recognition for another thing. It is much more meaningful if someone can differentiate between the types of Japanese aircraft."

"I was going to suggest to the President that we set up a communications net using our own people to communicate within the COMINT community. There's simply too much technical information that has to be passed to avoid speculation about what all the hush-hush communications are about among the radiomen. If we set up our own we can be collocated with regular comm centers and not have to erect a lot of additional antennas," I said. "If that happens then I will have an excuse to visit MacArthur, or at least his command. That might provide an opportunity to do what you are talking about, but the only thing going for me will be my powers of persuasion. He is surrounded by a protective group who were with him in the Philippines, and I doubt that he will even talk to me directly. The one thing that is in our favor is that there are only a few people cleared for the MAGIC material, so I guess it is possible that I will talk to him directly."

"At least there is a possibility. That's more than I have been able to accomplish to date," Donovan said. "Another reason he will probably not give my people the time of day is my rank. I am but a lowly Colonel, therefore I could not add much to his esteemed group in terms of strategic guidance."

"I am in the process of remedying that problem. I have sent your name to the senate for confirmation of a promotion to Brigadier General. It should be approved before long," the President said.

The Ditty Chasers

"That brings to mind something I might want to discuss with Prime Minister Churchill. I don't know quite what they have left in the Far East as far as effective troops are concerned but I know the MAGIC information would be very useful to them if we have not already done something in that regard that I don't know about," I said.

"I had not put that on the list and it is definitely something to discuss with him. How hard will it be to set up the communications as you envision the network?" the President asked.

"Not hard at all. We will use the same radios as the regular communicators, just different call signs and a separate crypto center. We will simply take the responsibility from the regular communications officers. I am not sure how things work now in the Pacific, but on the way I can stop by Hawaii, which I would have to do anyway, and find out," I said.

"While you are in England Bill can work up something for the Pacific. Like Bill, I believe the best chance of getting any cooperation from MacArthur is through you," the President said.

"I am going to go ahead with the trip arrangements to England for Monday if you have no objections," I said to the President.

"That's fine. I have about exhausted my storehouse of things I want you to bring up."

J.C. and I left the Oval Office and returned to our small area.

"Did you get any additional information from the COMINT section while I was with Admiral King?" I asked.

"Some of the analysts seem to believe that the Japanese have a rather large number of troops doing something that we haven't gotten a handle on yet in the Southern Pacific," J.C. said.

"Define large number," I said.

"It's hard to quantify at the present, but several thousand as represented by the commanders of the units. You know how they name their units after the commanders; well on that basis it's somewhere in the neighborhood of 30,000."

I whistled. "That's a large force all right."

"Nothing can be done until we get additional information, but I talked to some of the analysts who feel they will contest the invasion of any of the Solomon Islands, assuming they get wind of the invasion before the fact. That is not as far-fetched as it sounds. A large task group will be required to transport, I think the number was more than 10,000 troops of the First Marine Division to the area. That opens them up to detection throughout the transit, and during the rehearsals, if they actually hold any. The Japanese have a COMINT section of their own and are not completely inept in that field. They probably also have spies all over the South Pacific, so while they may not learn the actual target of the landings, they will have a good idea of the area based on COMINT and reconnaissance," J.C. said.

"Did you know that the President had the lines of responsibility redrawn in the South Pacific to allow Admiral Nimitz to have command of the actual landings?"

"No, what was that about?"

"I don't believe MacArthur agreed with the strategy and while not actually refusing to conduct the operation wanted more material support than Nimitz was willing to supply. This way Nimitz will have responsibility for all the actions in the area of amphibious landings,"

"Not much we can do about that. Might as well start planning the trip back to England. You can get the orders cut tomorrow," I said.

Chapter 17

We took the same route to London we had taken some six months previously, but this time it was summer and we didn't have to carry so much luggage. The trip again took three days and since the government had reimbursed us for the stay at the more expensive hotel before we elected to stay there again.

A message had been sent to alert the British to our arrival and a copy had been supplied to General Eisenhower to grease the skids for a visit to his headquarters. He had only recently taken up residence at the headquarters, which was located just off Tottingham Court Road. A bomb shelter was just behind the building Eisenhower was using as his headquarters.

General Eisenhower's title was Commander of U.S. Forces in Europe. To that point in his career the General had very little experience commanding combat troops. Most of his assignments had dealt with logistics, planning, and administrative billets.

General Marshall had by-passed a lot of more senior officers to assign Eisenhower, who had no actual combat experience, to the job. The fact that he had been on Marshall's staff for his previous assignment played in his favor. Although he had been mentored by such illustrious personages as Douglas MacArthur, among others, who gave him glowing fitness reports, his academic achievements and political savvy seemed to be the deciding factors for his assignment.

There was no real precedent for combining various nation's military assets under a single leadership. Much was done by committee's to that point in history.

I was not aware of any of the above factors and only knew General Eisenhower due to the Presidential comments when talking about the overall allied war strategy.

After we got checked into the hotel I called Churchill's adjutant, whose name and number I had kept since our last visit, and asked for an appointment with the Prime Minister. He set it up for the following afternoon. Since we had the entire afternoon to kill, we walked to the building that housed General Eisenhower's staff.

We had both changed into uniforms and gained access to the staff administrative section.

When I told them I wanted to see Eisenhower the comment drew a good many chuckles from the staffers, until General Smith, Eisenhower's chief of staff, invited us into his office.

He, of course, was privy to the message from the President that we would be there.

"What can I do for you Commander? I understand that you work directly for the President," he said.

I showed him my letter, as did J.C.

"Prime Minister Churchill asked me to come back to brief him once we got our COMINT program on track. That has happened and here we are. The President also gave me a list of things to discuss with General Eisenhower. General Marshall is aware of our mission and asked me to courier any material that General Eisenhower might think to be too sensitive to trust to normal communication channels," I said.

"I try not to bother the General unless absolutely necessary with things of this nature. Can you ask me your questions and accept my responses as representative of General Eisenhower's thoughts?"

"I suppose I could if you will not allow me an appointment, but there are some things I need to discuss with Prime Minister Churchill that would be of interest to him and I wondered if he might be open to accompanying us to a meeting tomorrow with the Prime Minister," I said.

"You already have an appointment?"

"Yes sir. I called to set it up just before we came here."

"What is so important that the President feels he needs to send someone so junior on such a mission?"

"I was tasked to develop a COMINT program for all our services. My first visit to London was to coordinate our efforts with the British and outline the guidelines under which the program would operate with regard to who is allowed access to the materials, both ours and theirs. The Prime Minister asked that I come back and brief him when things were on track. We are now at that stage when we need to make some hard and fast decisions about who gets the take and who doesn't."

"And you will decide those things?"

"No sir. The President in our case, and the Prime Minister in the British case, make those determinations. My job is to set up the procedures for doing what they decide needs to be done."

"We don't really see much of that here. We have only been here a short time and are playing catchup to get a handle on what needs to be done," General Smith said. "I heard through the grapevine that COMINT had played an important role in the two major sea battles in the Pacific recently, is that true?"

"I can answer yes to the question, but I can't give you a blow by blow description of the contributions. That is one of the things I hope to discuss with the Prime Minister, which is the major reason I thought General Eisenhower might be willing to sit in on the meeting."

"Can you just invite people to such a high level meeting with a Prime Minister without his knowledge?"

"If General Eisenhower agrees to go along I will call and ask that he be added to the list of visitors. Admiral Leahy accompanied me during the first meeting when he was the Ambassador to Vichy France. I think the Prime Minister trusts my judgement that I will not waste his valuable time," I said.

General Eisenhower walked out of his office and glanced in our direction. The naval uniforms probably caught his attention and he walked into the office in which we were talking.

"You have to be Commander Ward. I got the message that you would be in the area and frankly wondered what a Presidential delegate would be consulting the Prime Minister about, especially since I have just been given command of all U.S. forces in Europe," he said.

I couldn't help it, I had to laugh. Before General Eisenhower could get mad I explained why I laughed. "General Smith just asked the same question. I suppose it is true that imitation is the truest form of flattery. This is Chief Radioman Carter," I said.

Eisenhower asked, "What can I do for you?"

"Attend a meeting with the Prime Minister tomorrow afternoon if you are free. I haven't asked his permission to invite you, but if you agree to come I will add your name to the list."

Eisenhower stared at me strangely for a few seconds, which seemed much longer. "General Marshall talked to me about you, believe it or not. When you came to see him about setting up the COMINT program he asked me why I thought the President would choose someone so junior for such a formidable job. I commented that rank was not necessarily the best indicator of the best man for a job. I think you impressed him with your knowledge and demeanor."

To General Smith he said, "This is the guy who predicted the attack on Pearl Harbor, Wake, Guam, and the Philippines a couple of days before it happened. I heard some of the Generals who were at the briefing he gave after the attack talking about his explanation about how he arrived at the conclusion, but I want to hear it first hand," he said.

"Then if you will offer a cup of coffee I will explain it to you," I said.

He turned and headed to his office, motioning us to accompany him. General Smith came along as well and pointed us toward the coffee pot on the way.

For what seemed the 20th time I went over the circumstances and the conclusions.

"I can see why the President would be impressed, but why are you a personal gofer for him?"

"You mean you didn't know that President Roosevelt has his own little group of spies?"

"You are kidding, right?"

"No sir. He had Admiral Leahy assigned as Ambassador to Vichy France for the express purpose of ensuring that he got the unvarnished truth about what was happening in Europe. After the briefing I gave on December 8th to the Cabinet he told me he was going to have me assigned as a personal aide to set up a COMINT program which included all the services. I asked for the Chief here and the two of us have been doing that, plus other things that he has tasked us to do. When I was with the Prime Minister he set up a tour of Bletchley Park for us and asked me to come back to see him after our program was underway. We are now at that point and here we are. Other things that the President asked me to discuss impact the European theater and I felt it only good manners to invite you along. I believe the Prime Minister will see it the same and should harbor no animosity toward me if that is a gaffe. I can plead ignorance to protocol and probably get away with it since I am so junior," I said.

"What sort of things might interest me?"

"War strategy in general. You do know that an amphibious landing is being planned, as a matter of fact, the troops are probably halfway to where they are going by now, in the South Pacific?" I asked.

"I knew they had been pushing for authority to carry out the landings, but our overall policy is to fight in Europe first."

"The First Marine Division under General Vandergrift is going to conduct the operation. That's something like 11,000 troops. In addition a lot of naval assets will be used. All those will come from the Pacific fleet, and operational command will be under CINCPACFLT. The geographical boundaries between SWPOA and CINCPAC were adjusted westward over sixty miles to get the landing areas from under SWPOA's area of responsibility. General MacArthur was opposed to the operation and rather than get into a row with him the President saw the adjustment as the solution to the problem. The entire operation will now be the responsibility of Admiral Nimitz, though it is much closer physically to General MacArthur in Australia."

"I worked for General MacArthur in the Philippines. If he was opposed to the landings he will have a good reason. I hope this doesn't cause a lot of dissension among the theater commanders over there."

"The one thing that General MacArthur did that impressed me mightily was to request COMINT support the minute he learned that the program was going to be greatly expanded. I will be making a trip to Australia after this to address some issues with him, that's assuming I can get an audience. Bill Donovan, who runs the OSS hasn't been able to get any of his people to even have a conversation with him directly and I might find myself in the same situation. The one thing I have going for me, in addition to the Presidential letter, is that very few people on his staff are cleared for either ULTRA or MAGIC. He obviously knows what part I played in building the program, and might deduce that I could possibly interfere with getting his people access to the information that is developed from COMINT."

"That is probably true. If he believes in something he will back it with all his power, and he obviously believes in it. I am a great believer as well. Maybe you can give me some advice about how to get my own efforts set up in that regard."

"That was on my list of things from the President to address with you. Another was setting up our own dedicated COMINT circuits to pass the analytical information on a day to day basis. I want to collocate with existing comm centers and use their antennas. We will provide the cryptographic and Morse code operators to copy our own traffic. I still need to iron out the details, and there are some out of the way places that could benefit from the COMINT take."

"Is there anything you intend to discuss that I need to be forewarned about?" General Eisenhower asked.

"I am going to lobby to get more of our people working at Bletchley Park on the German problem. I think those people should be army, or even a combination of all our services. Our COMINT program is not going to go away after the current war is over. I see it as expanding greatly based on advances in communication codes and other potential trouble spots. COMINT is here to stay and the more training and experience we can get for our people the better off we will be in the future," I said.

"I certainly agree with that observation. I guess I can see what the President had in mind for you two. I know the Chief isn't mute, but he hasn't said much since you have been here," the General said.

"I know when to keep my mouth shut sir. Besides, it's pretty hard to improve on anything the Commander says. I'm just along because he told me he could get me promoted if I agreed to tag along."

General Eisenhower laughed. "I don't believe he would have you along just as a conversation starter."

"Actually, J.C. is the guy who copied the message that twigged my interest in the Japanese problem before they attacked Pearl Harbor. It was something innocuous that many, in fact most, Morse code intercept operators would not notice. He recognized the fist of the guy sending a message on the Japanese propaganda circuit who was on the Japanese Carrier KAGA, which was supposedly under radio silence. His insistence that he recognized the operator was what led to the prediction about Pearl Harbor."

The General asked, "Can you actually identify an operator from the way he sends code?"

"Some of us can. It isn't something that can be taught. It's just small nuances in the way code is sent that you become familiar with just as you would someone's voice you talk with regularly," J.C. replied.

"He's being modest General. He is probably the best Morse code operator in the world. He can copy 40 words per minute and carry on a conversation with you while doing it," I said.

"That is quite a talent from the little I know about Morse code. At one time, I think just after the First World War, they gave us all a short period of familiarization. I never got beyond the ability to recognize a single letter if given a few seconds between characters. Is it just certain operators you can recognize, or a large number?"

"It's a matter of frequency. The more I hear a single operator the better the chance that I can identify him. I copied certain circuits day after day and came to recognize their style. I say that because the pauses, types of chatter and operating signals, along with the actual code make up a style. It is not something I thought a lot about until just before Pearl Harbor. When a message is sent it has a heading, which includes the identification of the sender and receiver as well as the precedence and time. After the heading there is a break, signified by the letters BT in Morse code, letting the receiving station know that the body of the message is coming. That's to allow the operator to get his typewriter set up to copy the message. Some variance in the break from a second to three or four seconds is normal. Some allow more time, others, usually newer operators just go directly into the body of the message, not allowing the receiving operator time to prepare to copy the message. Then the type of operating signals used by an operator becomes familiar. There are a bunch of those, which simply shorten the frequently asked questions related to operating the circuit," J.C. said.

"How long have you been in the Navy?"

"Only four years, but I have been able to copy Morse code since I was about eight years old. I was intrigued with the way radio signals were sent and received so I joined the Amateur Radio Relay League. That's a worldwide group of communicators who share common interests. It was a way to talk to people all over the world at no cost. We built our own equipment, helping each other over a circuit to solve problems we encountered. I simply loved the interface with others from foreign countries and we did stuff that the military picked up on. The ENIGMA machine that the

Germans use was actually invented in the early 1920's and was intended for commercial use. It had a lot of problems at first and it took several years to get a model that worked. Once the amateurs saw that the machine had some possibilities we all became obsessed with being the first to break a message sent using that encryption system."

"Did you have any success?" General Eisenhower asked.

"No sir, but that didn't keep me from spending a lot of time trying. Two Poles were actually the first to exploit the crypto system. I believe it was around 1933. They were very much afraid of what is happening now being accomplished earlier. When it became obvious that they were going to be invaded, either by Russia or Germany, they turned what they had developed over to the British and the French. I don't believe the French ever did anything with it, but the British dived in with reckless abandon. They are still not able to break all the German codes. The Germans upgraded the system to five wheels instead of three, which increases the odds of decrypting a single letter from about one in half a million to one in five million. It is still the most secure cryptosystem in the world but like anything else, if someone can build it, someone else can eventually exploit it. Sorry for the history lesson, but that's where my interest in radios came from."

"That's fascinating. We all tend to get bogged down in our own areas of interest and give little thought to what others are doing. I have always tried to get a feel for what others do. Basically I try to determine the complexity of their tasks so as to consider those things in a given military situation. In answer to your question regarding a visit to the Prime Minister, count me in unless you run into opposition."

"I will give them a call from here and see how that plays out if you have no objections," I said.

He pointed to the phone on the desk and I picked it up and dialed the number for the Prime Minister. "This is Commander Ward. I have an appointment with the Prime Minister tomorrow afternoon at 1400. Would you kindly add General Eisenhower to the list?"

After a short pause I said, "Thank you," and hung up.

Belatedly I thought about General Smith. "General, I'm sorry. I should have asked if you would be along before I made that call."

"I think you just assumed that General Eisenhower would tell me what I need to know. You seem to have a natural leadership style that would be the envy of many General officers I have met. I guess the President recognized that as well," he said.

"The driver was going to pick us up at the hotel, but if you would rather use your staff car it's no problem," I said.

"I will meet you at your hotel at 1330 tomorrow."

"By your leave sir?" I said.

"I will see you tomorrow," he said.

J.C. and I left the building and walked back to the hotel.

"Do you have any idea how to get the information to General Eisenhower, or where to set up intercept stations that would benefit his mission?"

"I think the best thing to do would be to assign about half a dozen communicators cleared for ULTRA and MAGIC to his staff with the sole responsibility of decoding COMINT messages to keep him abreast of things of concern in his area of responsibility," J.C. said.

"Then that is what I am going to suggest, in addition to getting some more troops assigned to Bletchley Park," I said.

We managed to get through supper before the air raid sirens sounded that evening, but still had to get dressed just after midnight to get to the bomb shelter.

John Buckner

Chapter 18

J.C. and I spent the morning exploring London. We walked for the most part, not looking for anything in particular, but gauging the mood and spirit of the British people. We were both in civilian clothing and were among the minority as far as the ages of the people we saw. Most were either very young or very old. There was a smattering of people in our age group and most of those were in uniform or were obvious survivors of earlier battles. It should have been a depressing experience but the people were upbeat and friendly.

We were back at the hotel for lunch and changed into uniforms and waited near the entrance of the hotel for General Eisenhower's arrival. He had a female British driver who was familiar with the habit of driving on the left side of the road and knew the streets of London. He arrived ten minutes before the escort from the Prime Minister's office was scheduled to be there and we waited on the street outside the hotel.

The driver was on time and Churchill was waiting for us when we arrived. He was very cordial and invited us into his office. Tea and coffee were on a tray on the conference table and we took our seats.

"I hope you don't mind my taking the liberty of inviting General Eisenhower. I thought that some of the items we discuss will be important to him in his role as Commander of U.S. Forces in Europe," I said.

"Not at all. Had I thought about it I would have suggested that he be included in our talks."

"To get to the heart of the matter, our COMINT program is up and running now. The President asked me to discuss dissemination of the product and see if we could come to some mutually agreeable method to ensure that the information could be delivered to concerned parties and still be under absolute control. I have some suggestions, but we need to talk about getting our information about the Japanese to your people in the Pacific Theater. I am woefully ignorant about the disposition of forces, especially in Southeast Asia," I said.

"The situation is not very rosy for us in places like Singapore, New Guinea, and even India. The Nips have given us a proper shellacking on almost every front. Of course our main concern is to keep the Germans from turning the country into a pile of ruins and that gets our priority but at the same time we can't simply write off the large number of troops in the Pacific and Indian Ocean's. I suppose you folks have given some thought to how to handle the security problem dealing with what you learn about the Japanese," Churchill said.

"We have found that a large volume of radio traffic is necessary to keep the COMINT effort at its peak. The technical data such as call signs, frequencies, schedules and such have to be passed to the operators so they have a better chance of finding and copying the radio traffic of circuits assigned to them. In order to do this we will need our own dedicated communicators and cryptographers. My idea was to assign about a dozen people to supplement our regular communications centers and have them use their own call signs and copy our own messages. The cryptographers can then decode and get the messages to the proper people. I envision sending analytical reports along with broken Japanese messages in this manner. We will need someone at the analytical centers to make determination about distribution so that only intelligence relating to a particular area of operation is kept in that area. The exception will be for both our intelligence centers to receive all of the product. The details aren't solidified yet since I wanted to get your input before trying to design something that might not be workable," I said.

"One of the major problems that I see is that our own troops are on the move so much that the security aspect will become a chancy proposition. How will we deal with that?"

"I am not sure at this point. I do know that some thought has been given to providing a General officer to liaise with the Chinese. I assume Chiang Kai Shek will be the recipient of the support but I don't know when or where this will take place. We definitely need to find some way to get information to that location once it is in place. As to the other players in the SWPOA area, I think General MacArthur will find a way to get that done if I can get an audience with him to present our combined thoughts."

"Have you added to the distribution of your broken intercepts since we last talked?" Churchill asked.

"Only the Commander of the coming amphibious operation in the Solomon Islands. That is General Vandergrift. He commands the First Marine Division which will make the landings. I imagine the two Admirals commanding the amphibious forces and the men-of-war will also be getting data from Hawaii and more importantly from the Coastwatchers' the Australians have in place on some of the islands."

"Where are the landings to take place?"

"The Japanese have a seaplane base on the Island of Tulagi as a result of their landings during the battle of the Coral Sea. We want to take that away from them to deny their ability to target the Australian landmass. The Marines will also occupy the nearby Island of Florida. That is still about six weeks in the future I believe."

"What part do you see me playing in your production?" the Prime Minister asked.

I wasn't sure if he was being flippant or if the question was legitimate. I chose the latter option and responded accordingly. "I would like your concurrence to liaise with the Australians about setting up a full blown COMINT site someplace in the interior of the country. I haven't discussed this with the President yet, but I don't see us closing down our COMINT efforts after the war is over. The communications spectrum is going to be a battlefield of the future and I believe we will be well advised to continue the effort at a pretty high level. If we build such a site during wartime the money will be much more likely to be provided without a lot of justification that will be required later."

"And how do you see your relationship with us at that time?"

"I think you are going to do the same thing as I suggested we will do. Germany and Japan are not the only bad boys on the block, and once they are defeated we both would be well advised to have a close look at others who might be able to contest either of us. I see our relationship continuing in the COMINT world indefinitely."

"What about our part of the world in the present?" he asked.

"General Eisenhower and I were discussing that yesterday. You are going to have to make the ULTRA information available to him for planning operations. I am not talking about tons of material, only those things that concern his area of operations. I suggest assigning more people to Bletchley Park to address his needs. A pretty senior staff officer and another ten to twenty men to handle the communications should be enough. The officer can screen the decrypts in conjunction with one of your people and select the information that the General needs to see. His communications people can handle the decryption and security of the messages. I don't know a lot about what is to happen, but in talking with Admiral King I learned that an invasion of North Africa in being planned. Once we get a toe hold on that part of the world I could see a dedicated COMINT site to deal with the Italians and the German submarines in the Mediterranean. A lot depends on how General Eisenhower wants to use them," I said.

General Eisenhower had not said much and now injected his thoughts. "Once we take care of the Germans in North Africa I see us moving on to Sicily and into Italy and then northward. My primary area of concern, other than the Germans in North Africa is what we will be facing on Sicily and later on in Italy. If COMINT can provide those answers then I definitely want that capability. I don't care much about the nuts and bolts, but I definitely want access to the data."

"What we do with the ULTRA information is pretty much as the Commander outlined it. We decide who needs to know what and then use the best and most secure mode to get the data to those concerned. In the case of radio traffic we use a special code with an identifier in the early section of the encrypted message to let the communications people know that the message is destined for a special cryptographer who then decodes the message and hand delivers it to the intended recipient. Essentially, the message is double encrypted. The message is never out of the sight of the cryptographer and he destroys it after the addressee has seen it. I am somewhat paranoid, but the source is so valuable that we must go to extraordinary means to protect it. I think what the Commander suggested is the best way to handle getting you what you need operationally," Churchill said.

"Then I will work on getting some more people to Bletchley Park and some more to General Eisenhower."

"How large a part did COMINT play in the two major naval battles in the Pacific?" Churchill asked.

"In the Coral Sea battle we knew days in advance what the Japanese planned to do. We scrapped all the assets we had together and opposed them as best we could. They landed the troops on Tulagi as they had planned, but because of the opposition they had not expected they canceled the planned invasion of Port Moresby. I guess you could call it a mixed bag. While we lost the tactical battle we at least discouraged them from attacking Port Moresby, which would not have been a good thing to have happen. The most important thing that came out of that was that the IJN asked Admiral Inoue if the operation had been compromised and he responded that such was not possible and that the allies had just been lucky to have a force in the area. We held our breath for a few days after that, but they never changed procedures. In the battle of Midway, we knew they planned an attack and we knew what units they had in the task force, but we didn't know the destination. They used a two element digraph to designate the target and the COMINT section and the Command section differed in their assessment about where the landings would take place. The brass seemed to lean toward one of the Aleutian Islands, while the COMINT OIC thought Midway was the target. As the invasion fleet got closer to their D-day something had to be done to determine their target. Midway has no fresh water and they produce their own with a desalination station. The OIC proposed that CINCPACFLT direct Midway to send a message in plain language reporting the need for new desalination equipment since theirs needed repairs. The Japanese apparently copied the message because the IJN sent a message to the task group commander instructing him to make sure he had desalination equipment. That confirmed the target as Midway and CINCPACFLT sent everything available to oppose the large Japanese task force. They had five carriers and more than thirty cruisers and destroyers in addition to the amphibious landing craft. When it was over, the Japanese had lost all five carriers and about half the other combatants. We lost two carriers and some destroyers and cruisers but turned back the invasion force. Many of the flag officers became instant believers in the role of COMINT in combat. I had very little opposition to the COMINT program from that point on."

"And has General Donovan tried to bring you under his influence?" Churchill asked.

I laughed. "It's funny you should mention that because I have been waiting for his attempt ever since the President assigned me to the task. The President made it very clear to both of us what the working relationship would be. That is that I am not subordinate to OSS in terms of the mission. Donovan is actually a very smart fellow. His primary focus is on what is best for the country, and frankly I don't believe he wants the headaches of trying to run something like the COMINT effort that he has little knowledge about. He has not made any attempt to take over, or even to undermine my efforts for that matter. Like you two I believe he recognizes the tremendous importance of what we are doing in the ether world," I said.

"I have frankly been pleasantly surprised at the reports I am getting from our special operations people about how they fit into the overall war effort. I think Bill Stephenson's working with Donovan in the early stages of building his command played a large role in the close relationship that is now evident. The people from both sides of the pond are very capable and I am pleased that it turned out so well," Churchill said.

General Eisenhower asked, "How large a group does he have now? I would dearly love to have someone on the ground in North Africa to get a feel for what to expect when we go ashore. Specifically, I would like to have some idea about how the French are going to react to an invasion."

"I am not sure of the actual numbers, but based on the number of people he runs through his training facility I would guess the number to be in excess of 2,000. How much above that figure I can't say, but he processes a lot of intelligence data and has some very sharp people doing the planning. He is really bothered by General MacArthur's reluctance to include his people in the Pacific theater. I am going to have to convince him to cooperate with Donovan to some extent when I go there. The President has made it clear that he wants the OSS involved, though he realizes that it would be hard for Occidentals to blend in with the Orientals. Donovan wants to put people on some of the other islands in the Philippines to train and equip the local population. That makes sense to me, and it is just possible that General MacArthur is already doing that. I could also see a role for them in China, especially if we send a command group there to work with the Chinese."

"The Japanese have invaded Burma, primarily I think because that was the route being used to get what few supplies to China that we could spare. The convoys use overland travel and the jungle of Burma is not the same as the A1 highway. The rain in the monsoon season makes it very difficult to travel at any speed above a snail's pace. Add Japanese artillery and infantry to the mix and it makes for a very dangerous assignment," General Eisenhower said.

"That's one reason why it is essential that we get some training and equipment to China. The more pressure we can get them to put on the Japanese, the fewer troops they will have to oppose the convoys."

J.C. had not said anything at all other than good afternoon to the Prime Minister when we arrived. I glanced at him and had the impression that he wanted to say something but was debating the pros and cons of speaking.

Finally he asked, "Have we had any success tracking their submarines?"

"Not to any great extent. Why the question?" Churchill asked.

"I was thinking that we might be able to establish a net with the right geometry to locate some of them. Iceland is pretty secure and we could establish a DF site there, another in the south of England, and maybe one in northern Scotland. If we could add Bermuda to the mix it could prove worthwhile. I realize that we will not be able to pinpoint them with any degree of accuracy but we can certainly determine the area in general terms. That might be good enough to send aircraft to search the area of interest," J.C. said.

"What kind of manning and equipment would be required for something like that?" Eisenhower asked.

"Probably a dozen men at each site. The standard radio receivers could be used, but the antenna system will have to be erected at each location. Maybe I can talk to the people at Bletchley Park and see if they have any idea about an antenna system that will give us some degree of accuracy in determining the direction from which the signal is being transmitted."

"We already have an effort going to accomplish those things. I do not know the particulars, but the effort started out to locate illicit transmitters of German spies within the U.K. I know that the effort has been expanded to exploit German air and submarine signals. You can get the particulars from our COMINT group," Churchill said.

We spent more than half an hour with Churchill. Eisenhower asked, "How will you get back if I part ways with you here?"

"No problem. The driver who delivers us to Bletchley Park can drop us off at our hotel. How far in the future is the North Africa operation," I asked.

"Probably another month or so. The exact date hasn't been chosen yet, but the sooner we get underway the better off we will be."

General Eisenhower returned to his headquarters and the same escort we had before drove us to Bletchley Park.

I explained the solution that Churchill and Eisenhower had agreed upon to the Commander of the COMINT operation. He seemed to agree with the methodology.

We then entered a discussion about locating German submarines by direction finding.

"We actually took care of two of them before you chaps entered the picture. One was off Iceland in 1939 and the other off northern Scotland in 1940. In both cases we captured the cypher machine and the code books. The subs were then scuttled and the German crew never realized that we had taken the goodies before the ships sank. That was what put us ahead of the game. Alan Turing is making some progress with his bombe. It increases the rapidity with which we can attack the encoded messages. He thinks that eventually he will be able to break a message in a little as a day. I know that doesn't sound like much, but once the method proves out we can produce duplicates of the system to handle as many as twenty per day."

"How effective is your direction finding efforts against the subs?" J.C. asked.

"The early effort was to locate clandestine transmitters within the U.K. Once we ironed out some of the wrinkles and saw how effective the procedure could be we expanded the effort to searching for aircraft and naval units. The system still leaves a lot to be desired, but we have achieved some bit of success. The limiting factor is the reliability of the antenna system. It gives us a bearing that is not much more accurate than ten degrees. As you know, that is a pretty wide swath of ocean as the distance enlarges the ellipse of the search area. We have been working on a better antenna but have not devoted a lot of manpower to the task."

"What if we set up stations someplace like Iceland and Bermuda, the north of Scotland and the south of England? Just the extra inputs would refine the probable location to some degree," J. C. said.

"As you say, that would be an improvement. We are competing for manpower with the other units and I don't hold out much hope for improvement in that area in the near future."

"If I can come up with people to man the stations will there be any problem getting the go ahead to set up a net?"

"I can't see that there would. It would certainly add to our capability to prosecute the users of the nets we copy. The plans should be run by the upper level of command in any event."

"We were just with the Prime Minister and he seemed to think that the issue was pretty much up to your people. If we can work out the details for the people and equipment we will notify you and you can coordinate finding locations for the stations. I would suggest jointly manning the sites since you guys have been working the problem from the start," I said.

"It is certainly worth a try."

"We are going to be sending you a small group of operators and an officer to coordinate the information that General Eisenhower needs. I expect that will be taking place within the month. The Prime Minister agreed with the procedure, so you should be getting some direction as to how to set that up pretty soon."

We were back at the hotel before dark and once again had to take to the bomb shelter in the early night time hours.

All in all the trip was very productive.

Chapter 19

We returned to the states via the now well established route, which is via Iceland and Newfoundland, then to New Jersey, or in some cases Maine. The trip took two days under normal circumstances, but was a lot easier than the trip to Australia was going to be.

When we got back I visited Bill Donovan. I wanted to give him a brief informal overview before talking to the President.

"Churchill is very pleased with the working relationship between your people and his Special Operations branch. He now seems to see both units on a level footing and thought that Bill Stephenson's assistance to your group might have been the primary reason for the way your group fit with his people."

"I talked with General Eisenhower before visiting the Prime Minister and he accompanied us for the meeting. When the subject of your people came up and Churchill had good things to say, General Eisenhower stated that he would dearly love to have some first-hand information about how the people in North Africa, primarily the French, are going to react to the situation when all the amphibious landings are taking place. I am going to put some of our people at Bletchley Park to be sure he gets any of the ULTRA data that applies to his area of operation."

"Did he have any specific thoughts on the matter of my people?" Donovan asked.

"No, just the statement that he would love to have all he could get on the opposition his landings would face in the initial stages. He says the operation is at least a month away, and I personally think that his primary concern is how the French are going to react to the invasion," I said.

"I will have someone over there brief him on our capabilities and see what support we can provide him. I appreciate your efforts on my behalf at any rate," Donovan said.

Back at the White House in the afternoon I asked the Secret Service detail to see when the President was going to have some free time. It looked like the afternoon schedule was pretty full and I didn't expect to get to see him until the following day.

J.C. in the meantime was trying to get some information on the availability of antennas to use for the direction finding units.

He learned that the Army probably had the best handle on antennas and was scheduled to talk with the Army comms people the next day.

That would also be a good time to bring General Marshall up to date on what we had discussed with the Prime Minister and General Eisenhower since the army would provide the people to support the North Africa invasion.

Somewhat to my surprise one of the President's detail came to get me just after 1700. "The President requests your presence," he said.

J.C. was visiting the Army and would not be back until the following morning.

I followed the escort to the Oval Office and he knocked on the door and waved me inside.

The President looked tired and he pointed to a chair and the Secret Service agent poured coffee for us.

"So tell me about the latest trip," the President said.

"It went very well. Just so you will know, I talked to General Donovan about some aspects of the visit already that concern his mission. I didn't know if he would be at this briefing and didn't want him to feel slighted," I said.

"Take it from the top please."

"We didn't have any trouble with the travel and once we got into a hotel I called the Prime Minister's office and requested an appointment, which was set up for the following afternoon. Since we had the time, and General Eisenhower's headquarters was not far away we paid him a visit unannounced. General Smith invited us into his office and while we were talking General Eisenhower came in, and of course wanted to know what two swabbies were doing in his headquarters. When we told him he invited us all to his office and we had a pretty frank discussion about the European situation, particularly the coming North African invasion. I told him what we were doing with regard to the communications intelligence problem and he asked questions about what part the discipline had played in the two major sea battles in the Pacific. I gave him a quick overview of the part COMINT played in both operations and Chief Carter provided the history lesson about ENIGMA again. He was duly impressed and I asked if he would accompany us to the visit with the Prime Minister. He seemed pleased with the suggestion, so I called and asked if he could be added to the list for the appointment with the Prime Minister."

"The appointment was for 1400 and we were escorted directly to Churchill's office. We found out something interesting that neither J.C. nor I knew. The British had very early on set up a group to try to detect and locate clandestine radio contacts with the Germans emanating from the U.K. They rode around in cars or trucks and tried to isolate the locations of transmitters used for that purpose. The operation was more successful than they had any right to expect according to the Prime Minister. The decision was made to expand the effort to try to locate German aircraft and submarines, and while not an overwhelming success, they did have enough to make the effort worthwhile."

"J.C. and I had been discussing the possibility of setting up a HFDF net using the South of England, the North of Scotland, Iceland, and possibly Bermuda as fixed sites to target the German transmissions. Churchill didn't know much about the nuts and bolts and told us to confer with the people at Bletchley Park, which we did later that same day."

"The Prime Minister expressed great pleasure with the way General Donovan's people have integrated with his Special Operations group."

"General Eisenhower asked about getting access to the take from ULTRA as the intelligence applied to the North African area and to a lesser degree, the Mediterranean. I suggested setting up a dedicated effort to support him with several analysts and a mid-grade officer to determine what intelligence would apply to General Eisenhower's area of operation. It will require dedicated communications to keep the data from becoming common knowledge among the communicators, but we are going to have to address that problem right away because of the high volume of technical data that is required to maintain the COMINT effort worldwide. Both the General and the Prime Minister agreed with the procedure and J.C. is already visiting with the army to see what can be done about improving the antennas used for HFDF. There didn't appear to be any opposition to the DF net so I am going to run with that while the rest of the problems are being worked. I also mentioned that we could really use a pretty sophisticated intercept site in the interior of Australia with the intent of keeping it up and running after the current war is over. I think the lessons we have learned, even this early in the war, are that the communications spectrum is going to require a lot of attention in the future and it makes sense to plan for the long term while we will have fewer problems getting funding to build the sites we need."

"I agree with that assessment."

"One of the biggest hurdles right now with trying to keep track of naval units in particular is that we don't have any antenna that is designed for the job. I expect that J.C. will have some ideas that he will run by the army. He will also most likely contact RCA to talk about the technical part of the problem."

"And that is about it," I said.

"I'm glad you feel we are going to be in the COMINT business for a long time. I was going to ask you to plan for the future in your dealings during the current war. After we defeat the axis powers we are still going to have to deal with a world with all sorts of people in power who covet what others have. The minute they think they can get away with armed robbery, which is what it amounts to, they will do just as Hitler and Tojo have done. We are going to need to keep a close watch on what every country that we believe might have designs on expanding their territory, and I can't think of any better way to do that than through a major COMINT effort."

"I want you to pay a visit to General MacArthur soon. Get together with Bill and see if between the two of you there might be some approach that will convince him to use the OSS. I think that is another avenue of approach to keeping the peace after this war is over. We simply must have better intelligence on our potential enemies than we have had in the past. I don't see any way to do that with the different services doing their own thing and not sharing the intelligence with others. We simply must have a centrally controlled intelligence collection capability. The time to set those things in place is now when there will be no major outcry about spending the money to accomplish what we need to."

"Be sure to get Admiral Leahy involved in the discussions with Donovan. That way he knows it has my blessings," the President continued.

"With your concurrence I am going to ask General Marshall to augment General Eisenhower's staff with eight to twelve communicators cleared for both ULTRA and MAGIC. I am also going to ask both the army and navy to set up dedicated circuits to pass the encrypted COMINT and technical data. The volume is becoming a burden for the regular communications channels. Every location that has intercept sites, or provides messages to senior officers will have about a dozen communicators and an officer in charge of the operation. I want to have special codes to use strictly for our operations and our own assigned frequencies and call signs. It might pique the interest of the Japanese and Germans, but I think that is the most secure way to deal with the passing of information. If we can't get the intercepts to the people who need to see them then we are much less effective than we would be otherwise."

"Again, be sure to coordinate with Admiral Leahy and Secretary Knox before setting things in motion."

"Yes sir, I had planned to do that."

Chapter 20

After briefing Admiral Leahy and Secretary Knox, J.C. and I spent several days coordinating the nuts and bolts of the COMINT circuits. Consultations with the Commanders of each branch of service resulted in the assignment of 50 additional communicators each from the Army, Navy and Marine Corps. The navy would control the assignment of these personnel based on the needs of each command with personnel cleared for the ULTRA and MAGIC material.

The Army was assigned the responsibility of developing and distributing the codebooks for use by the COMINT communicators.

J.C. coordinated the assignments for the Atlantic HFDF net. For the present time he would work the Atlantic area and I would concentrate on the Pacific.

Our biggest problem was with the clearance procedures. A security officer was assigned from each service to coordinate the effort to at least make sure all the people assigned were thoroughly briefed on the importance of what they would be doing, and the absolute necessity to keep the information to themselves.

It was the middle of July before I could arrange the trip the President wanted me to make to Australia.

Armed with travel orders certifying the highest priority for travel I headed west. Admiral King suggested I touch base with Admiral Nimitz on the way over and sent a message telling him that I would stop on the way through.

It took me two full days to get that far. The air transportation from the states to Hawaii was heavily overburdened and without the high priority I would have sat in the air terminal for heaven knows how long waiting for an open seat.

Most of the travelers were very senior, and my Commander rank was among the lowest to get aboard the aircraft when the flight was called.

I didn't have any idea when I would be able to get to Hawaii and had not been able to notify Admiral Nimitz's staff of my arrival time and date.

The over ocean flight was long but uneventful.

When the plane landed I was just about to start searching for a phone listing for the Admiral when a navy Commander wearing the aiguillette of an aid to an Admiral approached and asked if I was Commander Ward.

"Guilty," I said.

"I am Admiral Nimitz's junior aide, Martin Davenport. The Admiral's compliments and he asked that you attend him at your earliest convenience."

"Let me grab my bag," I said.

Once that was accomplished he said, "Just throw it in the trunk. We can have the car take you to your quarters later."

Before I had time to do the proper reporting procedure the Admiral came from behind the desk and shook hands. "I have heard a lot about you from mutual acquaintances. Let me get a couple of other people in here and we can have a frank conversation."

To Commander Davenport he said, "Get the Chief of Staff and Commander Rochefort in here and then make yourself scarce for a while."

The two must have been in the COS office because it was no more than a minute before they came into the office.

Cdr. Rochefort approached me and gave an appraising look. "You certainly don't look to be the genius I have heard about. Your hair is not curly and you don't have a lot of extra weight from sitting behind your desk constantly." He laughed when he made the comment.

"Corey Ward," I said.

The Chief of Staff introduced himself and we all got coffee and sat around the conference table.

"I am familiar with your exploits as well," I replied to Commander Rochefort.

"Can you give me a synopsis of where we stand now with relation to our COMINT program?" Admiral Nimitz asked.

I was probably a bit more thorough than he wanted, but I felt it was important to give him the thinking of President Roosevelt and others in the chain of command. I covered the visits to Prime Minister Churchill and what was happening with the ENIGMA traffic. I concluded with the assignment of people to process the COMINT for General Eisenhower's staff based on what he would need to see from Bletchley Park.

When I paused for breath Commander Rochefort asked said, "Tell us about the assessment you did just before the Japanese attack here."

I mentioned the anomalies with the circuits the information came from. "It wasn't so much what they did as what they didn't do. As you know when you study the same forces on a daily basis a pattern will emerge if you look closely. One of our biggest mistakes up until the time of the attack was that there was not much interaction between operators and analysts. We encouraged operator comments but for someone who has never sat a manual Morse position it is difficult to read the proper context at times. I made it a point to learn Morse code when I was at sea after the academy. I never reached the proficiency of our better operators, but I could copy maybe 25 words per minute and became familiar with the operating signals and how the process worked. When one of our best operators called me to his position he showed me a comment from one Japanese operator to another. Both ends of the circuit was from aircraft carriers who had been working up for quite some time. The reference was to meeting on a sunny beach. Shortly after that comment the circuit went dead. The entire group that had been working up went to radio silence. On that basis I concluded that the work-up was over and they were now ready to move to whatever location they had designs on. The logic was somewhere in the Southern Pacific, and the operator comment about the sunny beaches was, I felt, enough evidence to warrant an intelligence estimate. I didn't know what the target was, but extrapolated their needs, which was to control the approaches to the South Pacific. I charted the most likely locations and wrote the report."

"It wasn't more than eight to twelve hours when my same operator came to me and said that he had just copied the operator from one of the carriers that was in radio silence sending a message on the Japanese propaganda circuit. You know the one I am talking about?"

Rochefort nodded yes.

"How can you be sure it was the operator from Kaga?" I asked.

"I recognize his fist," the operator said.

"Do you all understand that terminology?"

Rochefort was the only one who acknowledged that he did.

I felt a short explanation was necessary and provided it.

"There's probably not one in a hundred that can read the individual operator characteristics to the point that he can identify individuals, but my operator was that one. I told him that his Captain would not allow such a message to be sent while under radio silence. He informed me that the operator was probably a member of the amateur radio relay league. The group was worldwide and they built their own transmitters and receivers and most were more advanced than normal operators. He surmised that the operator he had recognized was using his home made equipment and that the Captain probably had no idea he had sent the message. I translated the message in question and it was pretty much the normal family-gram, except that there was a reference to Gaijin, meaning westerners, in the message. Based on what we had been tracking about the task group and their work-ups I decided that they were not headed for the South Pacific but for the Islands where westerners had bases, namely the Philippines, Guam and Midway. I thought Hawaii might be an outside possibility but didn't think it was the major thrust for the action."

"I wrote a revised assessment, which got all kinds of high level scrutiny. I was asked to brief the President and had to go back the following day to explain the second assessment. This was less than 48 hours before the attacks were carried out. That sequence of events caused the President to assign me to his personal staff. He tasked me to set up a COMINT program to include all the uniformed service branches plus civilian participation. Bits and pieces were already in place. The navy, and by extension, the Marine Corps had done the most, which you know about. The army already had a language school of sorts and by combining the training we would be able to start a pipeline for training right away. I talked with all the service heads and came up with some numbers to get the operator and analyst training in gear. The hardest part was the analysis center. Our biggest weakness on December 7th was that we had no cohesive method for passing intelligence reports, and analytic data that the operators need to maintain continuity of the circuits they were copying."

"The President sent me to England to coordinate the British effort with what we had planned. I expected to talk to someone in their COMINT program but instead ended up with an audience with Prime Minister Churchill. I explained what we were attempting to do and inquired about consolidating our efforts in the European Theater. He bought the approach and asked me to visit again once we had our program laid out. That happened last month and we are now at the point of putting the plan into action. The first class of linguists, some 50 of them, has graduated and are now enroute to duty stations. The first class of operators have also finished their training and are now at their stations. The communications aspect is being implemented just as soon as the army can get the codebooks to everyone who needs them."

"Who's going to be in charge of that aspect of the operation?" Rochefort asked.

"The army will produce codebooks for all services and the navy will handle the communications management aspect. The analysis center will be located at Camp Meade, Maryland and will be the control station for all COMINT related communications. All the operator training will be handled by the navy and the language training will be done by the army for all linguists. The biggest single aspect will be maintaining security for what we are doing. We have to be almost paranoid about the security. Churchill won't allow his forces to act on any intelligence gained from ULTRA unless there is some way the information could be obtained in some other fashion. I believe we are going to have to emulate that tactic in the Pacific."

Admiral Nimitz asked, "What about our task group commanders?"

"I factored that into the overall structure for disseminating information. A small cadre of communicators, and probably at least one linguist will be assigned to each task group to handle the decryption of MAGIC and ULTRA intelligence. In essence we will have our own worldwide communication net strictly for COMINT."

"Will all this be in place by the time we conduct the amphibious operation now in the planning stage for the Solomon Islands?" the Chief of Staff asked.

"What date are we talking about?" I asked.

"Probably within the next six weeks. General Vandergrift is enroute to New Zealand with the task group as we speak."

"I am enroute to see General MacArthur and if you wish I can ask that he provide a couple of communicators and a linguist to the invasion force. Alternatively you can send people from here to augment the task group. The directive for setting up the comms will be out within a couple of weeks, but I don't know if all the wrinkles will be ironed out by the time the invasion takes place," I said.

"I think it would be best if we provided the people for the afloat operations," Admiral Nimitz said. "And no, Commander Rochefort, you cannot go."

"I agree that would probably be the best solution. The guys here have the largest operation and you will better know what sort of information will help the invasion force," I said.

"What else is going to impact our area as the program grows?"

"The number of operators will increase as the training pipeline turns them out. I talked with the President about making the COMINT effort a continuing discipline after this war is over. I don't see the rest of the world falling in line and promising to be good boys after we take care of Germany, Japan and Italy. I think our national security will be better served by keeping track of the stronger nations on a continuing basis. I am going to talk with the Australians about setting up something in the interior of the country with the objective of keeping the site up and operational after the war is over. Prime Minister Churchill seems to be in agreement with the concept and sees a joint effort between the two of us for the collection and dissemination of intelligence gained through COMINT. We are in the process of setting up a HFDF net in the north Atlantic to try to refine the ability to locate especially German submarines more accurately. The stations will be in the south of England, the north of Scotland, Iceland, and possibly Bermuda. The biggest hurdle to deal with in that endeavor is the development of better antennas to give us better lines of bearing to active signals. I have a Chief working that problem with the army and RCA."

"You think we will be able to do the same thing in the Pacific?" Nimitz asked.

"I don't see why not. The problem right now is that we don't have a lot of choices about where to locate the stations. The Japanese hold most of the islands and that is where we will need to locate the individual sites. Probably Central America, someplace like San Diego or San Francisco, then one of the Aleutian Islands, plus of course Hawaii and Australia. That endeavor is going to create a lot of radio traffic because the different stations will have to be informed of the active signals and the call signs and frequencies. The bearings from the individual stations will then have to be transmitted back to the net control so they can be plotted. A lot will depend on radio wave propagation as to which stations will be able to acquire the signals. Even if they only have ten signals of interest per hour, that will require the transmission of more than sixty messages with six stations operational," I said.

"What kind of crypto do you envision for that task?" Rochefort asked.

"Probably one time pads for the reporting stations. The net control will use a different code to alert the net stations that a target is active. The Atlantic area will be the test bed for working out the wrinkles. I really believe that good locating data can make a big difference in the tactical environment if we can get the data to the people who need it in a timely manner."

"Be sure to touch base again on your return trip," Admiral Nimitz said.

The meeting had lasted less than an hour and I was on another flight before 1800 the same day.

Chapter 21

The flight was long and boring. The aircraft was a PBY seaplane, which provided much of the air transport for the military during the early years of the war. The reason obviously was that the situation was so fluid that land based aircraft might have trouble finding a suitable landing site.

I had been told that the headquarters for the task force destined for the Solomon Islands would be located at Espiritu Santo in the New Hebrides Islands, and they didn't have an airfield. They could only accommodate seaplanes, and even that endeavor was problematic.

The flight was not one to write home about, unless one's interest was self-flagellation. The flight was through some rough clouds and sometimes reminded me of my days aboard ship in rough weather.

I had to catch another ride from there to Melbourne, which was almost equivalent to a cross country flight from Washington to San Francisco.

Tulagi was toward the northwest in the Solomon Island chain, while Guadalcanal was to the southeast and much closer to the islands of New Britain.

MacArthur's headquarters was located in Melbourne, which is on the southern coast of Australia in New South Wales. There was definitely not any danger of Japanese air raids there!

Flight manifests were obviously provided to SWPOA because my plane was met by a representative of the G-2 section of MacArthur's staff, which was presided over by General Willoughby, who is of German extraction and either affects a foreign accent by design or as a result of his upbringing.

I had no idea why I had been met because Willoughby wasn't on the cleared list for either ULTRA or MAGIC. I had a feeling I was going to be walking a fine line in my dealings with SWPOA.

The headquarters building was right downtown in a multi-story building that had been conscripted by the Australian government for the duration of the war.

General MacArthur's office was on the eighth floor, as was General Willoughby's.

My escort led me to the elevator.

I asked about my luggage and was told that it would be taken to the hotel where most of the staff had rooms.

The man who met me was an army Major and he led me directly to General Willoughby's office and knocked on the door.

The General motioned us inside. We both stood at attention until he put us at ease.

"What can we do for the navy?" he asked.

"I need to confer with General MacArthur; at the President's orders," I added a little belatedly.

"What do you need to see him for?"

"I'm sorry sir, but I am not at liberty to divulge that information," I said.

I had a feeling that I was about to get the equivalent of a navy keel-hauling when MacArthur himself saved my bacon. Much as had happened in London with Eisenhower, he happened by at a most opportune time from my viewpoint.

He noticed the navy uniform and detoured to Willoughby's office. "You must be Commander Ward," he said.

I came to attention again and replied, "Yes sir."

"I need to go to the dungeon. Would you be so kind as to accompany me?"

"Yes sir," I said, and followed him out of office.

"General Willoughby is not privy to MAGIC, but I don't suppose I need to tell you that."

"No sir. I was trying to figure out how to best deal with the situation when you appeared," I said.

MacArthur chuckled. "I know it isn't a laughing matter, but he has been my G-2 since early in my assignment to the Philippines and I hate having to keep him in the dark. He obviously is smart enough to figure out what is going on, and rightly figures he should be cleared for the information. Who makes the determination as to who is briefed in on the program?"

"The President," I replied.

"You mean he provides guidance to the program?"

"No sir. I mean he actually signs the authorization to brief anyone new into the program. The way he worded the directive was that he would make the final determination on everyone who is cleared for access to the program," I replied.

"What do you think is the reason for keeping General Willoughby in the dark?"

"I don't believe there is any reason, other than the fact that he wants to keep the list as short as possible. If you wish I will mention the fact and express your desire to have him briefed into the program when I return to Washington," I said.

"We are on our way to what my people call the dungeon. It's actually the crypto room where the MAGIC traffic is decoded. The reason I wondered about General Willoughby's status is because we had our own intercept station in the Philippines and he saw that traffic on a daily basis."

"I'm sorry I can't give you an answer, other than the President's orders were that operational commanders were to be the only recipients, other than the people doing the interception and analysis. His exact words were, 'I don't want this kind of information passed around on reading boards'."

"Well I think he has a legitimate need to know officially what he already knows unofficially," MacArthur said.

We had been talking as we took the elevator reserved specifically for MacArthur's use to the basement of the building.

I didn't respond right away because the guards were within hearing distance. One of them immediately picked up a telephone. He didn't dial any number but started talking when someone obviously picked up the other telephone to which his was connected.

"The General and a navy commander are outside," he said and hung up the phone.

Within a matter of seconds an army Major opened the door and the General and I walked into a vestibule where we faced a second door.

Once the outside door was closed we continued on into the room behind the inner door.

The Major said, "I don't believe the General would bring anyone not authorized into our humble working space, but would you mind showing me your identification?"

I took out my ID card and also the letter from the President. I handed the letter to General MacArthur and the ID to the Major.

"Okay, what does the personal representative of the Commander in Chief want to talk about?"

The major found chairs for us and we all sat down.

"I probably need to start at the beginning so you will appreciated how I became the President's gofer."

I related the intelligence assessments just before Pearl Harbor and how that resulted in my being drafted by the President. I talked about the order to set up COMINT collection sites for all government agencies and went through the visits to London with a general description of how the training was set up and the results we had achieved during the previous months since December 7th.

"Were you aware that the British have been breaking the German's encrypted radio traffic since 1939?"

"I heard high level rumors that they were enjoying some degree of success, but nothing specific," MacArthur said.

I went into J.C.'s history lesson on the ENIGMA machine and how the two Pollack's had reversed engineered the machine and then provided the results to the British and French.

"During the meeting between the President and Prime Minister Churchill last June Mr. Churchill neglected to mention to the President that they were reading part of the German radio traffic, just as the President neglected to mention to Mr. Churchill that we were reading the Japanese messages."

"I was dispatched to London where I met with Admiral Leahy, who was them the Ambassador to the Free French. He set up a meeting with the Prime Minister and the two of us met with him. The British are as circumspect with their handling of ULTRA material as we are with MAGIC."

"I knew from another source about the ENIGMA machine and used that knowledge as a way to arrange for some of our people to be assigned to Bletchley Park, where they do the decoding of the German messages that they can break, and in return we would provide what we learned about the Japanese."

"During the meeting I discovered that the British were not anxious to integrate the people of OSS into their European operations. I convinced Mr. Churchill to allow a small number of Donovan's operatives to work alongside the British until they were satisfied that the two groups could work in a beneficial atmosphere. I was back in London two weeks ago and the Prime Minister was pleased that the integration of the two components had worked out well."

"While I was there I visited General Eisenhower and made arrangements to have a small group of ULTRA an MAGIC cleared people assigned to his staff. The Prime Minister also agreed to add to the group at Bletchley Park strictly to extract any intercepts that would impact General Eisenhower's mission for forwarding using special codes, much as we are doing here."

"We are in the process of setting up intercept sites in Iceland, in the north of Scotland, and once General Eisenhower establishes a footing in North Africa, someplace there. These stations will also have a group dedicated to high frequency direction finding, primarily to track mobile targets, such as ships and aircraft. That part of the plan is a work in progress because we don't have antennas suited to the task. RCA is working to solve that problem now."

"What the President wanted me to do here was to get your ideas about how we can improve the COMINT capability in the Pacific area. Since the Philippines fell we only have the site on Oahu in the Pacific, and we need to do a lot better than that to keep on top of the Japanese problem when we go into the offensive mode of operations."

"I have been a believer in the value of COMINT since I first learned that we were able to read the Japanese codes several years ago. I wish I had the resources to set up a good intercept site here, but the situation is so fluid that it would be too difficult to set something like that up," MacArthur said.

"I don't believe the tactical situation has much impact on where a station is sited. The most important factor is the ability to hear the signals we are interested in. Further, the people doing the work need to be well away from any possibility of having to engage the enemy at close quarters due to security concerns."

"So what would you propose?"

"I would look for some site in the interior of the country that has ample space for erecting the needed antennae and build the site from the ground up with the intention of operating the station for a very long time, assuming we can get the Australians to go along with the plan. I don't believe the need for COMINT is going to disappear after the current conflict is over. There are always going to be countries that we want to keep an eye on, and COMINT is the less intrusive way to accomplish that."

"What about the people to operate the site?"

"We are training operators to the tune of 200 every six months. The training is conducted by the navy for all branches of service, and when they become qualified operators they are assigned where the need exists without regard to service. The army is responsible for the language training and handle all the services. I asked for 2,000 trained operators and 250 trained linguists for starters. I visited with all the heads of services and I believe everyone is enthusiastic about the value of COMINT, especially in light of the contributions to the Battles of Coral Sea and Midway."

"I certainly have to agree with that statement. What was the reference to the OSS? I know you didn't just throw that in for a conversation piece," MacArthur said.

"Another facet of the war in this area is the Chinese. The Japanese have been concentrating on Burma since they learned that was the route we were taking to get supplies to China. The President feels that we need to provide sanitized MAGIC information to the Chinese. I think he has directed General Marshall to start planning to send an advisory group under a flag officer to coordinate with the Chinese. That is going to require some coordination at higher levels. The OSS wants to get involved in the Pacific and General Donovan has made a case to the President that his people would be invaluable in training and supplying the native populations on various islands. You might very well already be doing that, but if not then that task could be undertaken using Donovan's people. At the same time you could use his people to augment the Chinese group to keep up to date about what the Chinese are doing."

"You mentioned 2,000 operators. How many intercept sites are planned?"

"That's still open for debate. My personal opinion is that we keep putting people on the task until we feel relatively certain that we are copying the majority of Japanese communications. We won't know that until we have enough operators in the field to build a data base for the analysts to reconstruct the different communication nets that are in use. I know for a fact that some of the lower echelon circuits are not getting a lot of attention simply because we don't have the manpower in place to exploit them. As we bring more intercept sites on line we will start to look at the communications of other countries as well. The way the world is aligned after the war will dictate the amount of effort we put into the task, but I believe that the assets we have in place at that point will not change appreciably when the combat arms start to draw down. It is just too important to skimp on the continued effort. The majority of high ranking officers in the military now recognize the importance of COMINT and those will be the people who have the greatest voice in shaping the structure of our peacetime forces. If our success in exploiting the communications of the Germans and Japanese continues, each battle in which COMINT played a key role will be documented and the weight of high ranking officers such as yourself, Admiral Nimitz and General Eisenhower will convince the Congress to keep the money spigot open for the continued effort. The President supports the effort and he can do some arm twisting to get what he wants."

"I have people near Townsville, where the Australian Coastwatcher group is located attempting to do exactly what you are suggesting. Unfortunately the effort has not been very successful because of the lack of antennae and linguists to decode what they copy. We courier their intercepts from there and try to translate here, where, as you might guess, we have few Japanese linguists. How can we rectify that situation?" MacArthur asked.

"By building an antenna field and sending additional operators and analysts to Townsville. I need to look at the site to get some idea of the needs while I am here. If you can grease the skids with the Australian Prime Minister it would make the job easier. A lot of the war is taking place all around us and it makes a lot of sense to have an intercept site nearby that can provide information quickly."

"I will arrange for a visit to Townsville for you. As to the OSS, I don't really see how they could be of use to me. They certainly can't pass themselves off as natives, and I am not sure that the natives will listen to them if they are used in a training role," MacArthur said.

"With your influence I am sure the locals will take the matter seriously, especially the islands of the Philippines. Besides, that would be a good way to keep them occupied and out of the decision making process. I tend to agree that they will not be able to blend in with local populations but if some could be infiltrated and a supply of weapons should follow, then the locals will be impressed and look more favorably on the effort. And the bottom line is that when we start taking the islands back from the Japanese every additional body will help," I said.

"I will give your suggestion some thought."

We went back to the eighth floor to MacArthur's office.

He motioned his administrative assistant into the office and told him to summon the Colonel in charge of his air assets.

The Colonel was in the same building and was there in a matter of minutes.

MacArthur said, "Please make arrangements to transport Commander Ward to Townsville. He will also require transportation back here within a few days."

"See me when you are finished here and I will give you the schedule," he replied.

"Is there anything else we need to discuss Commander?" MacArthur asked.

"No sir, I don't believe so."

"Just to set the record straight, the President wants me to confer with the Australians about setting up a large intercept site, which presents no problem as I am the Commander of the combined forces in this area. You, or I should say our military will provide the personnel to erect the antenna field and construct buildings to house the operation and personnel. A supply of operators and analysts will be ordered in to man the site and the communications will be set up to service the facility."

"Yes sir, and the site will also be part of the HFDF net," I replied.

"I think we can manage that. I hope it will not take long to get things up and running. I have been tasked to take Rabaul in conjunction with the amphibious operation being commanded by Admiral Nimitz and having some idea about the Japanese intentions will certainly make that job easier. If I don't see you again before you leave, it has been a pleasure meeting you," he said.

I left MacArthur's office and sought the Colonel who was making the transportation arrangements.

The next day I was on a B-17 headed for Townsville.

Townsville was not a thriving metropolis, though they did have a nice airfield.

The intercept site was nothing more than several large tents sited inside a double roll of concertina wire with a guard shack at the break in the wire. I didn't even see the antennas they were using until they were pointed out to me. They were well outside the wire and consisted of dipole and long wire configurations.

An army Major was in charge of the operation. MacArthur had apparently sent a message pertaining to my mission because the Major's first question was, "when are we going to be augmented and get some linguists?"

We went to his office in one of the tents and I laid out the plan for him.

"The wheels of bureaucracy move ever so slowly," I told him. "General MacArthur is going to get permission from the Australians to build the site. I am going to ask the President to dispatch a contingent of Navy Seabees to build the permanent buildings. I want it done in such a way that we can remain operational after the war is over, assuming we win of course. During the construction phase you will have some input into the design phase as the Seabees do the work. Keep in mind the security aspect. I want chain link fencing as the outer perimeter and concertina wire about twenty feet inside that. Fence the entire area, including the antenna field. I am going to try to get approval for at least 50 intercept positions and a direction finding station. The analysts will need dedicated spaces, and there are going to be a bunch of those, probably in the neighborhood of 40 to 50. The troops will start to arrive before the construction is finished. Use them to do the gofer work for the Seabees. We want this up and running within 60 days. You are going to have to close down your active operation until the Seabees finish with the buildings. I am going to send a Chief Radioman to give you a hand. He works directly for me, and we both work directly for the President, so keep that in mind if there is a need for some horsepower along the way."

"I understand," the Major said. "I was wondering how long it would take our leaders to grasp the significance of what we do."

"The two latest major naval battles cemented that aspect of the program. All the brass I have visited are now firm believers in the value of COMINT, so they will be falling all over themselves to get this done."

I spent two days in Townsville and made sketches of the terrain and between the two of us we decided the best way to lay the base out.

The trip back to Hawaii took me three days. I visited with Admiral Nimitz again and told him what was going on within MacArthur's area. Since he had operational control of a Seabee Battalion I asked if he could dispatch someone to Australia to oversee the construction of the base.

He readily agreed and asked when the construction would be started.

"It would not surprise me if everything is already in place as far as the coordination with the Australians is concerned. General MacArthur believes strongly in the role of COMINT and probably has seen to that."

"The amphibious assault in the Solomon's is probably going to take place within the next two or three weeks, depending on how the rehearsal goes. The tentative date is August 7th. You might tell the analysts back in Washington to make sure they provide anything that could impact the operation on a priority basis," Nimitz said. "I have sent four man teams to both Admiral Ghormley and Admiral Turner. They will handle the communication of MAGIC material to make sure they get anything pertinent to the operation. They will also keep General Vandergrift informed."

"Then I guess I am about ready to head back to the states."

The trip back took three days. There were restrictions on travel and everyone needed a priority before a seat could be reserved, even on civilian airlines.

I was not sure how productive the trip had been as it related to the OSS problem. I felt certain that General MacArthur would make full use of any COMINT resources though and that was my priority.

Chapter 22

When I got back to Washington I spent a late evening writing a trip report, trying to fix in my own mind how to present the information to the President.

J.C. had not spent much time in our little office while I had been gone according to the Secret Service detail. I assumed he was still dealing with the antenna problem.

I penned a note letting the President know that I was back and would report the next morning. I then went to the hotel and tried to get my body clock back on schedule.

When I arrived at the White House the following morning the Service guy said the President wanted to see me. He knocked on the door and then opened it. The President was alone and motioned toward the coffee pot when I stepped inside.

"How did the trip go?" he asked.

"Kind of a mixed bag actually. General MacArthur is a firm believer in the value of COMINT. He even has a rudimentary intercept site near Townsville with the operators he evacuated from the Philippines. They don't have much in the way of antennas and only a couple of linguists. They courier their intercepts to the headquarters in Melbourne where they have a small cadre of people handling the MIGIC communications. They do what they can, but it is very little in terms of usable intelligence. Some of the work probably duplicates what is being done in Hawaii and here because we have no way to assign circuit priorities at present."

"Before we get into a lot of detail let me see if I can get Secretary Knox, General Donovan and Admiral Leahy together this afternoon so you can brief us all at the same time."

"I am going to visit the navy yard this morning. When will I need to be back here?"

"After lunch will be fine. I will attempt to get everyone together around 1:00 p.m."

I left and headed out to see Admiral King. I wanted to see how the amphibious landing rehearsal had went.

I had to wait for about a quarter of an hour before he had any free time.

I explained about plan to build an intercept and analysis site in Australia and wondered how difficult it would be to get a Seabee Battalion, or at least part of one, to Australia.

"The people are not a large problem. The problem is getting the equipment they need for the job. I am assuming you plan to procure building materials locally," he said.

"To tell you the truth I had not even considered that aspect of the problem. I think the best way to handle that is to dump the problem in General MacArthur's lap. I feel sure he will be able to get what is needed from the Australians, but it will be a costly proposition," I said.

"How long to get the station operational?"

"I hope to have a fundamental capability in under a month. I want to divert some of the operators destined for other sites to Australia, and at least a dozen of the linguists in the next class. This is based on the assumption that the President buys into the plan. I am supposed to brief him this afternoon with Secretary Knox, Admiral Leahy and General Donovan in attendance. On the way back I asked Admiral Nimitz to send a senior Seabee to Townsville to work with the current OIC of the setup they have. He's an army Major and I think General MacArthur will leave him in place when the site is completed. Since the amphibious operation is so close at hand I want to send some people there right away, preferably some of the better operators and at least a couple of top notch linguists. Admiral Nimitz has placed people cleared for MAGIC on the staffs of both Admiral Turner and Admiral Fletcher. They will carry the codes with them and do all the crypto work in a separate space from the ship's crypto room, passing pertinent information to Admiral Ghormley and General Vandergrift."

"You feel pretty confident that the President will buy your suggestions?"

"Yes sir. We talked about it before I made the trip and he is in full agreement that we will need to retain a COMINT capability after the war is over. That is based on the assumption that we will come out on top," I said.

"I don't suppose you have seen it yet, but a message came in this morning from SWPOA. It was addressed to Admiral Nimitz and we got an information copy. Seems a reconnaissance plane got some pictures on one of the islands that was on the target list for General Vandergrift. It was not one of the major objectives, but was pretty much one of those nice to have things. The brunt of the force was supposed to invade the islands of Florida, Tulagi and Gavutu. The Japanese have an operational seaplane base on Tulagi and it is important to take that out of the equation. With the discovery of the information about Guadalcanal I imagine the plan will be modified to include that location as the main thrust of the whole operation."

"How far along are they with the construction?" I asked.

"From my understanding it is more than fifty percent finished. If they get it operational they can control the surrounding area, which routes we use to ship supplies to SWPOA, and also be able to reach Australia and Port Moresby."

"I am frankly surprised that we didn't get any earlier indications about the construction of the airfield through

COMINT. There has to a sizeable force there to carry out the construction work, not to mention keeping the natives in line."

"Well apparently that is the case, and I expect Admiral Nimitz will modify the operations order to include Guadalcanal."

"I assume that Secretary Knox will keep you informed, but I will get you a copy of my trip report so you will know the details of the plan, again, assuming the President approves it."

I swung by the intelligence spaces to do a quick review of what had been happening during my trip to the Pacific and went back to the hotel for lunch before returning to the White House.

As I walked by the hallway where the Oval Office is located I was motioned toward the office by one of the Secret Service agents.

"I need to grab a file from my office. Be right back," I said.

I rightly assumed that Secretary Knox, Admiral Leahy and General Donovan were inside.

The agent knocked lightly on the door and opened it after having a look through the peep hole.

After the greetings I took my cup of coffee from the Service guy who had poured it and sat down with the others on the couch.

"Okay, the floor is yours Corey," the President said.

"First of all, the situation has changed since I was there. I am referring to the message about the discovery of the Japanese efforts to build an airstrip on the island of Guadalcanal. I assume you have all seen that?"

Secretary Knox had seen it but Donovan, Leahy and the President shook their heads no.

"I have not seen the message itself but got the word from Admiral King. I believe that is going to require a modification to the operations order for the invasion to put Guadalcanal at the top of the list. It is toward the southern end of the Solomon Island chain, a good distance from the other objectives. I don't know how they will split the amphibious force, nor how many troops the Japanese have on that particular island, but I assume they have a substantial force. The island is also much larger than the other islands that are being targeted. We had absolutely no indication through our COMINT effort that the airfield was under construction. The discovery was made by a reconnaissance flight. From the descriptions I got it appears to be about halfway completed."

"I stopped by CINCPAC both coming and going and briefed Admiral Nimitz."

"When I arrived in Melbourne General Willoughby had sent one of his officers to meet my plane. I was very much afraid that General Willoughby was going to ask the nature of my visit and I didn't believe he would take the statement that he was not cleared to hear what my visit was about gracefully. As it happened, providence was on my side because General MacArthur came by at that time and invited me to accompany him to the dungeon, which is where they handle the MAGIC decrypts. We went into the spaces, which were manned by an army Major and a Master Sergeant. We held the major portion of the discussion there. The COMINT operators who were evacuated from the Philippines had been sent to Townsville, quite a distance up the coast, and told to try to set up an operation there. There were only about a dozen of them and the reason they were sent to that location was because that is where the control group for the Coastwatcher's is located. They operated out of large tents but had pretty good security with concertina enclosing the perimeter."

"I discussed the possibility of setting up a substantial intercept facility with General MacArthur and he is probably as anxious as we are to make it happen. I asked if he would coordinate with the Australians to get permission to build a permanent site there. In his words, 'I am the Commander of SWPOA and that gives me the authority to do what is necessary to defend the area'. He indicated that he would talk with the Prime Minister to assure that we didn't run into problems on the political side. He was concerned that General Willoughby was not officially privy to MAGIC since he regularly saw the reports when they were in the Philippines. He wants Willoughby added to the list, which I told him I would recommend. He does have a legitimate need to know."

"When I broached the subject of OSS participation in his area of responsibility he sort of brushed me off until I mentioned that there was a very real possibility that we would send a General Officer to China to provide intelligence to Chiang Kai Shek's forces, and that the OSS might be well suited to providing the liaison between the two headquarters. He was still noncommittal but said he would give the matter some consideration. He seems to believe that no worthwhile objectives will be achieved by sending small groups to work with native populations."

"I then went to Townsville and talked to the Major in charge of the operation. Since they have no linguistic capability to speak of the copy is sent by courier to Melbourne twice a week and left to the people there to do the translations. The Major and I looked the area over for possible locations that would require the least in the way of land preparation and got a general idea about where to place the antennas and living and working spaces for the troops."

"On the way back I mentioned the project to Admiral Nimitz and asked about the availability of Seabees to handle the construction. He has already sent a man to work with the Major in Townsville, based on my statement that the President was aware of the project. I probably overstepped my authority there, but based on our last conversation about continued COMINT resources after the war, I felt sure the project would gain your support."

"That's about it in a nutshell," I finished.

"Do you think we can get the proposed site in Townsville operational in time to provide support to the coming operation?" the President asked.

"I would hope so, but it all depends on how long it takes to achieve our objectives. If it is relatively quickly, then we probably won't be able to do much, but if it is a drawn out operation then we could very well provide some good intelligence about the plans and disposition of Japanese forces. It also depends on how quickly we can get the Seabees into position and equipped to build what we need. The antenna field can be constructed first and the tents currently in use can be used until more permanent facilities are completed."

"What about people?" Secretary Knox asked.

"I plan to divert at least 30 of the next class of operators to Townsville, and at least 12 linguists. The site can also provide support to the HFDF network as it comes on line."

"So where do you go from here?" Admiral Leahy asked.

"The official messages need to go out to set things in motion. I suppose a written directive from the President to the Service Chiefs with marching orders will be the first step. The services will have to be told exactly what their responsibilities are. I will work on that from this moment forward until everything is in motion."

Donovan was not too happy about MacArthur's continued reluctance to use his resources. "All he said was that he would give it some thought?" he asked.

"Yes sir. I got the feeling that he might decide to at least use your people to do the interface with the folks in China. I don't know why he is so set against working with the natives on the various islands. As the Commander of the Philippine army for so long he must surely have some appreciation for what can be accomplished with native troops."

"Is the amphibious operation still scheduled for August 7th?" the President asked.

Secretary Knox replied, "To the best of my knowledge. I am not sure what the latest change will do to set the time table back, but I believe everything will be in place on schedule."

"If you don't have anything else for me I will get back to work. I have to find out where Chief Carter is and see where we stand about antennas. I will do the rough draft of a memorandum for the service chief's and have that to you by the end of the day," I said.

The President nodded and I left the office.

I checked with the navy department to find out when J.C. had left and when he planned to be back. I also needed a phone number to reach him if possible.

I was told that he had been gone for nine days and that he had expected to be gone for as much as two weeks. I called the army and got a number for RCA in Princeton, New Jersey, which is where J.C. had gone.

I managed to track him down and left a message for him to call.

He got back to me before an hour had passed.

I told him that we needed enough antennas to set up the site in Australia and that the army would be directed to set up the contract.

"You can give the okay to start building them now if they don't have anything in stock. Make sure we get enough to handle fifty positions. After you do that come on back home so you can get ready for another trip."

I then started working on the memorandum for the President outlining the actions required of all the players.

General MacArthur was told to secure the permission of the Australians to build the site and to arrange for purchase of materials. He was to find out what the Seabees would need in the way of equipment and rent or lease it from local sources.

Admiral Nimitz was directed to deploy a Seabee Battalion on a priority basis to Townsville, Australia where they would be provided further instructions about the task.

The navy was directed to send 30 of the next intercept operator graduates to Townsville, and the army to dispatch not less than ten linguists to the same location.

The navy was also tasked to set up circuits between Townsville, Oahu and Washington.

The army would provide the code books.

Chapter 23

I had the tasking memorandum roughed out by the end of the day and got it to the President. He added a comment that the orders were to be implemented immediately and that any delays or funding shortfalls should be identified as they occurred.

The message was delivered the following morning to the concerned parties.

J.C. returned that morning and we sat down for a discussion of both our trips.

"RCA has better antennas that what is currently in use for shortwave reception. They have come up with a two element one that allows its use across the entire spectrum. We currently use two different types depending on whether it is day or night. I think this one will work much better and the antenna field won't have to be too large. They also have developed an oscilloscope that displays the signal in a butterfly pattern. It isn't terribly accurate and will depend a lot on the operator lining the incoming signal signature properly. I think it will be a big improvement over the way we do things now. I asked for one to experiment with here to see just how good or bad they are. They will ship it tomorrow."

"I got a chance to play with one of the superhetrodyne receivers and didn't have any problem picking up signals from either side of the world. I believe we need to outfit all the stations with them until something better comes along, which they tell me could happen at any time. They are constantly experimenting to improve the product."

"How large are they for shipping purposes, and can they be broken down into components and reconfigured when they get to the destination?" I asked.

"The antennas are about thirty feet tall, maybe eight inches in diameter, and can be broken down into four sections. I don't know if they will be able to airship them or not, but I think they will fit inside the fuselage of some of the larger aircraft."

"I would like to have them shipped by air if possible. You are going to Townsville, Australia to help set up the station there. A few of the operators who were in the Philippines are operating a very rudimentary intercept site but without linguists and analysts they are pretty much hamstrung. The amphibious operation in the Solomon Islands is scheduled for August 7th, and it would be nice to have at least a better capability than is there now before that happens. That's less than two weeks away. What about the receivers?"

"If the planes are available, RCA has the antennas in stock and probably could ship them right away. The same goes for the receivers. I don't know if they have the quantity we will need on hand, but they surely have enough for Australia," J.C. said.

"Okay, find out how to get the funding in place and I will make arrangements for shipping after you are on the way. The Major in charge of the outfits name is Dawson, and Admiral Nimitz sent a Seabee Chief to start with the layout and material list. Keep in mind that the only people on SWPOA's staff cleared for ULTRA and MAGIC are General MacArthur, and probably General Willoughby by the time you get there."

J.C. gave me the contacts for RCA and was on a plane the following morning for the west coast and then on to Australia.

I got a message saying he had arrived and the Seabees would be arriving just as soon as transportation could be arranged.

I got the funding data from the navy and visited RCA to assess the situation with the antennas. It was as J.C. had said and I judged that they could fit inside aircraft. I had to check the weight limits and size specifications but managed that chore in a single day. The navy would fly the antennas as far as Espiritu Santo where the army would take them the rest of the way.

As the days passed I monitored the status of the items shipped and the state of the building project. Admiral Nimitz dispatched three planes loaded with the Seabees immediately after receiving the tasking. That was not the full battalion but was judged to be adequate to the task by the project commander.

General MacArthur's staff lined up the supplies and equipment that would be needed and the Seabees only beat the material to the site by a couple of days. I had never seen a military project move this swiftly, but the site would definitely not be ready for use by the time the amphibious landings were to occur.

The Seabees went to work on the antenna field right away and only took two days to get that done. They ran the wiring to the tents currently in use so the troops could use the antennas while the remainder of the construction was taking place.

Daily updates were provided by the Seabees to CINCPAC and J.C. sent me informal wire notes to keep me up to speed.

As August 7th approached I kept an eye on the intercepts from both our site in Washington and the one on Oahu. So far there was no indication that the Japanese suspected anything. They did have indications of a large U.S. force somewhere in the area, but Admiral Yamamoto, the man in charge of all Japanese forces, with headquarters at Rabaul, stated that the heavier than usual message traffic probably meant that the U.S. was trying to reinforce Australia and Port Moresby as well.

The weather in the entire South Pacific area was lousy for almost a week commencing the 1st of August. The U.S. and Australian task groups slowly made their way to the Southern Solomon Islands. Due to cloud cover and white capped seas the Japanese did not discover the large allied force until it was too late to oppose the landings with outside air and sea assets.

I followed the message traffic closely to see if the operation was going to be successful, as did most of those in positions of leadership in all the services.

The islands of Tulagi and Florida were attacked by part of the task force, while the remainder landed on Guadalcanal after a heavy bombardment by naval ships and carrier aircraft.

The invasion commenced at 0900, August 7th. By the end of the day we were in possession of Guadalcanal, and more importantly, the half-finished landing strip at Lunga Point. The opposition had been very light. When the bombardment and air raids commenced the Japanese construction engineers and the conscripted Korean's doing the work vacated the area immediately. The first message indicated that the landing on Guadalcanal received very little opposition.

The operations at Florida and Tulagi were contested to a much greater degree. The after action report indicated that the Japanese had approximately 1,000 troops on the islands and they were well entrenched. It took two days to secure Florida and Tulagi. The marines lost 122 men in the effort while the Japanese defenders were totally eliminated.

Once the cat was out of the bag the Japanese sent planes from Rabaul and naval units under the command of Sadayoshi Yamada to oppose the landing forces.

During the first sea action the Japanese attacked the landing forces several times. USS George F. Elliot was sunk and USS Jarvis heavily damaged. During the days of 8 and 9 August the Japanese lost 36 aircraft according to after action reports. During the same period the U.S. lost 19.

Admiral Fletcher decided that the loss of the aircraft lowered his carrier support to a degree that his entire fleet was threatened and that he dare not remain in the area. To be fair, his ships were reportedly dangerously low on fuel when he decided to leave the amphibious area, even though the marines only had half the supplies they were counting on. He had his people work through the night on August 8th to maximize the amount of supplies getting ashore. While the supplies were being unloaded a sea battle was taking place between a Japanese convoy of cruisers and destroyers and a similar group from the allied forces under British Rear Admiral Victor Crutchley. The Japanese force was commanded by Vice Admiral Gunichi Mikawa. The forces were about equal in terms of firepower. The Japanese forces dealt the Allies a stunning defeat in what is now called the battle of Savo Island.

The Allies lost four cruisers while another was badly damaged and a destroyer also suffered damage. No damage to Japanese naval units could be confirmed. For whatever reason, the two forces disengaged, the Allies to lick their wounds and pick up survivors, the Japanese back to Rabaul for fear of being caught in the open seas by Allied carrier based aircraft the next day. Had they known that Admiral Fletcher had withdrawn they would surely have pressed the attack. Their failure to do so allowed the Allies time to deliver more supplies and troops to Guadalcanal.

As the messages came in detailing the action that was taking place thousands of miles away the intelligence sections kept track of what was happening with maps tacked to wall board or taped over chalkboards.

I looked at all the intercepts we had to see if any worthwhile information was getting to the task force conducting the operation. Admiral King, Commander of the U.S. Fleet was getting information copies of all the message traffic.

There were several messages from CINCPACFLT alerting the Allies to Japanese movements but no defining information was included. Basically they were telling the Task Force Commander that the Japanese were active, and sometimes even including the identification of the ships involved, but little was known about their locations and intentions.

The Australian Coastwatchers' were more effective in detailing when the Japanese planes from Rabaul would be in the combat area based on when they were spotted from the various islands where they were located. This at least allowed the Allied forces to get planes in the air to repel the attacks.

General Vandergrift was extremely displeased with the fact that Admiral Fletcher had sailed away with about half the marine supplies still aboard the ships. While he didn't make any personal accusations, he let it be known that he didn't agree with the decision.

The navy had gotten the COMINT sites in San Francisco and San Diego equipped for HFDF and were working on setting up stations in Central America and on Adak in the Aleutian island chain.

Locating data started to flow after the first few days of the action in the Solomon Islands. The data was not very precise, but was better than nothing. When the site at Townsville came on line on the 22nd of August the additional line of bearing greatly affected the geometry of the fixes.

While the data was still not as precise as everyone preferred, the closer cut improved the accuracy of the locations to the point that reconnaissance aircraft could then be sent to search the area to determine how accurate the locating data was.

The navy was sending people and equipment to the locations we had decided on in the Atlantic area and that system became operational during the first week of September.

In the meantime, the action on Guadalcanal was shaping up to be one of the fiercest battles of the war in the Pacific to that point.

The marines had used the captured Japanese equipment for the most part to finish the runway on Lunga Point. By the 18th of August, 1942, the runway was completed and ready to accept aircraft.

Once the Japanese realized the enormity of the situation in the Solomon's the Imperial General Headquarters sent a message to the Imperial Japanese Army, based at Rabaul, assigning the Japanese 17th Army the task of retaking Guadalcanal. Admiral Yamamoto, who commanded the Combined Japanese Fleet from the island of Truk was directed to provide naval support for the operation.

Both messages were intercepted and the decoded version transmitted to Admirals Fletcher and Turner. General Vandergrift was informed and wanted to know exactly what the Japanese 17th Army consisted of in the way of manpower and firepower.

If someone answered that message the reply did not make it to Washington.

By the beginning of September what was affectionately dubbed The Cactus Air Force, was in possession of in excess of 60 F4F fighters and bomber aircraft. The timely notification by the Coast Watchers allowed the Marine pilots time to get into the air and position their forces optimally to repel the Japanese aircraft, which had in excess of a 1,000 mile round trip just to get to the battle area.

As the message traffic heralding the intense battle piled up it became apparent that the Guadalcanal campaign was shaping up to be an epic battle. The Japanese had hoped to have total control of the South Seas with the additional airfield there. The Allies recognized the strategic value of such an airfield and both sides poured men and equipment into the area at prolific rates.

The fighting was intense. The Japanese resorted to delivering supplies and troops during the hours of darkness down a slot from the Shortland Islands in order to avoid exposure to the aircraft from Guadalcanal and U.S. carrier aircraft. These supply runs were dubbed the 'Tokyo Express'.

For all intents and purposes the Japanese controlled the seas at night and the Allies during daylight hours. The Japanese could make the run to Guadalcanal and be back in the Shortland Islands to their base before daylight.

The intercept site in Townsville was operational, and new operators and analysts were arriving daily. The HFDF locating data provided constant updates on Japanese naval units, and the command circuits the Japanese used had been documented and a major effort was made to copy everything they sent over the airwaves.

The Seabees did a masterful job on the construction project and by the first week in October had the facilities about 90 percent completed.

The fierce battle for Guadalcanal raged on through the month of October, with each side reinforcing, and constant battles taking place at different points on the island.

The Japanese intent was, of course, to retake the airfield at Lunga Point. The perimeter was controlled by the bulk of General Vandergrift's troops. As more troops arrived the perimeter was expanded.

COMINT provided information that five Japanese destroyers carrying 300 ground troops were enroute to Koli Point, which the Japanese controlled, on the night of November 3rd. General Vandergrift dispatched a battalion of marines to intercept the Japanese at Koli Point. The battalion met heavy resistance and retreated back toward the Lunga perimeter.

In response, General Vandergrift ordered three more battalions to counterattack the Japanese at Koli Point. The battle raged for a full week, with the allied forces making progress slowly.

Another intercepted message from General Hyakutake to General Shoji, who was commander of the troops at Koli Point, ordered Shoji to abandon his position and rejoin the Japanese group at Kokumbona in the Matanikau area.

The information was late getting to Colonel Puller, who commanded the allied force, and Shoji was able to evacuate as many as 3,000 if his troops through a swampy gap in the jungle to the south. The allies quickly overran and killed remaining Japanese troops in the area. Approximately 500 Japanese troops were killed in the action, but most importantly the marines captured most of Shoji's heavy weapons and other provisions.

On November 11th a message was intercepted and decoded which directed another concerted effort to retake what was now named Henderson Field on Guadalcanal. Though the specific units were not identified, the information spurred the allies into reinforcing Guadalcanal. That task was undertaken on November 11th and 12th, with most of the men and supplies unloaded without serious opposition from the Japanese, though they did attack the screening destroyers on both days. Though the allied naval units were annihilated, they inflicted enough damage on the Japanese force to cause the Japanese task force commander to depart the area without bombarding Henderson Field. As a result the Japanese attempt to reinforce the island was pushed back another day by Admiral Yamamoto. The attempted reinforcement, which occurred on the 14th of November, revealed another blunder on the part of the Japanese. Henderson Field had been attacked by a heavy bombardment from Japanese cruisers and destroyers.

Assuming that the allies now had to rely on carrier aircraft the Japanese went ahead with the landing of troops and supplies down the slot. Four landing craft were beached on the morning of 14 November and unloading commenced. The aircraft from Henderson Field made short work of destroying the craft and most of the heavy equipment never made it into the hands of those who needed it.

On November 26th, a message was intercepted from IGH placing General Hitoshi Imamura in charge of the Japanese Eighth Army in Rabaul, New Guinea. Imamura's first objective was to retake Henderson Field on Guadalcanal.

His first order was to resupply the forces already on the island and he dispatched a force of destroyers with supplies encased in fuel drums which were then resealed and tied together. Each of the four destroyers would carry approximately 200 of the drums. The ships would approach the beach, make a sharp turn and release the barrels, which would then be retrieved by swimmers from ashore and the drums would be hauled to the beach and opened.

COMINT early warning of this proposed operation allowed the U.S. to intercept the force off Guadalcanal. A naval battle ensued, in which the U.S. lost several ships, cruisers and destroyers. However the interdiction foiled the attempt to resupply the Japanese on shore.

By the time December rolled around it was obvious, at least to me, that COMINT was playing a very important role in the battle of Guadalcanal.

The station at Townsville was doing a great job with the addition of operators and analysts. Chief Carter sent me informal messages at times keeping me abreast of the progress.

In early December the 1st Marine Division was withdrawn for recuperation and replaced by the U.S. 14th Army Corps under the command of Major General Alexander Patch. His troops consisted of the 2nd Marine Division and the Army 25th and 23rd infantry divisions.

On the 18th of December General Patch initiated an attack on fortified Japanese positions in an area called Mount Austen. There were also two additional Japanese strong points surrounding Mount Austen. The attack was stymied by the Japanese fighting from dug-in positions. The battle continued until January 4th when the U.S. withdrew from the area to regroup and reassess the effort.

On January 10th the attack was resumed with a greater force, yet it still took two weeks to rout the Japanese defenders. It was the 23rd of January before the U.S. forces were in total control of the mountainous area. More than 3,000 Japanese were killed during the two weeks of action while the Allied forces lost some 300 personnel.

An action that probably contributed to the retrograde movement by the Japanese was the decision by the Japanese to abandon Guadalcanal and concentrate their forces in badly needed areas that they already held on the islands to the west of the Solomon's, specifically

Bougainville and the areas around the southern portion of the South China Sea.

The HFDF net was doing an acceptable job considering the circumstances. The net control was getting much more adept at finding signals belonging to ships of the South Sea fleet of the Japanese and the time it took to decrypt bearings and plot fixes was a limiting factor in how much data they could provide.

Heavy Japanese movements of ships in the area had been noted by both the station in Townsville and Hawaii. The item of intelligence missing was the reason for the almost frantic movements of IJN assets.

The logical assumption was that the Japanese were getting prepared for a concerted effort to retake Guadalcanal. HFDF fixes placed the majority of the units between Guadalcanal and the Japanese naval base on the island of Truk.

What happened was that once the Japanese high command decided to evacuate the troops from Guadalcanal they sent an officer courier to deliver the orders to Admiral Yamamoto.

The stepped up activity noted by COMINT operators was in fact a task group transporting a battalion of troops to act as a rear guard for the evacuation of sick, tired and hungry Japanese troops who had endured the tropical jungle for many weeks, and in some cases, months.

This action was misread by all our intelligence assets and rather than push the advantage after taking Mount Austen, General Patch held in position to allow his troops time to rest and regroup for the expected Japanese offensive.

Admiral Halsey, also believing a new Japanese offensive was in the making, sent a resupply convoy to

Guadalcanal with a screening force of cruisers and destroyers.

The convoy was detected by Japanese aircraft and attacked by torpedo planes. The cruiser Chicago was heavily damaged, reattacked the following day and eventually sank.

The remaining ships were withdrawn to the Coral Sea area, south of Guadalcanal.

While this was happening, the Japanese were withdrawing to the West of Guadalcanal in preparation for evacuation of their remaining troops on the island. They sent a force of 20 destroyers to the western side of the island and evacuated nearly 5,000 troops on the night of February 1st.

The evacuation was completed on the nights of 4 and 7 February. It was the 9th of February before the forces on Guadalcanal realized that the Japanese were gone, with the exception of stragglers, which were hunted down after the island was declared secure on the 9th of February.

While the role of COMINT was not as apparent as it had been during the battles of Coral Sea and Midway, the senior commanders nevertheless were impressed with the kind of information provided and the timely manner in which the messages arrived.

If the battle of Midway was the turning point of the war at sea, the Guadalcanal battle was the equivalent for the land offensive.

Chapter 24

While the battle for Guadalcanal was raging the situation in Europe was beginning to take on a different complexity.

The British Prime Minister was pushing for the invasion of North Africa rather than the European mainland at that stage in the war. For his part, President Roosevelt didn't believe a full scale invasion of Europe would be successful at that time, mostly because America had not had time to ramp up the manpower training requirements, nor had the industrial sector begun to operate smoothly. For this reason he supported Churchill's wish to attack North Africa first to cut off the unrestricted use of the Mediterranean by the German navy. The thought was that the choke point at the Straits of Gibraltar would allow the Allies to detect German movements if they could expel the Germans and Vichy French (those who supported Germany) from North Africa.

Probably more important to the British at the time was the Suez Canal. The British were very dependent on oil shipped from the Middle East and control of North Africa would ensure the continued delivery of that commodity without having to sail around the Horn of Africa.

The politics of the situation with regard to how U.S. forces were employed was a pretty constant fight between those who insisted on 'Europe first' and those who wanted some immediate action in the Pacific area.

Admiral King was a very outspoken proponent of some meaningful action in the Pacific. He had gained enough support to convince the President to approve the action that resulted in the lengthy battle of Guadalcanal.

So even while the Marine 1st division under General Vandergrift was battling on Guadalcanal, the forces of

Operation Torch were executing the plan to take North Africa. The specific countries selected for the initial landings were Morocco, Algeria and Tunisia, mostly because of the force composition of the adversaries.

Those opposing the allied landings were mostly the Vichy French. A considerable number of French citizens supported the free French, which was under the tacit command of General Charles DE Gaulle.

They had been active as saboteurs and guerrilla fighters for many months.

It was hoped that the Vichy French would capitulate without a fight when they viewed the much superior forces arrayed against them. That didn't happen, at least not to the degree that the Allies hoped.

Many of the U.S. troops were fresh out of basic training and were transported directly from the United States to the Horn of Africa.

The Vichy French had some 125,000 troops, over 500 aircraft and 210 tanks, many obsolete.

The Allied forces outnumbered the Vichy French by a large margin, but the intent was not only to defeat the Vichy French but also the Germans and Italians occupying the continent. Hitler was sure to send reinforcements from both Germany and Italy to bolster the defenses in the area.

The effort was dubbed Operation Torch and commenced on November 8th of 1942.

It must be remembered that the Allies had been engaging Italian, German and Vichy French forces for at least the previous year in North Africa.

In addition to the normal intelligence gathering capabilities exercised during the North Africa Campaign this was the first true test of tactical utilization of the ULTRA decrypts.

Unfortunately, in retrospect, captured German COMINT collection facilities proved how much the Axis powers relied on the discipline as well.

Because of the paranoia with which the British guarded the ULTRA secret it took longer to deliver the information to the battlefield than would have been the case had they used codes more aligned to tactical requirements. Many times the battle was already underway before the intelligence predicting the action reached the participants.

When the British captured the German field radio intercept site in Tunisia they learned that the Germans had been successfully employing COMINT derived information for the better part of the campaign, which had been underway for more than a year at that point.

The Germans deployed the intercept troop contingent along with the supply sector, to the rear of battle formations, but close enough to get the intelligence to combat units in a timely manner. This led to the Allies revising procedures to get the decrypted information to the battlefield in a timelier fashion.

The single most important intelligence to come from ULTRA intercepts was the logistic plans of the Germans for resupply of the North Africa deployed army. This allowed the Allied forces to position assets in such a way as to interdict the shipments to deliver crucial supplies as they crossed the Mediterranean, whether by air or sea.

The after action reports coming from North Africa cemented the belief in COMINT in the European Theater much as the Battle of Midway had done in the Pacific.

The HFDF net was having much greater success in isolating the locations of German submarines once enough sites were activated to provide better geometry for the position fixes. The operational commanders now felt much more confident in deploying scarce assets to search in the areas identified through the COMINT discipline, and their success rates for interdicting German U-boats was much greater.

From that point on the opposition to requests for manpower and equipment for COMINT utilization completely died. The numbers of operators and analysts increased greatly, and communications nets were activated to streamline the delivery of intelligence to operational commanders.

With the successes of the North Africa campaign and the Solomon Islands, President Roosevelt became convinced that the U.S. could support battlefronts in both Europe and the Pacific. Strategic plans incorporated that philosophy for the remainder of the war.

Chapter 25

The Japanese attack on Pearl Harbor was a bitter pill to swallow for the American population at large. It was probably even harder for the senior military community.

The architect of the plan was Admiral Isoroku Yamamoto, a very influential member of the Imperial Japanese military hierarchy.

The army and navy components of the Japanese military were very competitive for prestige and leadership. The army was by far more aggressive in their thinking than was the navy, especially Yamamoto.

Yamamoto had studied at Harvard University from 1919-1921 and had two subsequent postings as naval attaché in Washington. He spoke fluent English and studied the American customs and business model exhaustively. He was also a part of a Japanese delegation visiting the U.S. Naval War College in 1924.

As it became clear that the Battle of Guadalcanal was successful, and that North Africa would soon be in the hands of the Allies, U.S. thinking turned from the defensive mindset to the offensive.

Guadalcanal opened the door to interdiction of Japanese shipping from the South Pacific to the home islands, while the taking of North Africa provided the control of the Mediterranean necessary for invasion of the European mainland through Italy.

Most Americans were still incensed by the sneak attack on Pearl Harbor. The newspapers had chronicled Yamamoto's previous ties to the United States and identified him as the brains behind the attack. As a result he was the most hated Japanese on the planet, with the possible exception of Hideki Tojo, Japan's Prime Minister.

I could not believe that the Japanese continued to use the JN25 code, even after it should have been obvious that we had to be reading their mail due to the way the two major sea battles, Coral Sea and Midway, turned out.

After the stunning defeat the Japanese suffered at Guadalcanal, Admiral Yamamoto was anxious to reassure his troops that the world would not end because of the setback. He planned an inspection tour of his bases in the South Pacific.

A message was copied from his headquarters to a number of action addressees. The message told of Yamamoto's coming inspection trip and laid out the itinerary, including what type aircraft would carry the inspection party and what escorts they would have for the trip.

That message was decrypted on April 14, 1943.

At first it was thought to be disinformation, designed to lure U.S. aircraft into a trap.

We had enough experience with COMINT by this time to accept the fact that it was a valid message and that Yamamoto was indeed placing himself in a very compromising situation.

The message was copied in Hawaii and Australia. General MacArthur sent a message to the President very eloquently worded which lobbied for the shoot down of Yamamoto's aircraft.

The President had seen the message and already discussed it with me, General Donovan, Secretary Knox, and Admiral Leahy.

The consensus of opinion was that Yamamoto had to go. There were several reasons, but the overriding opinion was that he was by far the most capable Japanese leader and his demise would at least cause confusion in the Japanese command structure as they sought to replace him.

His complicity in the Pearl Harbor attack was far from the least factor in the decision to shoot down his plane if possible.

The decision to attempt to 'get Yamamoto', as the President worded it, was not made until the 16th of April. The flight was scheduled for the morning of 18 April, which did not provide much time to get planes in place to take care of the chore.

A telephone call was made by Admiral King to Admiral Nimitz implementing the decision. It might become obvious that the only way we could have known about the flight was through their communications, but the rewards were worth the risk.

Admiral Nimitz, CINCPACFLT, ordered Admiral William F. Halsey, Jr., Commander South Pacific to attempt to shoot the plane down.

The best pilots from a squadron of P-38 Lightening planes were assigned the task, taking off from Guadalcanal. They were the only assets with the range to intercept the Japanese flight.

On the morning of April 18, 1943, despite warnings from his staff that his plane could be ambushed, Admiral Yamamoto left Rabaul aboard a Mitsubishi G4M bomber, configured as a transport aircraft. His plane was escorted by a second G4M aircraft and six A6M Zero fighter planes.

Sixteen P-38 Lightening's intercepted the flight over Bougainville and shot down both of the transport aircraft and two of the Zeros.

Though several pilots of the P-38's saw the plane go down in the jungle there was no way to verify that Yamamoto had perished. The after-action report stated that it was likely that he had died but there was no way to verify the fact.

It was not until late the next evening that confirmation of Yamamoto's death came, and that information was gained through the interception of the message sent to the Imperial Japanese leadership. The body of the Admiral had been found near the wreckage in the jungle. Yamamoto had taken two .50 caliber slugs, one in the upper left back and one which entered his lower left jaw and exited above his right eye. The autopsy reported that death was instantaneous.

Yamamoto was something of an enigma within the Japanese military hierarchy. He opposed the invasion of Manchuria in 1931, the land war with China in 1937 and the alliance with Germany and Italy in 1940. It is even said that he apologized to the American Ambassador for the 1937 attack on USS Panay in the Yangtze River.

His opinions made him a target of the hard line military segment of Japanese society, and he became a target for assassination threats by supporters of that group.

He reportedly received a constant stream of death threats and hate mail because of his radical views of what Japan could and could not accomplish through military action.

He believed that the only way to win a war with America was to deal a fatal blow to their military forces in the Pacific and quickly sue for peace.

The attack on Pearl Harbor was actually timed to occur after a letter from Japan to the U.S. severing diplomatic relations was delivered. The letter did not arrive before the attack and didn't receive a lot of attention considering the gravity of the Pearl Harbor attack.

Though Yamamoto did not embrace the prospect of war with the United States he carried out his duties to the best of his abilities. His loss proved to be a blow that the Japanese would not be able to overcome.

The American high command held their breath, waiting to see if the Japanese would now go to a more sophisticated code. It didn't happen.

The discovery that the Germans were employing tactical COMINT in North Africa caused the Allied leadership to rethink their methods of using COMINT.

More attention was paid to tactical use of the information derived from that medium. In addition, when the Allies learned in North Africa that the Germans had been intercepting reports made by an American Embassy official based on briefings by the British Military it became apparent why the Axis powers had met with so much success prior to the U.S. entry into the war.

That incident also led to greater emphasis on Communications Security (COMSEC), and resulted in more abundant use of tactical codes, which sometimes caused chagrin at the command level because the messages, though mostly of the short variety, had to be decoded. This procedure could take precious minutes and that might make the difference in the decision process.

The Marines solved the problem by using Code Talkers. Many people associate the Navajo Indians with the term, though in reality the concept had its birth during WWI.

The Navajo are certainly the best known of the groups comprising that function, but several other Native American tribes performed the same function in other theaters of the war. Most prominent after the Navajo were the Choctaw and Cherokee tribes.

The concept was much like the Japanese use of a little known language to secure their communications. There were major differences of course, because the Japanese system first had to develop code groups to equate to the different symbols used in the Katakana language. The

Navajo system used simple substitution for alphabetic letters, adding code words for common terms used in tactical combat, such as rifle, airplane, ship, etc. The preponderance of message traffic the Japanese had to send was also infinitely greater than the simple messages used in tactical combat.

The lessons learned presented a great challenge to my little corner of the world. As proof of the value of tactical COMINT mounted more of the Admirals and Generals conducting the war lobbied for COMINT personnel assignments to their staffs to have ready access to the intelligence that affected their operations.

The only way to do that was to assign special communications personnel to the staffs and feed the specific intelligence related to an area via the communications channel.

This necessitated a much wider distribution of the code books used for the sensitive programs. It also meant that in the case of ships the CRYPTO center would need to be segregated between the regular communications and special communications.

The most logical solution in the case of ships was to develop supplementary radio spaces for the decoding of COMINT.

That action occurred before we got serious about island hopping our way to Japan, and the logical first step was to add to the communications net already in place for operational commanders.

We still needed to develop guidelines relative to safeguarding those who knew about COMINT to assure that they were not captured by the enemy.

Each branch of service was tasked to develop procedures for the added assets.

Most of the decryption and analyses of intercepted communications was still done at the major locations in Hawaii, Washington and Australia.

One of the hardest problems to overcome was the fact that intercept operators and analysts were ill equipped to put some of the intercepts into the proper perspective. The import of the information derived from decryptions sometimes escaped notice by the analysts who had no training relative to battlefield tactics.

This was more noticeable as the problem related to ground and air combat.

Experience taught us that we needed to have people with knowledge of battlefield tactics available to help fit the decrypted messages into the proper perspective to get it to the people who needed it.

This of course led to more military officers being briefed into the program.

Management of the program became a full time job. All requests for additional personnel had to be processed, which meant special background investigations. Hoover, the FBI director complained to the President about the amount of extra work to process the many requests.

The friction between Donovan and Hoover with regard to their different areas of responsibility was such that each had spies in the others camp to keep abreast of what the different branches of our government was up to.

As the allied landings in Sicily and then the Italian mainland, got underway General Eisenhower was made Supreme Commander of European Theater forces, which essentially made him responsible for the fighting of the war in Europe.

The master plan had to be coordinated with input from all the Allied force commanders participating in the operations. Since many of the countries in Europe were under Hitler's thumb each lobbied for action to retake their own homeland at the earliest opportunity.

Several meetings were held by the big three, Stalin, Churchill and Roosevelt to discuss the strategic aspects of the war in Europe. Stalin pushed at every opportunity for an invasion of Europe proper to relieve the pressure being put on Soviet troops by the Germans.

Churchill and Roosevelt countered that a European invasion was not a smart move until the forces and material necessary to the success of the operation could be assured.

The war in the Pacific didn't have any really strategic goal, other than the unconditional surrender of the Japanese.

Since many of the Japanese occupied islands were in the SWPOA area of responsibility General MacArthur commanded the bulk of the Pacific action, coordinating with CINCPACFLT for ships and air power.

Names like Rabaul, Malaya, Singapore, Wake Island, Gilbert Islands, New Britain, Guam, Iwo Jima, Okinawa, Vella Lavella, Tarawa, Kwajalein, Eniwetok, Saipan, Pele, Tinian, Leyte, Samar, Luzon, Borneo, Manado and Tarakan became household words during the Allied offensive in the Pacific.

Even the Aleutian Islands of Kiska and Attu had to be retaken. As American industrial production got into high gear in mid-1942, the U.S. was building landing craft and airplanes faster than the adversaries could destroy them.

Though the soldiers, sailors (including Coast Guard) and marines fought valiantly, the single greatest accomplishment of America was the prolific rate at which they produced the needs of the military in terms of weapons and equipment throughout the war.

COMINT played a significant tactical role in many of the operations once the Allies went on the offensive in all theaters of the war.

The Ditty Chasers

Chapter 26

My White House job turned more toward other tasks as the individual services administered their own programs. The analyses were performed at the Army Security Station in Washington.

The number of officers outside the technical COMINT field swelled to nearly 100 in Washington, Hawaii and Australia. Their job was to determine the value of information recovered through intercepts of which analysts failed to grasp the significance.

As more operators and analysts were assigned to fleet and field units the number of people in the COMINT category increased to nearly 5,000.

Although by 1944 I was essentially out of the loop as far as the nuts and bolts of the COMINT business went, it was obvious to me that the numbers were not going to decrease after the war but would further increase.

I mentioned this fact to the President and he wanted to know how I arrived at the conclusion.

"Right now we are concentrating all our efforts on Germany and Japan. After the war we are going to start to worry about any country large and powerful enough to cause us heartache as a potential adversary. We are going to want to keep tabs on almost every large country in the world other than North America and the British Empire. That is going to take a concerted effort that will require thousands of operators around the clock. Analysts are going to need to incorporate more language skills into the mix, and command and control of the effort is going to become a large problem," I said.

"That might be your new job after the war is over, but is something I don't want to think about at the present time. Just out of curiosity, have you heard any scuttlebutt about any highly classified programs for which you are not cleared?"

"If you are referring to the Manhattan Project, I have heard enough to understand what it is all about, but nothing substantive. Most of what I picked up was because people thought that a direct representative of the President would be cleared for the program. I did not pry, and rather than cause a stink, simply informed the people who slipped up that I was not on the list for that program and that they should be more certain of the person's status they are talking to in the future."

"I hate to hear that. I believe this program is the single most important thing we have going on right now. If we are successful we will be able to end the war with Japan on our terms, which is their unconditional surrender. I am informed that the work looks very promising and that we should know if the concept is going to work or not in as little as three months. I wondered if you had run across anything that would indicate that the Germans are further advanced than we are."

"I can't answer that because I don't have the knowledge of how far we are along, or even what the overall concept is all about. As far as the Germans, the logical place for that kind of information to show up would be from ULTRA intercepts."

"I am thinking about getting you briefed into the program and sending you to England to see if you can learn anything about the German efforts. We are using a couple of scientists we got out of Germany and they feel that those they previously worked with will not be far behind us in developing a bomb of enormous power. A couple of them, used strategically, could end the war overnight," the President said.

"Do the British know anything at all about the project?" I asked.

"They actually know quite a bit. They were way ahead of us from the start. The theory goes back to 1939 actually. They learned that the Germans were working on a very secret project which required special materials. From what I have been told about the concept, and I must be careful to call it a concept because nothing physical has come of the program yet. However, the theoretical calculations are generally agreed upon by scientists who should know what they are talking about. The way it was explained to me is that they need to extract an isotope called Uranium 235 from the base element of Uranium 238. I don't understand how even the theoretical process works, but I have been assured that once the mechanics are worked out that a bomb no larger than a 500 pounder will devastate an entire city."

The President continued, "Albert Einstein got together with a scientist by the name of Szilard and produced a letter in August of 1939 outlining the concept and the potential for development of an atomic weapon. The strange part of the story is that the British were far ahead of us when we decided to pursue the concept. We formed a working group with them and the Canadians as early as 1940, but the letter convinced our scientists that the concept was within reason and we set up a group to look into the possibilities later that year, so the project has been going on for that long. A very tight lid was placed on the security of the research, second only to the code breaking work."

"I suppose that is why I didn't know more about it. But then, I haven't really attempted to learn anything outside my own area of expertise," I said.

"The project has a large number of people working at different locations around the country, something in the neighborhood of 20,000 from my understanding and I fear that our security is not as tight as it should be. I am surprised that you haven't run across anything from the ULTRA intercepts to do with the German program. They have been exploring the theoretical possibilities even longer than we have. I don't know for a fact, but I assume that the British got wind of the German program through their codebreaking efforts early on and put their special operations people to work trying to learn everything they could about the German efforts. I know that the Uranium which provides the raw element upon which the concept is based is not available just anywhere, and it takes special instruments to locate the material within the earth's crust. I have been told that the most likely location to find the material is in equatorial Africa."

"So what exactly do you want me to do?" I asked.

"There's another element that is crucial to actually producing a bomb. It is called 'heavy water' and is very scarce. I know that some is present in the North Atlantic, somewhere along the Norwegian coast. The British Spec Ops people and our own OSS have conducted raids to hamper the German efforts to get the element they need. I want you to have a look at our own operations and determine how vulnerable we are to others spying on our programs."

"When do you want me to start the effort, and where will the manpower come from?" I asked.

"You and Chief Carter can look into the program and figure out how to approach the problem. We will then determine where the manpower will come from," the President said.

"Do the Russians know anything about the project?"

"I don't know, and that is one of the things you need to find out. We are allies with them in this war, but I trust them just about as much as I trust the Germans. I have received reports of widespread massacres of Jews in their own territory, and even greater atrocities in Poland. Whatever form their government takes after this is over, it will not be a democracy," the President said emphatically.

"I will need to talk to our own people to get a better understanding of what is involved in the process before I can determine what to look for," I said.

"I will have you and Chief Carter added to the list and ensure that those in charge of our project give you what you need."

Chief Carter and I were still ensconced in the Willard Hotel and we had a long conversation about the new assignment that evening.

I briefly outlined the President's orders and, not surprisingly, J.C. knew more about the secret project than I did.

"I don't know anything of the fine points of the effort, but I do know how the command structure is set up and where the field activities are located," he told me.

"How did you acquire what you know?"

"Just through observation and common sense mostly. The organization is so large that they can't very well operate in a vacuum. I have heard that there are as many as ten thousand people employed on the project, and that the budget is in the millions. I learned a bit when I was working on the HFDF project a couple of years ago while I was at the RCA facility in New Jersey."

"How did that happen?"

"I was talking to one of their engineers about our radio and antenna needs and he mentioned that he was looking into some miniaturized circuits for another government agency. The agency was in the engineering segment of the Army and the request was so unusual that he wondered what they could possibly be looking at that required what they had asked for. When I asked what kind of engineering he was talking about he told me they build bases like our Seabees do. That didn't make a lot of sense to me and he looked up the paperwork and told me it was top secret, but the request had come from some General in the area office in New York."

"Since we know about almost everything going on with our own forces I deduced that this was a special program into which few people were briefed. I didn't pursue the matter any further with him but made a mental note to check into the engineering procedures the army used. I found that they have regional offices to oversee major construction projects in different areas. They usually name the projects after the area they occupy. For example, something in Washington would be dubbed the Washington Project. The General who asked for the work with RCA was in the Manhattan Project, which would lead one to believe that the facility he was in charge of would be in New York. I did some more discrete research and found that the location for which he wanted the items was in Oak Ridge, Tennessee. That's out in the middle of nowhere on a major river and has no military significance. I deduced that having a General in New York in charge of a project in Tennessee didn't make much sense unless the base was to support some highly sensitive program."

"Knowing the location gave me a starting point and I poked around the army assignment section some. I never told anyone that my inquiries were official and I assume they knew of what position you and I hold with the President and they gave me some figures on the number of army troops assigned to the facility, even before the construction was completed, and the numbers were very high. They have additional facilities in different parts of the country. I think I heard New Mexico mentioned and the state of Washington."

"I guess I must have had my head in the sand to not know about something this large. I did know that something special was going on but didn't pursue the matter."

"I think most of the work in the beginning was done by scientists in the academic community. I know that we managed to get our hands on a couple of Germans who were working on the program for them during the early stages of the war. I imagine Donovan had something to do with that. That might be a good place to start. He has to know more about the effort than we do," J.C. said.

"I think I will mention that to the President in the morning.

"Are we just going to look at the communications aspect of the program?" J.C. asked.

"I would expect that the FBI would look at other aspects. I imagine they had to vet the people working on the project just as we did for our operators. I also imagine the army has CID people assigned to the different places where the work is being carried out. So I guess the answer is yes we will look particularly at the communications, but at the same time if we identify any physical vulnerabilities we will address the issues," I said.

"I have a suspicion that we should look at the Russians more than the Germans. With the war starting to turn in our favor in Europe the allies will be looking for indications as to their efforts. The Russians on the other hand probably have not devoted much effort to what we are talking about. We would be naïve to even consider that they haven't had spies looking at both the Germans and our own efforts."

"I suppose the best approach is to learn what we can about the process and then concentrate on the more important aspects of the research."

We left it at that and went to bed.

Chapter 27

When we went to work the following morning I asked the President's detail if they had any indication that General Donovan would be in the area that day.

He checked the schedule and told me that he was penciled in for 10:00 a.m. but he might or might not show up on schedule.

"If he shows up would you send someone to get me?"

"Will do," he replied.

J.C. and I started to get some facts on paper, at least insofar as we could deduce locations and a timeline on the work. The outline was very skeletal since we were working from our own perceptions.

We had no idea what form any weapon they produced might take. It could be shaped like a regular bomb, or it might be a lot larger and take a different shape based on how they planned to get it to the target and how it would be armed.

One of the Secret Service agents came to let us know that Donovan had just arrived at 9:45.

We made our way to the Oval Office and joined Donovan and the President.

The President told Donovan that we were to be briefed into the Manhattan Project and the reason for the action. "I want to make sure the Germans do not beat us to the punch if what we are attempting ever comes to fruition," he said.

"The briefing will take days to make sure they understand all aspects of the program," Donovan said. "How in-depth do you want the briefing to be?"

"Thoroughly enough that they can understand the concepts and goals of the project," the President replied.

"I will have my deputy brief them. When is it convenient for you?" Donovan asked me.

"As soon as possible," I said.

"Let me give him a call and you can go out this afternoon," he said.

Neither J.C. nor I mentioned any of the things we already knew about the program.

After lunch we went to the OSS training facility and got the briefing by Donovan's second in command.

We were taken to a briefing room that had all the latest gadgets for sound suppression and security.

The briefer was BG John Magruder, Donovan's intelligence director.

Magruder had brought in a very thick folder with diagonal red stripes and TOP SECRET in bold letters top and bottom of the cover page.

"Where do you want me to start?" he asked.

"I guess at the beginning," I said. "Neither of us have had any connection to the program and the President has directed us to evaluate the security of the project. We assume that both your people and the FBI have looked pretty closely at the physical aspects of the effort. We are primarily concerned with the electronic aspects if someone might be perhaps passing information to others via radio. I majored in mathematics, so I have a pretty good understanding of the sciences," I said.

"The concept goes back to the late thirties. Scientists had been working for several years on the theoretical aspects of what we are attempting to do. The discovery that chemical elements are made up of neutrons and protons led to the work in developing spectroscopy to determine the molecular make up of each element. Each element is cataloged by the number of protons and neutrons contained within an atom of a given element."

"It was postulated that a bomb of great power could be developed with the right element and the proper fission material. The Germans in particular have been working on a program since 1939, which is just about the time the British got interested in the concept. Most scientists agree that the concept is viable, but the secret is getting the right isotope of the right material to use for the bomb."

"Uranium ore, which is found in most of the earth's crust, is not plentiful, but is common enough that it can be mined just like coal, gold, silver, and so forth. The problem is that the Uranium cannot be used as it comes out of the earth. A method to change the structure of a portion of the uranium ore, which is called Uranium 238, to an isotope of the ore called Uranium 235, has to be devised. Basically only about two to four percent of the uranium 235 isotope can be extracted from pure uranium."

"The major challenge is to devise a way to extract the isotope, which generates tremendous heat during the process. It takes a large plant and some very specialized equipment to do this. Our major effort is taking place in Tennessee, on a river near Oak Ridge. The water is necessary to act as a cooling agent during the manufacture process."

"The best method to do what they are attempting is to use what they call heavy water in an enclosed system to remove the heat during the separation process. Heavy water is a form of water with a unique atomic structure. If regular water is subjected to electrolysis, that is sending an electrical charge through the water, some of the water changes to what they call heavy water. The heavy water has two hydrogen atoms and one oxygen atom, where regular water has one hydrogen atom and two oxygen atoms. The heavy water, which is called deuterium oxide, slows down the reaction of the depletion process when the uranium is treated and the isotope, ^{235}U, is extracted. The regular ^{238}U is not fissionable, which means that it cannot explode, therefore cannot be used to make a bomb. The isotope can be used and the major task in designing a workable model of the theoretical is the separation of the isotope."

"Because the danger in the process is immense, a rather sophisticated separation plant is required. The chamber has to be isolated and strict control procedures in place to assure the safety of those operating the equipment. The process is manpower intensive and a huge number of people are involved in the project."

"How large a number?" I asked.

"The plant at Oak Ridge has more than 5,000 employees. The plant in Washington State has roughly the same number, and the proving ground in New Mexico has a couple of thousand. In addition several universities work on the theoretical aspects in their science departments. To my way of thinking the greatest vulnerability is within the scientific community. They tend to collaborate more on a personal level without much regard to the nationality of their correspondents. All have been cautioned to keep their work to themselves but how effective those admonitions are is a matter or speculation."

"Where do we get this 'heavy water'?" I asked.

"Make it I suppose. Regular water can be used and the process takes multiple procedures to gain even small amounts. There was a plant in Norway, in the town of Telemark, which produced the item to use in fertilizer. The Germans took over the plant in 1940 and we have been trying to take it out of action since. I believe we finally managed to do that with the help of the Norwegian resistance movement just a few months ago. I have no idea what the Germans are using now, but there are a couple of other theoretical methods to extract the isotope from uranium. I assume they are taking a different path now."

"The heavy water method is by far the best option for removing the isotope but the plant to produce the heavy water is very expensive. Even an efficiently operating plant can only produce about ten tons of the stuff per year."

"How close are we to having an operational weapon?"

"Your guess is as good as mine. What I have gone over so far is only the process to extract the isotope. Once they have enough of the material to make a bomb they still have to design the triggering mechanism. Add to that the fact that the material they produce is what they call, 'radioactive' and it is not an easy task."

"What do you mean radioactive?" J.C. asked.

"The element gives off some invisible form of energy that tends to make people sick who handle it, and some have even died. Very strict procedures are in place for working with the material and that makes it more difficult to fashion the material into something usable."

"Have any models been tested yet?" I asked.

"We haven't come up with enough of the material to run an operational test, but the scientific calculations, which were arrived at by collaboration of our scientists, seem pretty certain to work."

We spent that afternoon plus the entire next day going over the material the OSS had. I was particularly interested in the scientific community and discretely copied the names of scientific department heads at each educational institution working on the project.

J.C. and I spent the next month at various places where work on the project was taking place. The plant in Tennessee was by far the largest of the facilities and the people who worked at the plant, mostly women, were like a herd of stampeding cattle at shift change. With a four shift rotation that put roughly 2,000 people at the plant at any one time. The physical plant was crawling with security people, both within the confines of the property and outside the fences.

We looked at all aspects of the operation and concluded that the actual work site did not provide a very favorable circumstance for spying. It would be almost impossible to steal anything of value from the plant. The isotopes were dangerous to handle and a spy was not likely to try to walk off with any of that. The fact that the Germans already knew how to isolate the isotope also mitigated against such action. The Russians might be in need of some actual material, but again, it was almost impossible to remove the isotope from the plant.

The heavy water aspect might be something the Russians were interested in, but again, it was not a very likely scenario for them to put a lot of effort into acquiring samples. The process was widely known within the scientific community and the Russians certainly had scientists capable of extracting the deuterium from regular water if they were willing to invest in the plant to handle the extraction.

The most likely place for any spying to take place was at the academic institutions. That is where the brains of the project were concentrated, and not all in one place, but at their individual institutions of higher learning.

By our count there were in the neighborhood of 200 scientific people who had knowledge of the project scattered around the nation. In addition, there were Canadian and British scientists involved and the data was readily exchanged between the scientists.

J.C. and I both agreed that the Russians were more likely to concentrate on the methods of the calculations that the scientists came up with. Remember, everything was theoretical at this juncture. While everyone with a scientific mind could look at the data and understand the principles, the proof of the pudding was yet to be realized.

J.C. said, "I think we are going to have to retrain some operators to copy Russian communications, especially those originating at their embassies. I have a bit of experience with their communications and there are four or five additional letters in their alphabet. Our guys will need to work on that for a while before they become comfortable with the additional characters. Even then we are not going to be able to do much unless we can determine what codes they use and hopefully get our hands on some of their codebooks."

"First things first. We will go to work getting some people trained up. We can work with Donovan's people and see if they might be able to come up with Russian code books," I said.

"How large a group of operators are you thinking about?"

"Since we are not going to worry about their military comms we can probably get by with maybe 20 ditty chasers per section. Using a four section watch that means 80 operators. We will probably need at least twenty analysts, at least half of them Russian linguists," I said off the top of my head.

"And where will be operate from?"

"Start looking for a location. I would think someplace on our east coast would be best. If there is any spying going on they will most likely coordinate the effort over the air waves. I imagine any of the scientific data will have to be physically delivered, and that would mean working though the Russian Embassy. I believe our best shot will be to review all the personnel files on the scientific people and pull all those with ties to Europe or Communist countries.

We can then have either Donovan's people or the FBI keep tabs on those we select and see if they come up with any associations that tie to the Russians," I said.

"I believe we should try to get the Russian phones tapped at the Embassy too. If we can identify the trunk lines which connect with the Embassy we can listen in on their phone calls and see if anything comes from that. That means we are going to need a lot more linguists. It will probably take at least half a dozen men for each watch section, and we will also need a location from which to work that part of the effort."

"Let's rough up a plan and see what the boss thinks," J.C. said.

That was what we did over the next several days.

Chapter 28

The plan we came up with called for the monitoring effort to be located near Baltimore, Maryland because it was more convenient to the Washington area. The antennas for the radio station could be used for our purposes, and J.C. found a vacant building on government property to set up the receivers. It only took three days to get a contract in place to renovate the spaces to our specifications, which is a minor miracle within the bureaucracy.

We also had good luck with the phone monitoring part of the plan. The phone company had schematics of the trunk lines and provided the plans for the lines leading to the Russian Embassy. We would rent a nearby storefront building to house the operators who would listen to the phone calls.

We had more trouble locating the linguists than one would think. We looked first at the graduates of our language school and came up with a dozen that we could pull from other assignments.

I instituted the paperwork to have them transferred to Washington. Additional research located five others and we got them assigned as well.

J.C. listed those people he knew from his operator days who would be able to transition to the Russian alphabet very quickly.

"We need to get thirty Cyrillic typewriters. These guys aren't going to be able to hand copy fast enough to keep up with the transmissions," he said.

The requisition went in that very day.

I truthfully expected it to take 60 to 90 days to get everything in place, but it was done in 32 days.

The Ditty Chasers

The operators quickly incorporated the additional Cyrillic characters into their repertories.

The area we found for the phone monitors was much too large for such a small function and we decided to use the space for the analytical effort as well. The security was beefed up and some major changes were made to the interior of the building.

The guard force was almost as large as the working force. We had an entire company of military police, which totaled about 80 people.

Divided into a four section watch, that gave us 20 per shift. Only four wore military uniforms. Those were the ones who controlled entrance to the building. The rest were assigned watch posts within sight of the spaces but in civilian clothing. All were armed with both rifles and pistols. The uniformed ones carried sub-machine guns.

The Normandy invasion had taken place while J.C. and I were occupied with the new project.

Both of us spent a lot of time at the operations facilities, J.C. with the Morse code operators, and me with the analysts.

Donovan's people spent a lot of time trying to get us a copy of the Russian code books. In addition to the efforts to subvert Embassy personnel in Washington he put the word out to all his field people to make a concerted effort to obtain the Russian codes no matter what country they were in.

We were getting a good deal of traffic and isolated the circuit which handled the coded traffic from the Russian Embassy in Washington.

The operation was given a code name, which was VENONA. Within three months, in which the Allies made much progress in pushing the Germans back toward their homeland, our COMINT effort had amassed a very large amount of message traffic from Russian circuits. Without some way to attack the crypto system the best that could be learned from the Morse code circuits was what traffic analysis revealed. Schedules, call signs, operating signals and some locations were discerned, but the effort was relatively useless without being able to read the messages.

Five months into the effort Donovan paid a visit to the analytic facility bearing gifts. He did not reveal how he came by the codes, but he had a complete set of Russian diplomatic codes.

The telephone monitoring program had yielded some good results, which helped identify some suspects in the scientific community as being on the payroll of the Russians.

With the codes our people went to work on all the back logged traffic and we went to a three section watch, which essentially meant that our people worked every day unless they got completely burned out and need some recuperation time off.

All the messages could not be read but we got enough to learn that the Russians were indeed trying to spy on our nuclear efforts.

The information was provided to the President only, and he determined who needed to be briefed about our success. The list was very short and included the senior man in each service, the Secretary of the Navy, Secretary of Defense, and the FBI Director. I feel sure he briefed other selected political figures but that was not my business.

The Presidential election in 1944 brought some surprises. President Roosevelt's health was declining rapidly. Every time I was in his presence he looked more and more frail. His weight inched downward and he did not attempt to get on his feet as much as he had in the past. His suits had to be altered so that he didn't look like a scarecrow. He had not been happy with his vice president during the war years and searched for a replacement on the political ticket who could help garner votes and would not be as vocal toward his war policies as had been his wartime second in command Henry Wallace.

Harry Truman was selected by the DNC to replace Wallace on the ticket for the 1944 election. I was not a politician and paid scant attention to the behind the scenes maneuvering of various people.

After the election results confirmed the Democratic ticket for an unprecedented fourth term for President Roosevelt it soon became a matter of general opinion that the war was going in favor of the Allies and that Germany couldn't hold out much longer against the combined might of Russia, Britain and the U.S.

Japan was also reeling backward with the loss of one of their occupied islands after another as General MacArthur's forces relentlessly pursued the Pacific war.

Roosevelt's primary concern was how the world would be shaped after the war. Churchill was very adamant that the Russians could not be trusted and tried to bring Roosevelt to his side of the argument. Roosevelt felt, and voiced, the opinion that as long as we continued to help the Russians they would be more likely to embrace a democratic form of government.

That had been one of the times when Roosevelt was completely wrong.

I did not put much time in at the White House in the final year of the war. I was too busy trying to structure our COMINT program for after the war.

With the success of our efforts against the Russian diplomatic codes we uncovered enough hard evidence to state with assurance that Russia was trying to get enough intelligence about the Manhattan Project to start or I guess more appropriately, to enhance their efforts to manufacture their own atomic weapons. All this even before the concept was proven to be viable.

Some say that Truman was never briefed about the effort we were going through to produce an atomic bomb, but I personally find that to be a rather ludicrous statement. Truman was no dummy, and with the size of the effort and his place in the governing body, it would have been unbelievable that he would not have known about the effort.

Roosevelt's health continued to decline after the 1944 elections and many wondered at the wisdom of even putting a person in his state of health on the political ticket.

For his part, Roosevelt downplayed his health issues and made sure to never be photographed in a standing position, which by that time was an impossibility unless he was supported on at least one side of his body.

His new term began in January of 1945 and two prototype atomic bombs had been constructed, code named 'Little Boy' and 'Fat Man'. The terms were descriptive of the destructive power of each.

Unfortunately, the President didn't live long enough to witness the success of the program.

Roosevelt died on April 12, 1945. Less than a month later on May 8, 1945, Germany surrendered and the European war was over for all intents and purposes. A lot of work still had to be done to bring war criminals to trial, and to administer war devastated Germany.

The roles of the major allied countries had to be negotiated and administered. The Russians wanted all of Berlin but the other Allies were having none of that game and Berlin was divided among the major powers for administration of government.

When Truman ascended to the Presidency and was briefed on the war effort against Japan he was told that it was going to be a very costly proposition in terms of American lives to invade the islands of Japan as they had done on the march north from the South Pacific Ocean area.

Truman was told that prototype devices had been manufactured in the atomic bomb project and that testing could be done within the next sixty days.

Truman approved the tests and on July 16th, the first atomic explosion took place at Alamogordo Bombing and Gunnery range in New Mexico.

The test was obviously successful and less than a month later the first atomic bomb was dropped from a specially configured B-29 on the Japanese city of Hiroshima. That weapon was one of the cigar shaped warheads constructed from Uranium 235. Three days later a larger weapon was used against the city of Nagasaki.

Within a week after those two events the Japanese capitulated. The surrender document was signed on the deck of the battleship Missouri in which the Japanese agreed to an unconditional surrender.

The U.S. would govern the Japanese homeland for some seven years.

The aftermath of the war caused some turf wars within the military and intelligence organizations.

The military wanted the OSS broken up completely so that they could get back to managing their own intelligence collection efforts.

The COMINT program came under the same scrutiny but the military didn't have a very favorable positon with regard to that organization.

While all the heavyweights in the military were firm believers in the value of COMINT, they knew that no one service component was capable of managing the program.

Truman had some hard decisions made relative to the drawdown of forces after the war. There were enough civilians in the analytical section of the COMINT program that most on both sides of the aisle could see the wisdom of civilian management of the future COMINT organization.

Our success against the Russians in our abbreviated effort taught us that the COMINT organization was going to go in the opposite direction from the regular forces. Instead of doing away with the program the wisest of our leadership recommended growth and expansion of the effort.

Chapter 29

Upon the death of President Roosevelt, J.C. and I were assigned back to the regular navy. We vacated the rooms at the Willard, which we occupied during the entire war years. I was asked if I wanted to remain in the naval service and continue working in the COMINT field.

At the time the war ended we had intercept sites scattered all over the world. Some were bare bones with only a handful of people working on specific tasks. Others, such as Hawaii, Guam, the Philippines, the Azores, Morocco, and a couple of sites in the United Kingdom had upwards of 100 people at each location, and these were only the navy sites.

The army security station, which had been the major analytical facility during the war could no longer accommodate the large number of analysts and the storage of the huge amount of paperwork that was generated to keep continuity of the different communication circuits that we were trying to exploit.

Soon the decision was made to build facilities at Camp Meade, Maryland to house all aspects of the program. Each service would still retain the responsibility for training and assigning operators based on perceived needs. Analysts were trained at a joint school, as were linguists.

Surprisingly, at least to me, was the fact that very little about the successes of the program during the war years came to the attention of the general public. I suppose the fact that everyone in the program had top secret clearances and had signed non-disclosure agreements which threatened stiff penalties for running off at the mouth to anyone not cleared for the information played a vital role in the continued secrecy.

During the ten years after the war the COMINT discipline grew by leaps and bounds.

As it became apparent that Russia and China in particular were destined to become communist countries our leaders sought to keep tabs on what was happing in those locations. The most non-intrusive way to do that was through COMINT. We could pick the signals off the air waves without their knowledge and determine a lot about what was going on within those countries.

Communications became more sophisticated with new discoveries and required better ways to exploit the signals. Robust crypto systems became the order of the day and it was rare that the important messages were broken.

Reliance on analytical tools to keep track of order of battle and location of mobile units were the most important aspects of the program.

With the Soviet Union in possession of nuclear technology, and other countries to follow, the emphasis was on locating and tracking any potential enemy units that were capable of delivering nuclear weapons to a target.

From its modest beginning in the early 1930's COMINT became SIGINT, or signals intelligence, to more accurately describe the discipline. In addition to looking at communications circuits we started looking at other signals for characteristics that could be used to tie a transmitter to a specific unit.

Radar signals in particular could be viewed visually on a spectroscope and the characteristics peculiar to that transmitter analyzed to a degree not even thought about during the war years.

In short, the modest COMINT program from the 1940's has grown to such a degree that more than 50,000 people are employed in the occupation full time.

The Ditty Chasers

Upon creation of the National Security Agency in 1952 all COMINT operations were placed under a single entity.

To catalog the advances in communications technology since WWII would require volumes.

The silent war has been going on relentlessly and any time a new communications system was recognized work was immediately started to exploit that new system.

With the advent of computers the world took on an entirely different complexion. The operators of the old days would not recognize the signals intelligence discipline today, but those familiar with the work of the British to break the ENIGMA code actually were at the forefront of computer technology. The Bombe machines that Alan Turing built in the early forties were computers, though very fundamental ones, in all respects.

Someone once said that the more things change, the more they stay the same. The challenges in the intelligence field are just as relevant today as they were in the early days.

All but a very few of the COMINT operators from the early days are now gone, but the contributions they made to the security of our nation at a low point in our history cannot be overstated.

At a time when our nation was at a point of distress to rival the war of independence and the civil war our citizens again proved that we could rise to any occasion.

The silent war continues, but on a much grander scale.

Will our nation rise to meet the challenge, or will it take some major calamity to wake us up again?

Only time will tell.

www.ingramcontent.com/pod-product-compliance
Lightning Source LLC
Chambersburg PA
CBHW062122170626
46813CB00002B/540

* 9 780099 789492 9 *